EXPLORATION 2127

EXPLORATION 2127

THE FALSE FLAG WAR | BOOK 1

RAYMUND EICH

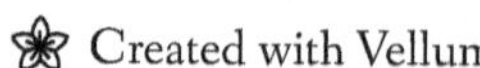 Created with Vellum

CHAPTER 1

*11 MARCH 2127 (EARTH REFERENCE FRAME) | 12 MAY 2125
(CONCORDIA REFERENCE FRAME)*

CONCORDIA BACKED toward the planet on a tail of fusion fire a
million miles long.

Harrison Jaeger sat at the propulsion board in the ship's control
room. His gaze darted over the screens showing fuel supply, flow
rates, fusion efficiency, speed, vector. His meaty hands rested on the
home row of the keyboard except when his hands darted to the other
controls at his station. Quick, precise motions despite the thickness of
his fingers.

Years of training on Earth, plus over three subjective years in
flight. He could run the prop system blindfolded.

Even so, his jaws mashed a stick of gum. Only tiny amounts of
artificial sweetener and fake watermelon flavor lingered. No time to

get a new stick. Bad idea to spit out the old one. Otherwise, he'd grind down his teeth four-point-three light-years from the nearest dentist.

It didn't help his nerves that straps bound him to his chair. Not just a lap belt, but a five-point harness, like a rider on a roller coaster where your legs dangled into air. The drive would turn off within moments. Free fall would return while *Concordia*'s lifesystem modules pivoted for spin gravity. Spin gravity for a year, until it was time to return to Earth.

If Earth would still be there by the time they got back.

The control room always felt cramped. Stark LED panels in the ceiling whitewashed everything. The closeness of the rows of control boards forced people to walk sideways around their seated colleagues. Now, making it worse, even more people than usual jammed the space. The climate control labored to cool them but couldn't overcome the musk of bodies and coffee. The final act of the outbound leg and all the joint mission's leadership teams, Traditionalist and Humanist alike, crowded in for the photo op.

Jaeger worked his jaws harder. Tasted nothing anymore.

Senior bureaucrats. At least he and the techs and scientists in the Humanist Alliance had a common enemy.

He gave his head a quick shake. Not the time for cynicism. He had a job to do.

The reason to do it well filled the main screen.

The feuding factions hadn't agreed on an official name for the planet Alpha Centauri Bc. The Humanist brass labeled it Four Freedoms. The Traditionalist authorities referred to it as New Eden.

Everyone on *Concordia* called it Bravo Charlie.

The planet's slow rotation now turned a hemisphere almost entirely of land to the camera. Blue sea fringed a broad continent. Based on prior observations from Earth and *Concordia*, Andrew McIlroy, the Humanist geologist Jaeger played UltraHistory with, a good guy and a fellow Texan, called the continent a pangaea.

Whatever the geologists called it, colors banded the landmass. Deep green near the ocean, dotted with white clouds. Paler and yellower shades farther inland. Night shadowed the interior of the continent, but from prior observations, Jaeger knew how it looked. Five thousand miles from the sea, reached only by the scantest of rains. Shades of red as desolate as the surface of Mars.

Jaeger's jaws stopped working. His jaws gaped and his fingers stilled for a moment.

A new world. Full of plant life, plausibly animals too. No sign of intelligence. A treasure trove for the hundred scientists from Earth's two main factions on board the ship.

Maybe this mission would be what the politicians back home pretended to agree it was. The first step in getting Earth's warring camps to beat their swords into plowshares. Work together for the common good of all humankind.

A new world, and they would orbit it within minutes.

Sandford, the Humanist co-commander, spoke in her usual high-pitched British accent. "Propulsion?"

Jaeger tore his gaze away from the main screen to the displays on his board.

Too slowly for Sandford, apparently. "Bloody hell, Jay-ger, what's your damned status?"

He'd learned years ago not to rise to the bait of her crass language or mispronunciation of *Yay-ger*. "Propulsion green."

Even without looking over his shoulder, Jaeger knew she gave him a cold look and a toss of her white hair. Wise crew called it platinum blond, if speaking aloud, where Sandford or her cronies could hear.

Before she could throw her rank around, Varanathan, the co-commander from the Traditionalist Coalition, spoke. His voice sounded as smooth as a tub of clarified butter, and the English accent he'd learned in India sounded more plummy than Sandford's. "Navigation, status?"

"Velocity and deceleration on target," said Cardenas, the nav officer. "Updating time till end of burn."

A countdown timer appeared next to the image of the planet. Fourteen minutes to go.

Bravo Charlie grew larger and larger, overfilling the top and bottom of the screen, finally blocking out the stars on the sides.

Jaeger watched his controls. He'd scripted the end of burn commands. Manually, he'd only need to hit the enter key on the keyboard. Still, as the time ticked down, he held both hands ready to flip any switch or turn any dial. Just in case.

The timer reached 00:00:00.

"Now!" said Varanathan and Sandford in ragged unison.

Jaeger ran the script. The drive cut off. The low throb of fusing hydrogen and immense thrust had permeated the ship almost every moment for years. Now it was gone.

The silence of the stopped drive rang in Jaeger's ears. His stomach flopped and his torso floated against the straps.

Free fall.

The co-commanders took turns asking for the ship's status. Orbit safely entered. The six crew modules girdling the ship preparing to pivot for spin gravity.

Jaeger worked his way through the drive shut-down checklist. About a standard year in orbit, with the reactor fusing a trickle of stored hydrogen to power the ship's systems. A faint candle to the energies the ship had consumed getting here, when the particle spin magnets sucked hydrogen from trillions of cubic kilometers of inter-stellar space into the maw of the Bussard ramjet.

Do each step right. You want to power it back up when it's time to leave, don't you? Don't get distracted by the world on the main screen.

His fingers paused on the sculpted keycaps at his station. He couldn't help himself. On screen, glittering rivers meandered across a landscape of thick jungle. Clouds like cotton candy floated through the sky. The late afternoon light of Alpha Centauri B cast the shadows of low hills miles across the terrain.

Three and a half years of subjective travel time. Four-point-three light-years from Earth. Now just two hundred klicks away.

A warm glow eased his flopping stomach. He'd done everything right to get the mission to this point. Untold discoveries to be shared with all mankind.

The presence of Sandford and Varanathan and their staffers behind him suddenly pressed on him. A shudder ran through his shoulders.

Untold discoveries for all mankind, if the senior bureaucrats on both sides wouldn't foul it up.

CHAPTER 2

11 MARCH 2127 (EARTH REFERENCE FRAME) | 12 MAY 2125
(CONCORDIA REFERENCE FRAME)

AN HOUR after his shift ended, Jaeger made his way to the lounge in Module 4 to play the next round of his UltraHistory game.

When he left his sleeping closet in Module 2 after changing into off-duty khaki cargo pants and a blue polo shirt with the mission logo, *Concordia* spun at its target rotation rate. Spin gravity planted his feet to the floors, at about 0.9 g near his sleeping closet. But something felt wrong. Not just less apparent gravity compared to the ship's 1.0 g thrust. He walked past the changed navigation signs and took five steps along the main corridor on Deck F before he remembered.

Airtight tubing no longer connected the F decks of neighboring modules. To get between modules, crew members now had to take the steep and narrow open stairs deck by deck up to A, climb a ladder, and go around an accessway circling the ship's spine.

He bounded along the accessway like the Apollo and Chang'e

astronauts had on Luna long ago. This close to *Concordia*'s spine, the rotation rate gave about as much spin gravity as Earth's moon. The floor of the accessway curved up to meet his feet.

A pipe across the ceiling loomed in front of him. He ducked to avoid banging his head.

He took smaller bounds after that.

When he made it to Mod 4, he had to go all the way down to Deck H. He got heavier the farther down the module he went. Not like thrust gravity at all. And when he got to the lounge and asked the beverage dispenser to pour him a bock beer, he watched the stream of honey-brown liquid curve down into his cup. Coriolis force, he knew that, but the floor still seemed slanted at odds with the sensation in his inner ears. His stomach felt queasy and he had to look away until the trickle of beer into his mug stopped.

He ordered a slice of pizza from the snack oven and made his way through the lounge. Blocky couches with thick cushions and upholstered in earth tones formed half a dozen seating areas. Walls that didn't reach the ceiling, with flat screens displaying the live camera feed of the planet below, separated the seating areas.

The Coriolis force no longer bothered his stomach. Instead, the usual off-duty social dynamics of the crew soured him. Humanists sat with other Alliance members, Traditionalists with Trads. Everyone drank the same coffee drinks from the barista machine, everyone spoke English from the same palette of accents, everyone sounded excited to have finally arrived. Yet still the Humanists glanced at him and their brows clouded, while the Trads looked up and gave him smiles.

Was *us versus them* as much a law of nature as Coriolis force? Jaeger tightened his grip on his beer. With luck, the planetary scientists from the two sides would work together better than this when they got down to the surface.

He rounded the last corner and breathed easier. The UltraHistory gaming club bridged the Coalition/Alliance gap going back to the first days of the mission, when *Concordia* fused hydrogen mined from

Jupiter before it got enough speed to power up the particle spin magnets on the Bussard ramjet. That's when he'd first spoken in depth with McIlroy. A fellow Texan, he and McIlroy could talk about slow-smoked brisket, craft beer, and timeless songs by Waylon Jennings and Willie Nelson, and forget about the border of razor wire and armored vehicle patrols that made the hundred miles between their home towns seem like a million.

McIlroy waited with the other four players, two from each side, in their usual seating area at the back of the lounge. The couches were shades of yellow. The video screen on the wall cycled through still photos of man-made terrestrial landmarks. Someone had overriden the camera feed of the planet. The screen now showed a red sunset silhouetting the four minarets and the central dome of the Taj Mahal.

Jaeger looked at the time projected into the lower left corner of his vision by his wearable computer onto his optic nerves through the neural stim patches on his temples. 1711. They weren't scheduled to start for twenty minutes. "What are you guys doing here so early?"

"Big day," McIlroy said. He held a glass of a hazy IPA in one hand, and with the other, stroked the wiry brown beard over his jutting chin. He projected his usual benevolent uncle vibe. "Lot to talk about."

"You're not going to get approval for your side expedition." The cold male voice belonged to Amundsen, a botanist from the Humanist Alliance. He shook his head slowly enough to keep his off-duty tweed cap over his bald spot. The schools in Denmark had done a good job flattening his accent, but his voice was cooler than usual. Scandinavian reticence, or some dislike for McIlroy? Jaeger had never figured him out.

McIlroy gave a wry grin. "We'll see what Sandford and Varanathan say."

Jaeger took an empty seat next to Regina Smalley, the only woman in the group, a zoologist and a fellow Trad from a small town on the Coalition side of the inner Australian border. She pushed a strand of brown hair behind her ear and said "G'day, Harry," in a lilting tone.

They'd dated, briefly, early in the acceleration phase, but disentangled without any hard feelings. Jaeger set his pizza plate and beer on the coffee table next to her froth-topped coffee drink.

"Good to see you," he told her. He might want to reentangle with her some day when they were both between relationships. He turned to McIlroy. "What side expedition?" He bit off the front corner of his pizza slice. Hot cheese burned the roof of his mouth. He opened his mouth and huffed breaths in and out while McIlroy replied.

"When we were coming in, the IR, visual, and UV scopes all picked up some odd surface formations in the deep interior of the continent."

Jaeger swallowed. The hot bite went sluggishly down his throat. "You said something about it the other day. A lava bed someplace it shouldn't be?" He took a sip of his bock to cool his mouth more.

"Near there, but something else. A bunch of small features spread across the surface."

After another swallow of beer, Jaeger asked, "What's odd about them?"

"They're dark." To McIlroy's side, Amundsen shook his head again. McIlroy backhanded the air in Amundsen's direction and kept his focus on Jaeger. "At every wavelength we looked at. They don't trap just visible light, like soot or coal. UV rays too."

"There will be plenty of rocks in the forested zone," said Amundsen.

"But none like these." McIlroy's face lit up. "Their albedo is under 0.01. That's practically a blackbody. Except their IR emissions are less than we'd expect for a blackbody at ambient temperatures in that part of the continent."

"Okay," Jaeger said, to show interest, but not understanding.

McIlroy's hand left his beard and clawed at the air. Frustration crinkled his eyes. "They absorb almost all radiation that hits them and emit much less than they should! No one expected that. And they're only found in one small region, about eight klicks by five."

Jaeger did the conversion in his head. Five miles by three.

"One small anomalous region isn't enough for the co-commanders to waste resources on your side expedition," Amundsen said.

Jaeger moved his head in a slow, arcing nod. *That* explained Amundsen's coldness for McIlroy's idea. A bureaucratic turf war.

One advantage of being a cynic was never being surprised at human behavior.

Much as you might hope to be.

Jaeger rubbed his eyes. Too downcast a set of thoughts for a day like this. They'd reached their destination after years. He had beer and a slice of pizza. And the next turns of their game to play.

Regina Smalley leaned forward and gave McIlroy a wrinkle of her small brown eyes. "We've got a bonzer lot of plants and animals to take a squizz at first. Your rocks won't go walkabout on us. Will they?"

"No," McIlroy grudgingly said. He glanced at Jaeger and hope sprung into his eyes. "Harrison, what do you think?"

"I'll tell Varanathan. Next time I see him."

Smalley piped up. "You won't be on the bridge much, too right."

"I got us here. My job's done for the next year. Unless we find aliens."

A chuckle went around the table. Even Amundsen showed a grin. Everyone on board had at least one secondary assignment. Jaeger's was xenology. So was McIlroy's. People on both sides had joked for years about how useless those assignments would be. A speculative science. A minuscule chance intelligent life had arisen on Bravo Charlie but not progressed enough to make its presence known to radio astronomers back at Sol System, or the telescopes mounted on *Concordia*'s hull that had pivoted to watch the planet for over three years.

After the mirth died down, Jaeger hammed up a Texas accent. "But since the rest of y'all are heading down to the planet soon, and I'd like to finish our game, maybe we can get started?"

McIlroy, president of the UltraHistory club, nodded. "Teeing up tonight's session now."

Projected into everyone's vision, the augmented reality game board covered the coffee table. A map of Earth, with scores of territories and dozens of marked-off oceans and seas. The board conformed to the food and drinks on the table. Regina Smalley's coffee drink towered thousands of scale miles above northern Scandinavia, and Siberian territories lay on top of Jaeger's pizza plate and crust.

A rainbow array of virtual playing pieces, foot soldiers, horsemen, ships, fortresses, and cities covered the board. Thirty empires large and small, old and new, growing or declining, after dozens of hours of play and four thousand years of simulated history.

A scoreboard hung above the map, showing each player's victory point totals and control shares held in each active empire. McIlroy led by twenty points, with Jaeger and Smalley neck-and-neck for second and Amundsen five points behind them. The other two players were much farther behind and probably had no chance to win.

The scoreboard also showed the game turn. *1200 CE.*

Jaeger always wrinkled his nose that the game used *CE* instead of *AD*. Not that he was particularly religious. Twice a year, Easter and Christmas, he attended services out of habit. Just the alternative acronym, for *Common Era*, sounded stilted, like something a Humanist college professor would say. But the Trads used it too, to paper over the differences between the Coalition's religious communities.

Instead of the acronym, he focused on the number. A grin smoothed out his face.

This turn, the game engine should generate the Mongols. A massive army of light cavalry would pop up in Mongolia, just the other side of his pizza plate. A force that could conquer most of Asia.

A lot of victory points to its primary controller.

Which meant he'd need a large victory point bid to win the control auction.

Jaeger had other plans that didn't require him to overpay for the Mongols. He looked at his hand of event cards, projected next to the scoreboard but privately, only onto his optic nerve, to refresh his memory of his options.

The Mongol horde would fall apart as abruptly as it would rise, simulating the death of Genghis Khan. Jaeger had a card in his hand to help seize control of one of the successor khanates.

On the other hand, a Mongol invasion of China would promote feuding Chinese factions to unify for their own survival, and he could bid for control of the Ming Dynasty in about three turns. Another card would give him a discount on that bid.

Could he do both?

The glint in McIlroy's eyes across the table told Jaeger that the Alliance geologist had similar plans.

The scoreboard winked out, replaced by a swirl of rainbow colors coalescing into a bright white point. The sign of a new empire being born. The point drifted toward Mongolia.

McIlroy's eyes danced with excitement. Was he going to try to take control?

When Regina Smalley opened the bidding for the Mongols at eighteen victory points, a shockingly high bid, Jaeger leaned back and sipped beer. He gave her a sidelong glance but couldn't gauge her plans. Yes, he would bide his time.

Other people, some of whom had played in one of the many earlier games during the mission, others who were just curious or bored, drifted over to watch. The watchers were an even mix of Alliance and Coalition, chatting among themselves, occasionally asking questions of the players.

Jaeger responded, politely but distantly. His attention stayed on the game. Regina Smalley took control of the Mongols. Surprisingly, she directed the horde away from the Great Wall and the rich territories of China behind it. Instead, she aimed west, following the Silk Road trade route and invasion paths into India and the Near East.

Mouth quirked, Jaeger cracked the knuckles on his thick fingers.

Into his vision popped an icon of an ancient phone, the wired kind with a handset and a base. The handset jumped and a low chime sounded through his earbuds. Text across the base read *Andrew McIlroy.*

Jaeger reached for the virtual handset, curious about what private message the other wanted to share.

A word balloon appeared in the air next to McIlroy's head. A wry smile creased his brown beard. *Harrison, you know as well as I do that without Mongol pressure, the Ming Dynasty won't be worth a plugged nickel.*

Jaeger put on a poker face. He rested his hands on his thighs and moved his fingers across the denim fabric. His wearable interpreted the finger movements as touch typing. *Maybe I'll save my Soldier of God card for 1400 and play it as Joan of Arc, for France.*

McIlroy rolled his eyes. From the gesture, Jaeger could tell McIlroy thought he bluffed about having that card. Jaeger kept his poker face as McIlroy replied, *Which Mongol successor kingdom do you want?*

I'll take.... Jaeger stopped typing. His gaze landed on two spectators behind McIlroy.

Tsai, a Coalition molecular fabricator tech, had a buzz cut of black hair, plus acne that some mean-spirited Alliance crew joked he squeezed into the food extruder. In the face of the distrust through which most crew members, Trad or Humanist alike, viewed Chinese from the former superpower's balkanized successor states, he kept his voice low and his gaze on the floor. He'd played a game early in the mission, then given up after getting trounced by ruthless players like McIlroy. Yet still he watched, drawn to it.

Next to Tsai stood Biala, a Humanist on one of the life science teams, in brown trousers with a pressed crease down the front. The crease and cut of her trousers made her look taller and thinner. Broad face, blond hair in a pageboy cut, curling toward her chin. In her fist, she held a vape pen. She exhaled some flavor between banana and bubble gum. She'd never played UltraHistory. She wasn't there with Tsai, either. From her mannerisms the times she came by, Jaeger guessed Biala had a romantic interest in Amundsen, hard as that was to believe.

The presence of spectators didn't distract Jaeger. What puzzled him was how Tsai and Biala ignored the game and shared wide-eyed, questioning glances.

"What's come up?" he asked them.

Biala snapped her head around. She glanced over all the seated players. Her eyebrows arched high and her voice bubbled. "The ship received a radio signal!"

Jaeger squinted. A message from Earth? But why would she be happy?

In his usual voice, barely above a whisper, nasal, and heavily accented, Tsai added, "Not from home. From Bravo Charlie."

CHAPTER 3

ALPHA CENTAURI B SYSTEM | CONCORDIA | BRAVO CHARLIE ORBIT

12 MARCH 2127 (EARTH REFERENCE FRAME) | 13 MAY 2125
(CONCORDIA REFERENCE FRAME)

THE ULTRAHISTORY GAME, and many parts of the mission timetable, paled in importance over the next days. In the lounges and labs, in the public corridors, everywhere crew members ran into one another, conversations invariably turned to the signal.

In the cafeteria near the end of the lunch hour the next day, under the bright glow of Sol-spectrum LEDs, Jaeger found McIlroy and a mix of people at the long table near the back. Five Humanists. The only other Coalition members were the Finkelshteyns, Shimshon and Hannah, husband and wife. Jaeger sat down and started eating seared slices of tuna-flavored protein on a bed of hydroponic arugula with balsamic vinaigrette.

"Are we sure it's artificial?" asked Mercy Mwengi. A young Alliance woman, dark skin, high cheekbones scarred by a chi-pox not fully eradicated after the war, lilting accent. A hydroponics tech.

"Absolutely," Jaeger said. Nods and grunts around the table revealed most others agreed. The most palpable dissent came from Shimshon Finkelshteyn rolling his eyes.

Mwengi regarded him. "How so?"

He didn't need to replay it through his earbuds to remember how it sounded. "It turns on or off like a switch." He knifed his hand up and down through the air. "When it's on, it's always at the same strength. And when it turns on or off, it stays that way for multiples of, I don't remember the exact duration, about three seconds."

"3.2454 seconds," said Finkelshteyn, the highest-ranking Trad geologist. He wore a graying beard, a long-sleeved shirt, and a yarmulke.

"How can that be natural?" piped up Robertson, a male ecologist with a soft look. Like he never lifted weights, or gave up meat years before the mission left Earth.

"How can it not be?" said Finkelshteyn. "Do you see alien cities? Factories? Power plants? Radio towers? We should assume the signal is natural."

McIlroy waggled the synthetic cheeseburger in his hand. "Do you see a quartz oscillator? A rotating ball of neutronium?"

"The universe isn't stranger than we suppose, it's stranger than we can suppose."

McIlroy grinned at Finkelshteyn's banter. "I could quote a famous dead scientist to support my point, too."

Finkelshteyn gave him a wry look. The two head geologists often squabbled, but worked well together.

"If the universe is so strange," Jaeger added, "why shouldn't there be intelligent life other than us?"

"Why are you taking his side?" Finkelshteyn said. "There might be intelligent aliens out there, but here?"

Jaeger gave a wry grin and shook his head. He jabbed his fork into his greens.

Down the table, Robertson turned to Mwengi. If he meant to

speak quietly, he failed. "Finkelshteyn's going to say God sends the signal."

The wry look turned to flinty eyes. "Who the hell are you to tell me what I'm going to say?"

Robertson quivered. "I—I didn't mean—"

From flinty eyes, Finkelshteyn's entire face turned stony. "The hell you didn't mean! I believe in something more than living for today and that makes me a bad scientist?" He slammed his forearms on the table next to his plate.

Hannah, one of the ship's physicians, with a long and glossy black wig, rested her palm on his arm. He brushed her off and held his glare on the ecologist.

Robertson scowled back. "I do too believe in something. Something more than ancient tribal customs dressed up as divine revel—"

"Hey now!" Jaeger leaned forward and raised his arms. His biceps hardened, visible past the sleeves of his short sleeve shirt. He'd club both of them if he had to. "Think what you want but treat each other with respect." He glowered at Robertson and Finkelshteyn in turn. "Not just the two of you. All eight of us here. All hundred and fifty of us on board."

Cardenas, who'd work as a meteorologist now that he'd finished his navigation duties for the next year, lifted his shaven head. "Jaeger." From Spain, he pronounced the *J* as an *H*, *Hay-ger*. "Did you give us the key to decode it?"

"I'm sure I did." Jaeger put on a lazy smile. "Mind telling me how?"

Laughs went around the table. A little nervous, a little forced, but the tension slackened.

"You said *eight*." With a grin, Cardenas tapped the air with his index finger. "As you say, when the signal is on, it is a multiple of the three-point-two-four seconds your colleague said. A multiple from one to seven. And when it is off, it is off for either that duration, or three times that duration."

"Clearly artificial," said McIlroy.

"More than just artificial. Meaningful. After one duration off, there are between zero and seven durations on. These could be digits in octal, how does one say, base-eight?"

Shimshon Finkelshteyn leaned back and crossed his arms over his chest. "Hmm."

"*Now* you listen to them?" Hannah muttered.

Cardenas ran his hand over his smooth scalp. "A base-eight number of exactly one hundred digits? That begins three, one?" His eyes widened. "Three-point-one? Is it the first hundred digits of *pi*?" He pulled his hand from his scalp. His index finger tapped the number keys of what Jaeger assumed was a virtual calculator.

The extended finger closed. Cardenas fist-pumped the air. "Yes! Here, I share it with you all."

A shared file appeared in the air above Jaeger's salad bowl. He reached for it, then noticed his fork still in his hand.

With a gesture of his other hand, he opened the file. Three rows of data ran from side to side. At the top, the square waveform of the signal. Base-eight digits derived from the on/off durations in the middle. At the bottom, a string of digits familiar decades after middle-school math class. 3.14159....

Silence filled the room. Not even a fork clanked on a plate.

"Okay," Finkelshteyn said. "It's not natural."

"A transmitter needs energy, yes?" asked Mercy Mwengi. "Where does it come from? We see no artificial structures. Yes?"

McIlroy put down the last of his plant protein burger and swallowed. "We do see some artificial structures. The extremely low albedo formations in the middle of the continent. What if those are high efficiency solar energy collectors?"

Jaeger's mouth hung open, speared arugula and tuna slice nearby. "Powering the transmitter."

"Exactly. And sensors, too? Watching the skies for an inbound interstellar ship and transmitting the digits of *pi* after that ship enters Bravo Charlie orbit?" McIlroy's eyes lit up. He turned to Cardenas. "Do we know where that signal originated?"

"We can't get good triangulation from different sides of the ship. *Concordia* is too small—"

"Doppler shifts? The velocity differential between the ship and any spot on the planet's surface will change throughout our orbit."

"I shall look into this," Cardenas said. "I will need some time."

By late afternoon, Cardenas found the time to track tiny shifts in the incoming signal's frequency as a function of *Concordia*'s orbits of Bravo Charlie. He posted his findings to the crew's public forum. A 98% probability the signal came from a circle fifty kilometers across and including McIlroy's energy-absorbing features.

When the six players gathered in the lounge for that night's Ultra-History session, where the video screen now showed the Arc de Triomphe with all the usual cars spiraling around it photoshopped out, McIlroy settled back in his plush seat. He gave a little flick of the wrist in Jaeger's direction, then gave Amundsen a mocking look.

Voice extra slow, McIlroy said, "I reckon we'll get our side expedition after all."

CHAPTER 4

ALPHA CENTAURI B SYSTEM | CONCORDIA | BRAVO CHARLIE ORBIT

11 APRIL 2127 (EARTH REFERENCE FRAME) | 12 JUNE 2125
(CONCORDIA REFERENCE FRAME)

IT TOOK a month to prep the expedition to the signal source. Unlike the two planned excursions, which used equipment packed by the team in Sol system, Jaeger, McIlroy, and the others had to dial up hardware from the molecular fabricator. People like Amundsen had a checklist to follow, collect this sample, gather that data. The xenology team had no checklist. Live aliens? Dead ones? Robots? They faced a thousand contingencies and couldn't prepare for them all.

Sometimes Jaeger caught himself staring at the bulkhead, grinning like a holy fool. Another intelligence had made its mark on the galaxy. And he would be among the first to learn about them.

They knew damn little so far. From the use of octal numbers in the signal, they assumed the intelligent life behind all this had eight appendages. Which could range from two hands of four fingers each to a land octopus. And told them nothing about how the aliens might *think*.

McIlroy leaned back from the ground-penetrating radar set he demoed to Jaeger and the others. "Even if we don't know what to expect, we're prepared," he said and scratched his brown beard. "Remember that UltraHistory game last year where the Celts obliterated Rome in 400 BC?"

Jaeger chuckled. He remembered instantly. Because the Roman Empire never happened, the game engine generated unexpected kingdoms and empires. All the players scrambled to reassemble strategies. By the 20th century, Jaeger's Cherokee-Inca alliance fought Buddhist Slavs played by McIlroy for dominance of Europe. "I almost beat you."

A grin showed through the brown beard. "Almost."

The prep for the expedition continued every day and deep into the night. No time for UltraHistory, but Jaeger played a bigger, real game now. Which wore him out like he trained for the Olympics.

On the final night before departure, Jaeger made it back to his sleeping closet after 2200 hours. The mission specs called it a PQ-S, *Private Quarters - Single*, but that made it sound like the one-bedroom off-campus apartment in College Station he'd lived in while getting his Ph.D. in nuclear fusion.

In the hallway outside, he aimed his thumb at the scanner and tapped in his access code.

The door unlocked with a mechanical clank. He pushed it open and swore at himself under his breath. He'd left the desk down.

Yes, he had to fold the chair of aluminum rods and rubbery black webbing into its niche on the bottom of his desk, then the desk into the wall. Only then could he flip down the Murphy bed and get some shuteye. The morning would come early, with eight, maybe ten hours needed for final prep, before *Gagarin* shuttled down to a landing spot near the transmission source at the energy-absorbing rock formations on the surface.

Sixteen hours till departure, but it seemed like sixteen minutes.

Too much to think about now. Jaeger folded up his desk, then trudged into the sleeping closet.

The toe of his slip-on sneakers kicked something on the thin tan carpet.

He rubbed his eyes and looked down. Yes, a piece of paper, kicked by his sneakers toward the back wall of the closet. The paper had the mottled look of something that came out of the molecular fabricator. Folded in half, indentations of blocky handwriting bulged on the plain side facing up.

Some girlfriend, old or new, wanting a roll in the hay the last night before he went down to Bravo Charlie?

Jaeger pulled the door shut and locked it behind him. Then he picked up the paper. Tape secured the edges except for a quarter of an inch at the corners.

He pulled his pocketknife from a zippered pocket of his flight suit. He cut the tape and unfolded the paper with a snap of his wrist.

Not a request for a tryst. Unless the male writer had kept a secret from the psych reviewers on Earth and everyone on board for years.

Need to talk urgently before you leave. Mod 1, chapel, after 2100. Will wait all night. Varanathan.

Jaeger swayed from side to side. What the hell did Varanathan want? The Traditionalist Coalition co-commander had visited the docking port and inspected *Gagarin* earlier that day.

Inspected overstated it. Cursory glances at stowed equipment, a few high-level questions, shuffling his feet when the answers got too detailed. A hearty backslap here, a vague nostrum there. *We'll work together for the good of all humankind.* Exactly what Jaeger expected when Varanathan announced his impending visit to the ship on the xenology team's subforum that morning.

More than the request to talk puzzled Jaeger.

Why the chapel?

Varanathan wanted to wish him Godspeed? Krishnaspeed? Jaeger scrunched up his face. Despite his high position in the Coalition's science bureaucracy, Varanathan seemed to pay little more than lip service to Traditionalist spiritual movements. And even if he felt a pang of piety, Varanathan could have wished him well in the control room, or one of the lounges.

Someplace around other crew members. Probably including Humanists.

The chapel should be empty at this hour of the night.

And why hadn't Varanathan send the invitation electronically?

Because it would generate signals intelligence, sigint, that *Concordia*'s IT team could track.

The IT team included Humanists.

Jaeger hurriedly folded his bed down from the wall opposite the desk. He dropped Varanathan's note on the bed, then unzipped his flight suit and tossed it next to the unfolded paper. After a longing glance at the soft, ivory cotton, he changed into workout shorts and a sweat-wicking shirt. The weight room was in Mod 1, two decks below the chapel. Good cover.

He hesitated a moment, then pulled his wearable computer's chain from around his neck and dropped it on the firm memory foam mattress. Now, no one could track his location through it.

He kicked off his sneakers and pulled on thin shoes, like gloves for his toes. He reached for the door handle, but the paper caught his eye. Message received, best to recycle the paper. What were the odds that Tsai, the molecular fabrication tech, or his Alliance counterpart, might happen to read it before their machines rendered it to atoms?

Jaeger picked it up and tried tearing it into pieces. The tape around the edges resisted his meaty fingers, leaving him with partially torn paper, like an art project his nephew had done in kindergarten.

The boy would graduate high school by the time he returned. Probably done playing football, still learning how to flirt with girls. Growing into the next stage of his life. Running his leg of the relay race of their family. Their culture. The human species.

With a pang, Jaeger groped in his pocket for his multitool knife, unfolded the tiny scissors, and cut Varanathan's note into about fifty confetti-sized squares. He mixed the tiny pieces of paper in his hands. A third of them went into the recycling bin in his sleeping closet.

In the nearest kitchenette, he dropped another third into the hopper, barely deviating from his path to the refrigerator for a bottle of water. Cameras and microphones hid in the kitchenettes' walls. The psych teams supposedly reviewed the data, though they denied the cameras even existed.

He shoved the final third into a recycling bag of thick plastic hanging on the wall of the central, curving accessway. He pulled the bag's drawstring tight and jostled the contents with a squeeze of his fingers.

Jaeger descended the ladder into Module 1 and made his way down steep and narrow stairs. He passed the shut doors of sleeping closets and the lingering smell of overcooked broccoli from an empty kitchenette. Saw no one. Sipped water like he really went to the weight room.

The chapel was on C deck, on a rarely-trafficked corridor. He peered through the stained glass window in the chapel door. The video wall at the front of the chapel cast a faint glow in stained glass panes of sunbeam and rainbow.

He wanted to peer left and right and make sure no one in the corridor saw him. He stiffened his neck instead. It would look more suspicious to see if someone watched him than if he went straight in.

The door was never locked. Jaeger turned the handle, pushed it open. Went in and closed the door behind him.

Dim lighting. Off-white walls with accent strips of synthetic wood running vertically. Artificial flowers, graceful leaves longer than his forearm and white petals Jaeger couldn't identify, near the front. Silent, luckily. If low organ music coming through the speakers, the chapel would remind him too much of his grandfather's funeral service.

The chapel had reconfigurable rows of theater seats on wheels. Now, the rows faced the video wall in the standard orientation, like pews in a church.

Unless one of the religious communities on board used the chapel for a worship or meditation service, the video wall at the front, flanked by the artificial flowers, usually showed a generic image of natural beauty on Earth. Now, though, it showed a sunlit slice of Bravo Charlie's continent. Winding rivers fringed by pale green meandered across yellow grasslands. Ahead on *Concordia*'s line of flight, the rivers shrank and the grasslands grew duller in color.

In a few minutes, tomorrow's landing site would come into view.

"You're a lucky man, Yeggs, to walk the surface of New Eden."

Varanathan's smooth voice came from the back corner of the chapel, to Jaeger's right. He emerged from the shadows. His black hair was parted down the middle and swept back on the sides, like a boy band pop star's. Light from the video wall glinted on his low forehead, but his small eyes remained in shade.

"Thanks, but boss, can we get down to business? I've got a pillow with my name on it."

"I know it is late and you have worked hard to prepare. I don't wish to keep you long. I find it is at times helpful to come here, free of distractions—" Varanathan touched his fist to chest, then pulled it away and spread his fingers wide. "—to take another look at our higher purpose."

The gesture meant Varanathan's wearable computer was somewhere else. Or is that what the co-commander wanted him to think, so he would talk freely and get recorded?

Jaeger peered at the IIT Bangalore logo on Varanathan's off-duty, untucked polo shirt. No wearable bulge underneath. No sign Varanathan lied.

When in doubt, tell the truth. If nothing else, it's easier to remember.

"I took off my wearable computer, too," Jaeger said.

"We call our higher purpose different names, but we turn our gazes to it with the same reverence." Varanathan sounded pleased. He extended his arm toward the front row, as far from the door as possible.

Jaeger trudged that way. Every step forward meant an extra step on the journey back to his sleeping closet.

Varanathan walked behind him down the center aisle. He said over his shoulder, "What do you expect to see when you land?"

"McIlroy's energy-absorbing geological formations," Jaeger said around a nugget of sarcasm. He showed his palm in apology. "I've worked sixteen hour days getting ready for this expedition. I'd like you to get to your point so I can rack out."

He flipped down the theater seat and settled on it with a creak. The video wall now showed the red desert in the middle of the continent below.

The co-commander took the seat next to him. He put on a breezy smile. "I am getting to my point. I want your guesses as to what you might see, but I don't want to color your perceptions by telling you what I think you might see."

"You want my guess about the source of the signal? I've been too busy to speculate, but I can take a stab at it. We're going to find an automated station. No live aliens."

"What clues show you that answer?"

Jaeger ticked things off on his meaty fingers. "One, the signal is the only radio transmission we picked up. Live aliens on the planet would presumably contact each other over the radio spectrum and drop sigint all over the place."

Varanathan said smoothly, "Another explanation for the lack of signals intelligence is, they might be so advanced they stopped using radio."

Jaeger shook his head. "Two, we found no signs of settlement or agriculture anywhere around the signal source."

"On the surface."

"Three, McIlroy's formations couldn't generate enough energy to power an underground settlement—"

"You're certain of that?" Varanathan's voice quickened.

"McIlroy ran some back-of-the-envelope numbers of how much solar energy his formations could be absorbing. I know how much our fusion reactor has to generate to keep the lights on while we're in orbit. Reasonable to guess intelligent aliens would need a comparable amount. McIlroy's formations absorb maybe one part per thousand of what a settlement of live aliens would need."

"So you expect you will see an automated station," Varanathan said. "Or a tomb. I expect this too. My next question. Where did this station's builders come from?"

Jaeger squinted at Varanathan. The red desert on the video wall tinted his face, but not enough to reveal what the co-commander drove at.

He answered truthfully. "I've been too busy prepping to think about it."

"Please think about it now. There are only two answers. Either they came from Bravo Charlie or they came from elsewhere."

"The simplest answer is they're from here."

"The simplest, yes. But if they're from here, why is there no other sign of them?"

Jaeger sucked in a breath through his teeth. The video wall showed vast desert, brushed in a palette of ten thousand shades of red and brown. Hills, mountains, plains. Rock and sand. Tiny flecks of green in the nooks and crannies where water would flow on the rare days when clouds dropped rain.

All natural.

Just like the grasslands. And the rainforests.

"Maybe they built the station to last." From the sound of his own voice he didn't believe that answer.

"I think we all see they did that," Varanathan said. "But why only one station in the middle of a desert? The terrain we're flying over now, dry as it is, is far more hospitable than the transmission location." He lifted his hand from the armrest. Greenish-black splotched the winding line of an arroyo, now arid. Maybe five inches of rain fell there in a standard year. Cardenas and the other meteorologists estimated the transmission site might get five inches in a century.

Varanathan went on. "Why not build their cities, their factories, their transport to the same standard?"

"Maybe they expected the dry climate to preserve it longer."

Varanathan smiled. Jaeger briefly wondered how often the co-commander whitened his teeth. "It appears you can see they aren't from here."

"*I'm* keeping an open mind. I get the feeling you think they came from—where?"

"Look around the Alpha Centauri system and tell me where you can see them coming from." The glow of the desert on the video wall glinted in Varanathan's smile.

Jaeger leaned against the padded backrest. The hinge of his seat creaked. He barely heard.

After half a decade of training and flight, he knew the bodies orbiting Proxima and the two stars of the Alpha binary system about as well as he knew Earth and the planets of Sol. Mostly small and rocky worlds, like Mercury, orbited Alpha Centauri A and B. Icy like Pluto if they had formed far enough from their central stars to retain small volatile molecules. One gas giant, Bravo Foxtrot, orbiting B while surrounded by moons like Jupiter's. One moon a sulfurous volcanic hellhole like Io, three moons cloaked by ice or liquid methane.

Maybe life existed on those moons. Near subocean vents under the ice, or using liquid methane instead of water as a solvent for biochemistry.

Neither type likely to give rise to high tech, intelligent life as human beings might know it.

One slim possibility remained. "Alfa Echo?"

"The greenhouse world?"

"Maybe it was a garden world like Bravo Charlie until they fouled it up. A handful of survivors made it here—"

"—and only left signs of their presence in the most inhospitable desert of this planet?" Varanathan's smile returned. "This leads us back to where we were."

Jaeger took a deep breath. "You think the alien presence came from an interstellar mission. They built this base, in this desert, on purpose."

"Why not? We came here on an interstellar mission. This shows it is possible."

Possible. Another mission, like *Concordia*'s, crossing light-years of space from some other star. A thrill ran down Jaeger's arms.

He pivoted in his seat with another creak of the hinge, then rested his forearm on the backrest. "You could have given me your guess about the aliens by text or call. What did you bring me here to tell me in person?"

"The American, the Texan, always eager to get down to brass tacks. Here is my point. If they came from another star, their technology is, or was, as advanced as ours. If not more so."

"Obviously."

"A technology more advanced than ours could give a huge advantage to whichever of the Traditionalist Coalition or the Humanist Alliance could monopolize it."

Jaeger slowly drew in a breath. He dropped his gaze to the carpet, as reddish-brown as dried blood in the glow of the desert in the video wall.

For two centuries, Earth had been divided into armed camps, each with weapons that could kill billions of people and devastate vast swaths of the planet. A-bombs, H-bombs, neutron bombs, dirty bombs. Nerve gas, tailored plagues, engineered psychosis. Electromagnetic pulses to cripple all the electronics on a continent. Back doors in hardware and software to trigger power planet meltdowns or drive fifty million cars into head-on collisions. Space rocks nudged toward enemy cities.

An unstated purpose behind the *Concordia* mission had been to test new fusion power technologies. A drive powerful enough to accelerate a huge ship to 0.04 c, the speed at which a Bussard ramjet could kick in, could obliterate a small country, if used as a weapon.

The weapons had mutated. The armed camps had reshuffled.

Hell, the original two superpowers had long since shattered. Some of those weapons saw action, in the war that shattered the hegemony of the third superpower, China, forty years prior, and raised up the fourth and fifth, the Traditionalists and the Humanists.

But though the empires had changed, the world remained under threat. Hubris, ignorance, brinksmanship, or bad luck might disregard the likelihood of mutual assured destruction and bring about Armageddon.

A damnable set of affairs. A cloud of death hung over billions of people, while a few insiders profited, in money, prestige, and power.

Insiders like Varanathan.

All the skullduggery to set up the meeting now made sense. "You got my attention," Jaeger said, mouth dry.

"It would be better if we were the ones to derive an advantage, rather than the Alliance. Wouldn't it?"

Part of Jaeger recoiled. But what more might Varanathan tell him if he feigned agreement? "I am an officer in the Army Reserve of the Federated States of North America."

Varanathan's teeth gleamed in the reddish glow of the rusty desert passing by on the screen, as if stained by blood. "I knew I could trust you. Some of my subordinates on our leadership team don't. They say you are too chummy with McIlroy."

Jaeger shrugged. "He had the bad luck to grow up on the wrong side of the inner Texan border. Can't hate a man for that."

After a long peering look, the co-commander's eyes eased. "Well said. If McIlroy were in charge on their side, we needn't be having this talk." Varanathan winced. "Sadly, you know Sandford. Vile woman. She is licking her chops at the thought of what her team might find down there. And give to her, for her to give to her masters back on Earth. She was vehement about keeping silent about the alien presence in our transmissions to Earth, you know. It is clear why."

"Both sides have personnel at mission control," Jaeger said.

"And don't forget, each side has monitoring stations across the southern hemisphere and throughout Sol System. An open transmission would alert both factions to the possibility of advanced alien technology. It would deny the element of surprise to whichever of our factions might monopolize it. Hence her vehemence for silence."

A silence Varanathan agreed to. Or was first to propose, and the only vehemence Sandford exhibited came in how quickly she agreed.

"Most personnel believe the official reason for staying silent," Jaeger said.

"Most personnel are naïve. 'We don't want to panic the masses on Earth.' 'We need to learn more about the aliens before we report.'" Varanathan shook his head and smiled with closed lips, like an adult indulging a child's belief in Santa Claus.

He waggled his hand at the red desert on the video wall. "Perhaps there is nothing of advantage to either side to be found down there. Then my concerns about the Alliance seizing the upper hand are merely me jumping at shadows. But if there is an item of advantage, can I rely on you to do the right thing?"

"The 'right thing?' Spell it out for me."

Varanathan looked like he suffered mild heartburn. "Secure that item for us, and let me know privately."

Jaeger drummed his fingers against the padded backrest. "If there's any tech worth a damn down there, McIlroy and the Alliance personnel will find it too and send back their own secret messages to Sandford."

"They might, yes." Varanathan reached toward the small of his back and under the untucked tail of his shirt. "Unless your team discovers something dangerous and only Coalition members survive."

Varanathan held out his flat hand. On his palm and fingers rested a pistol.

A sour feeling exploded in Jaeger's gut. He kept it off his face.

"You are a reserve officer in the army of a Traditionalist member state. I assume you are competent with...?"

It had been years since he'd discharged a firearm. Hunting with his father and uncles. His national service year jumping out of the back of an armored personnel carrier with a rifle in his hands, patrolling the inner Texan border. He'd gotten a passing score in pistol shooting as part of the reserve officer training program mandated for all male citizens seeking Ph.D.s in the hard sciences of a university in the FSNA.

Years, but as familiar as riding the proverbial bike.

"I can hit a target." Jaeger made no move to take the pistol.

Varanathan moved his hand with the pistol a few inches closer. "Stow it with your personal items and take it to the planet."

Jaeger studied the pistol. New Eden had its apple, didn't it? If he took the pistol from Varanathan, he would still have the power to never pull the trigger. And if he refused to take the pistol, what sort of grudge would Varanathan nurse? Not just for the next ten months in orbit, or the three-plus years returning home, but for the rest of Jaeger's career. And life.

He reached for the pistol. Gray plastic rough from the 3d printer. At least his finger wouldn't slip off the safety catch. Or the trigger. He gauged the caliber with the pad of his index finger across the barrel mouth. A 9 mm or a .357. Short barrel, low accuracy. Enough stopping power if you got close to a hostile.

Hostile? A fellow scientist from the other side of a demilitarized zone.

"You'll need these, too." From the back of his waistband Varanathan pulled out four magazines. "Fifteen rounds each. The pistol is rated for two hundred rounds before the barrel melts into uselessness. That should be enough."

Jaeger swiped his hand over the magazines and shoved them in his pocket. The pistol lay across his other hand. The video wall showed thin yellow grassland now and gave a sickly tint to the weapon's barrel and handgrip. He stared at the pistol, hoping for an objection to come to mind. And finding one.

"It would look suspicious if an accident killed only Humanists."

Varanathan nodded. "I'm sure some number of Traditionalists might die too. Tragic, but affairs of state, yes?"

Jaeger's gaze met the co-commander's small dark eyes. Then he filled his voice with all the agreement he could fake. "You can't make an omelet without breaking eggs." He closed his hand around the hunk of plastic.

"I'm glad you see what we must be prepared to do."

The heft of the pistol in his hand sent a thought fleeting through his mind. Slot home a magazine and shoot the co-commander now. Two rounds in the chest, point blank. The man would be dead within ten seconds.

And security would arrest him, the psych techs would rewire his brain, and the Trad number two would deny Varanathan had any plans to steal alien tech for the Coalition. Then the Trad number two would send someone else down to the planet. Someone willing to steal valuable tech and kill anyone in the way.

"How do I get you a message? Especially if the biotelemetry coming up here from the other expedition members tips everyone off that *affairs of state* happened?"

"Before you act, send me a text with the word *chakra* in it."

"*Chakra.*" A grad school girlfriend had used the word when talking about her yoga class. "Like I'm balancing my *qi* or something?"

Varanathan's heartburn face looked more sour than before. "The alignment of *chakras* is ancient Hindu science, completely different from the Chinese folk magic about energy flows and whatnot. I'm sure they stole the concept of *qi* from ancient India, in fact."

Jaeger drew in a long, slow breath. His culture had its blind spots and hobby horses too, didn't it? "I'll text that I could use a *chakra* alignment. Then what?"

"I will reply with the word *karma*. Within minutes, at most an hour. This is your signal that our people have taken control of the data feed from the surface. Then you will do what you must." Varanathan's smile failed to reach his eyes. "I trust you grasp the great autonomy you have?"

With a word, Jaeger could play a *Palace Revolution* card. He swallowed thickly. Varanathan's plan wasn't a stratagem in an Ultra-History game. He plotted a coup, with violence, and God knew how much spilled blood and how many dead bodies. Of their fellow crew.

Jaeger relaxed his grip on the pistol. "Great power, great responsibility."

"You Americans and your comic books," Varanathan said in a light tone. He rose from his seat. "I wish you and the entire expedition the best of luck."

"I can tell."

Varanathan gave a last gleaming grin. The red glow from the screen glistened on his teeth. The memory of crimson stuck with Jaeger long after the co-commander left the chapel.

Jaeger waited. He had to. It wouldn't do to be seen leaving the chapel minutes after Varanathan did the same. He tried to ease into the seat, but the cushions seemed less plush and the curve of the rigid backrest kept his back and shoulders from relaxing. Uncomfortable, he sipped water and watched the planet scroll by beneath the ship.

He prayed, too, though no higher power answered.

Srinivas Varanathan strode at comfortable pace down the corridors from the chapel. Out of habit, the muscles in his face held an expression of calm, confident leadership.

But as he climbed the stairs to lighter levels near the ship's spine, it sank in that no one stirred. He stalked forward, brow creased, as he mulled over Jaeger's words.

Not the bit about *chakras* and *qi*, infuriatingly ignorant though it was. Yeggs couldn't help himself. American civilization had shallow roots. A mere five centuries on its continent. During the five decades of Chinese hegemony, the occupiers had ripped out large swathes of American culture and planted their own. Inevitable, for any civilization lacking five thousand years of transcendent Hindu wisdom.

He had lied to Jaeger, of course. A leader who never lied did his job incorrectly. Two lies of omission. The first was mandatory, for need-to-know reasons.

The code phrase had been worked out months before *Concordia's* departure. A simple and innocuous phrase, in line with his casual statements to Earth about all the old books he would supposedly read on the journey. *I finally started reading the Raj Quartet.* So innocuous, the ship transmitted it in the clear back to Earth. Only a handful of senior officials at Coalition headquarters in St. Petersburg would understand it to mean they'd found signs of intelligent life. He would select from further sets of code phrases, relating to some novels about India written by an Englishman nearly two centuries prior, as his people learned more.

Sandford had no such code phrase. His people monitoring her transmissions back to Earth confirmed she'd said used no new words or odd phrasings since she had officially agreed with him to hold off on informing Earth about the signal from the surface. Coarse and domineering woman, but her handlers back home had failed to prepare for every possibility.

He smiled with self-satisfaction. Pictured himself in a corner office overlooking a research park leafy with red cotton and jackfruit trees, where technicians would exploit alien discoveries and politicians would offer him plum positions at higher and higher ranks in the Coalition's science bureaucracy....

The grin faded. Much as the image pleased him, it at best lay five years away. And required Yeggs to do the right thing, here, now.

The second lie was that only his subordinates harbored misgivings about Jaeger's chumminess with the Humanist, McIlroy.

Varanathan did too.

Yes, Yeggs had said the right things. He had no quarrel with rank and file Humanists, but if conflict broke out, his unreserved loyalties lay with the Traditionalist Alliance.

Though come to think of it, he'd only spoken of his duties as a reserve officer for FSNA. Did he carve out some mental space for himself, that he would follow only lawful orders issued by his superiors in that chain of command over three subjective years ago?

Varanathan climbed the ladder to the inter-module accessway.

Despite the low spin-gravity this close to the ship's spine, he paused to catch his breath.

At least Yeggs took the pistol. Recognized that affairs of state sometimes required extralegal action.

Varanathan loped along. He asked his wearable for his notes and it projected them onto a virtual screen in front of him. Pasted excerpts from reports by the Trad psych officer, and a member of his command staff, scrolled along, matching his reading speed.

Harrison Jaeger affects a cynical demeanor, which masks an idealistic streak that sees little difference at the highest levels between the Alliance and our Coalition.

His UltraHistory opponents tell me he is quite good at pretending to ally with them, only to pursue his own agenda.

Bright red paint, touched up a month ago in preparation for spin gravity, caught his eye on the wall ahead, near an alcove where a ladder came out of a hole in the floor. *Mod 5.* His spacious quarters, where he could leave both desk and bed open and have room to sidle around them, lay five decks down.

He scowled at the painted sign, then nodded to himself.

He had a contingency plan. Time to activate it.

Varanathan moved past the ladder to Module 5. Calm confidence formed in the muscles behind his face.

CHAPTER 5

15 APRIL 2127 (EARTH REFERENCE FRAME) | 16 JUNE 2125
(CONCORDIA REFERENCE FRAME)

THE CHUG of the oxygen compressor kicking in outside of the tent
woke him.

Jaeger shifted on his cot, then opened his eyes. A moment of
confusion—only his third sleeping shift on the planet, the arrange-
ments not yet burned into his subconscious. He placed the sound
from the compressor, his position in the tent.

Tent? More inflatable house than tent. They relaxed and slept in
greater comfort than Genghis Khan's most luxurious yurt.

Which did Jaeger no good now. A pale tinge coming through the
translucent window told him he wouldn't have enough time to get
back to sleep. Dammit.

But on the other hand, the first sunrise since their landing crept
toward them. Might as well see it.

Quietly, he slipped out of thin sheets and pressed his thumb to the sensor on the locker standing up behind his cot. The locker door opened noiselessly. Working by the feel of fabrics, he pulled on his cargo pants and a T-shirt.

The pistol and its magazines lay at the bottom of the locker, hidden under extra underwear and a grooming kit. Though concealed, its presence radiated to him every time he opened the door.

Boots in hand, Jaeger tiptoed in his socks around the three other men still asleep in this room. Feng, a Humanist from one of the Chinese successor states, snored lightly. Like Tsai on the Trad side, he mostly kept to himself. Ulanovas's arms jerked and his closed eyes twitched. Dreaming about basketball or ancient aliens, Jaeger guessed. Maybe both. The Lithuanian's sandy blond hair would have a serious case of bedhead when he woke.

Both Ulanovas and Feng were pilots, rated for everything from the shuttle that brought them here to the off-road vehicles they'd use to get around.

McIlroy, the last man in the room, slept on his back, navy blue sleep mask and bright orange earplugs in place.

Jaeger slowly zipped open the flap to the public room, stepped through, and pulled the zipper down inch by inch. Let them sleep. The other three men would need to be sharp. So, too, the two women, Marie d'Arbaud—*dar-BOW*, almost four years in and he finally pronounced it to her liking—and Annike Ingvarsson, asleep in the room they shared to the left.

He filled his insulated water bottle of rigid plastic in the tent's kitchenette. The stink of burned garlic bread from Ulanovas's botched cooking of dinner lingered around the microwaves.

Jaeger sat on the airlock's floor and put on his boots. The tent wall flexed and squeaked when he leaned against it. He zipped shut the inner flap, took and held his breath, and opened the outer.

Bad idea. When he finally exhaled, he reflexively breathed deeply, but the partial pressure of oxygen in Bravo Charlie's atmosphere was lower than the Earth standard air in the tent. Like gaining two miles of altitude in a couple of steps.

He gasped for breath. Spots swam in his vision. An echo of the panicked feeling of the first time he got the wind knocked out of him on a football practice field.

He managed to sit on a flat-topped red rock without falling. Five feet wide, plenty of landing zone. Bravo Charlie's point-eight g of surface gravity gave him a little more control of his descent.

Head between his knees, he sucked air as crisp as a mountain wilderness back on Earth, until his head stopped swimming.

Jaeger looked toward the east. From his vantage point on a low rise, starting a hundred yards away, the field of McIlroy's formations spread below, across rolling terrain still colorless from the ebbing night. The formations looked like trees, with jutting branches reaching toward the sky. Despite the natural fractal shapes, no one doubted alien minds and tools had built them. Trees blacker than black, absorbing every photon falling on them from the stars.

Beyond the formations, crimson dawn smeared like trickling blood across the horizon. His stomach clenched. *Red sky at morning, sailor take warning.*

He took more deep breaths. The red came merely from atmospheric dust. Not an omen. He wasn't going to let his last meeting with Varanathan trouble him this shift. During the prior Bravo Charlie ninety-hour day, the team had spent its three waking shifts on post-landing checks, unloading *Gagarin*, and setting up the tent. Now, finally, they would explore McIlroy's formations, looking for clues about the alien installation they assumed waited for them beneath the surface.

No alien activity had come to them. Small desert creatures with six spindly legs and a dozen telescoping eyes crawled past the security cameras in the night. Nothing large. Nothing intelligent. Nothing artificial.

Jaeger knew in his gut the aliens were gone. The only question was, to another star system, or the grave?

The red streak along the horizon widened. Orange tinted the sky near where Alpha Centauri B would rise. He cleared his throat, coughed louder, spat onto the ground. He couldn't see red dust in his phlegm but he knew it was there. So too were bacteria, but d'Arbaud, the only microbiologist at Gagarin Station, assured him they would not contaminate Bravo Charlie. Native microbes had evolved for the planet's particular conditions for billions of years. Earth microbes lacked any chance of outcompeting them.

And as soon as Marie d'Arbaud had said that, she pulled her arms close around her and narrowed her soft, sad eyes at him. She did the same with all four men on this expedition. A nasty fight with her husband, rumor had it. Whether he reaction meant she now hated all men, or resisted the urge to get back at her husband by cheating on him, Jaeger couldn't tell and had been too busy to pry.

A faint sound trickled into his ears. The outer flap zipper. He didn't remember closing it. He tensed and turned.

McIlroy emerged from the airlock. He carried an insulated steel coffee mug and a foil pack of the standard-issue drug to prevent low-oxygen sickness. "Mind if I join you?"

Jaeger scooted over on the rock. "Sit a spell on the front porch."

"Thanks." McIlroy took a seat. The bitter scent of coffee came to Jaeger. Another human presence on this alien world. "Couldn't sleep?"

"Woke up early," said Jaeger. "The oxygen compressor kicked in. It's pretty loud."

"I'll add that to the list, next maintenance shift." Their one active shift during the planet's next night, about sixty hours away.

After two full shifts, thirty-six hours, exploring the alien presence.

Jaeger's gaze wandered to the vista below him. The deep black formations with their fractal edges punished his gaze, like an optical illusion of black and white stripes. So strongly did they contrast with the natural gray reflection of pre-dawn plus starlight off the rocky and sandy landscape.

Alien technology. Solar panels far more efficient than anything people had built to date. A boon to all humankind. Nothing worth killing for.

McIlroy's steel mug clinked against the rock. Jaeger glanced over. Behind him and across a dirt yard from the tent loomed the oxygen compressor, water condenser, and the food and waste processors. In the dim light, Jaeger couldn't read McIlroy's expression.

Had Sandford met privately with McIlroy, just as Varanathan had with him? Probably. But if Jaeger broached the subject, would McIlroy give a straight answer? *Yes, she asked me to kill you and steal alien tech.*

No way. He'd evade the question, like he did during in-game negotiations every UltraHistory session.

And if Sandford hadn't asked him, getting queried about it by Jaeger would lead him to figure out that Varanathan had asked Jaeger to do the same.

Jaeger swallowed water, but couldn't wash a foul feeling from his mouth. He cracked his knuckles and nodded his chin toward the alien formations. "I can't wait to get started."

"Off the driving range and onto the first tee."

Face scrunched, Jaeger turned to McIlroy. "I thought Humanists didn't golf. Watering that much grass is bad for the environment, or it promotes Scots privilege, or something."

McIlroy lowered his coffee cup. "Don't tell anyone." Enough dawn now showed to let Jaeger see a glint in his eye. "We're settled on today's plan?"

They talked it out as they sipped their beverages and shades of red seeped into the terrain around them.

One of the pilots had to stay near the tent. Orders from *Concordia*'s co-commanders. Their landing craft, *Gagarin*, which lay on a rocky plateau a mile and a half away, remained on call in case some other expedition needed it to redeploy.

Jaeger clamped his meaty fingers on his water bottle. Between pre-flight checks and the need to refuel back at *Concordia*, their landing craft couldn't get anywhere else on the planet for seventy-two hours. Some other expedition leader must have lobbied Sandford or Varanathan for this useless order out of envy.

McIlroy guessed Amundsen, but lacked proof.

Jaeger would violate the order, if need be. The co-commanders couldn't enforce their orders from orbit, and better to ask for forgiveness than permission. But the hassle of asking Varanathan for forgiveness at taking both pilots away from the camp meant he would need a very good reason.

Feng would stay at the tent this shift. Also, because Varanathan and Sandford didn't trust anyone, a Traditionalist had to stay with him. Which meant d'Arbaud. Jaeger had to join every trip hunting for clues to the aliens. More orders.

Not that he needed them. Not when he didn't know what Sandford had asked McIlroy to do. More importantly, when he didn't know what McIlroy had decided in his own mind.

Hence, he, McIlroy, Ulanovas, and Annike Ingvarsson would spend the shift scouting the area. The drone would fly two runs over the area, going back and forth each time like a farmer plowing a field. The first run, with normal radar, would refine the surface mapping done from *Concordia*. For the second run, they would swap in the ground-penetrating radar and the drone would look for subsurface discontinuities. Buried equipment. Tunnels and chambers.

Alpha Centauri B crept up the eastern sky. Lights came on in the tent's public room. Voices muttered over the buzz of the microwave.

McIlroy took another sip of coffee. "Time to head back in?"

"Unless Ulanovas is cooking breakfast."

They chuckled and went inside. Ingvarsson stared at one of the microwaves and didn't look up until McIlroy and Jaeger said good morning. Her blond ponytail bobbed across the back of her shoulders as she turned. She returned the greeting with a hint of her Swedish accent. She held a coffee mug near her mouth, but low enough to show off the mole on the lower curve of her high cheekbone.

If you have a beauty imperfection, don't hide it, lead with it. He remembered reading that in a magazine one morning in a girlfriend's apartment during graduate school. Apparently Alliance women from Sweden learned that too.

Her brown eyes met Jaeger's gaze for a moment and memories of ex-girlfriends faded.

Though he held her gaze, a voice inside said *careful*. He hadn't dated any Humanists on the expedition. He didn't need Varanathan to remind him that any Humanist woman might be an agent for the Alliance intelligence service.

The microwave dinged. Ingvarsson pulled out a cinnamon roll in a crinkly plastic bag. The break in eye contact gave Jaeger a chance to exhale without her noticing.

Over the next minutes, after they took turns at the microwaves and the coffee dispenser, the four people working this shift drifted toward the inflatable chairs and couch making up the tent's sitting area. They ate and continued to talk.

While Ulanovas monitored the drone, he would also drive one of the off-road vehicles parked behind the tent to carry the other three around the site. McIlroy was in charge of deploying ground thumpers and seismographs to augment the ground-penetrating radar survey. Which meant he decided where they should go and Jaeger and Ingvarsson would do most of the heavy lifting.

"Can't have you breaking a fingernail," Jaeger said to McIlroy through a lazy grin.

McIlroy laughed.

A good guy. For the thousandth time since *Concordia* left Sol, Jaeger wished they could have been on the same side.

They were, though. The side of humanity.

Jaeger hid his musings behind mouthfuls of breakfast burrito and chatter and banter about the plan for the coming shift.

Within half an hour, Jaeger, McIlroy, Ulanovas, and Ingvarsson left the tent. The pilot got the radar-mapping drone airborne with a few commands he tapped on the air, translated and forwarded to the drone. Four rotors and a spindly alloy body wider than a basketball player's wingspan. The drone buzzed straight up with a wash of dusty air. It bobbed a moment, then made a beeline for the nearest corner of the survey zone.

"Time to drive," McIlroy said.

Thin light colored their off-roader's knobby black tires and flimsy white panels. Thick gray fabric roofed the three rows of seats. Two open-topped trailers were hitched to it in series. On the gate of the rear trailer, someone had painted a spider, front legs pointing up and rear legs pointing down.

Jaeger frowned. He didn't remember seeing any figures painted on the trailers when they loaded them from *Concordia* into *Gagarin's* main cargo hold. And why did one of the spider's right rear legs have a line as long as it was, jutting from its foot to the side? It looked familiar....

"Ulanovas?"

The pilot shook his broad head to clear lank, sandy blond hair away from his eyes. Jaeger had gotten an ear for his Lithuanian accent. It couldn't obscure the smile in his voice. "Who could have painted that?"

Jaeger asked, "It's a Nazca glyph, isn't it?" Figures half a mile long, scraped across the Peruvian desert by primitive people two thousand years earlier.

"When the aliens see us coming, from that they will know we know it's them."

McIlroy groaned. "Not that ancient aliens crap again."

"You have proof aliens never came to Earth?" Ulanovas's grin showed gleaming teeth.

Jaeger rolled his eyes. Ulanovas didn't actually believe that nonsense, did he? "Get behind the wheel."

They climbed in. Ulanovas drove them around the tent and down the slope. The knobby tires found easy traction on hard-packed high ground. Gravel-sized rocks crunched into the dirt and against each other. Sand covered the bottoms of hollows and hissed against the undercarriage. The rear tires flung rooster tails of it into the air.

The Lithuanian drove one-handed, like he took a Sunday drive. He barely glanced at the nav display mounted in the dashboard.

Alpha Centauri B squatted on the horizon like a squished egg yolk. The star's rays overpowered the running lights on the off-roader. Going to be a hot day.

Only McIlroy's formations resisted the growing light and heat of Alpha Centauri B. Most of them rose ten to fifteen feet above rocky outcroppings in the red desert, spaced about twice as far apart. Not as thick as a forest but denser than a savannah. A few jutted farther, up wind-scoured spires of rock. The sandy bottomlands held none of the formations.

A breeze skittered grains over the surface. Like slow-motion waves on a sandy ocean.

A shudder went across Jaeger's shoulders. Just how old were the formations, anyway?

They'd find out in good time. With hard data, not hunches.

The tree metaphor held up to a closer look. Thick trunks spread into fractal branches that seemed to have flowed through the air before solidifying. Though no tree could be so uniformly and deeply black. Jaeger had to be careful how long he looked at any one formation. The contrast between a light-absorbing formation and the desert landscape behind it, red and rocky, dusty and shimmering with heat, threatened to combine with the low oxygen content to give him a headache.

Jaeger gulped altitude sickness meds and chased them with a swig of water. He patted his pockets for his sunglasses. And cursed when he found none.

At least this sun pumped out less ultraviolet and couldn't give them a sunburn.

Ulanovas squeezed the brake pedal at a patch of rock no different than any other. The first seismic thumper deployment site.

Between the meds and thirty seconds spent holding a mask over his mouth, Jaeger was ready to go.

And he was ready at the next one, and the one after that. Park, climb out, wrestle a solar-powered barrel into position. Make sure the piston aimed downward, to drum the ground.

He caught his breath and chugged water while Ingvarsson checked the thumper's battery charge and radio connectivity. She'd trained on these tasks upstairs, all the while apologizing for being a psychologist and a linguist, and lacking a knack for this work. But the training paid off. The unit's test sent a faint thud through his boots, then the piston ratcheted back to the top, cocking for live fire.

"Just a few more," McIlroy said as they climbed into the off-roader with him.

Jaeger lost count of how many made a *few*. Drive a mile. Radio status to d'Arbaud and Feng. Repeat.

The morning dragged on. From the low angle of Alpha Centauri B in the eastern sky, Jaeger knew in his bones they'd been out only an hour when they stopped for lunch, but the clock said six hours had passed. Human circadian rhythms hadn't evolved for a world of ninety-hour days.

The day had already gotten hot, sucking sweat from his body and gluing his shirt to the small of his back. They sat under the fabric roof, eating sandwiches of extruded starch, synthetic meat, and hydroponic lettuce, talking little. Wind stirred sand across the alien landscape. No other motion. No sign of life.

Making a joke felt laborious, but Jaeger tried anyway. To Ulanovas, he said, "Maybe they saw us coming and are staying hidden."

"We got to prove our worthiness," Ulanovas said, "before they will reveal themselves."

Ingvarsson squinted at him. "Did we not do so by crossing four light-years to get here?"

Ulanovas kept a serious expression on his broad face. "There must be animals in the galaxy capable of interstellar travel. Remember, some of the Nazca glyphs are of birds."

A snort from McIlroy. A buzzing high in the blue sky cut off the banter. The drone, surface mapping complete, homing in on them to swap parts. It descended. Jaeger coughed around a cloud of red dust and pulled the wrapper tighter around his sandwich.

Even before the drone landed, Ulanovas hurried to the front trailer and pulled out the ground-penetrating radar unit. A few deft moves, a couple of loud clicks, and the drone took back to the air with its new tool.

"Okay, folks," McIlroy said. He scratched at his brown beard. "Break's over."

Another six hours and they deployed the last of the seismic thumpers and the trio of seismographs around the region. Alpha Centauri B, as fat as Sol seen from Earth, hung about a quarter of the way up the sky.

After placing the last thumper on the hard-packed ground, he stepped back. Even though he shaded his eyes with his hand, he still had to squint at McIlroy. "Do you want to gather the seismic data now or wait till we get back to the tent?"

"Now. If we have to troubleshoot something, we're closer here to the problem site. And we have more time to crunch the data before the next sleep shift." McIlroy held up a hand.

Jaeger fell silent. The other two did the same. No one wanted to break the geologist's concentration. He tapped and swiped the thin, hot air.

The thud from the nearest one carried through Jaeger's boots. But the one he felt was less important than the ones he didn't. Twenty thumpers, sending vibrations through the ground to the three seismographs, and somehow McIlroy's software would extract an image from it.

The thud repeated.

"We're done for this shift," McIlroy said. He gestured for Ingvarsson and Jaeger to board the off-roader before him.

Although the seismic mapping continued on automatic, even after Ulanovas drove them back to camp and parked them in the shade of the open-walled garage tent, they still had tasks to do. Ulanovas connected the off-roader to the recharging cable connected to the polywell reactor, then retrieved the drone. The rest emptied trash, stowed tools, washed off dust in the lukewarm trickle of water allotted to each of them in the shower and restroom tents.

The sun in his eyes told Jaeger it was still morning, but his weary arms made it feel like the evening the clock insisted it was.

Finally, hands clean and the tent walls and roof increasing opacity to keep the sleeping chambers cool and dark for the sleep shift, they assembled around the coffee table in the sitting area.

It felt good to sit and breathe hyperoxic air. The microwave hummed. The scent of plant protein burgers and starch fries filled Jaeger's nose. His mouth watered and, even better, he hadn't lifted a finger to prep the food. Or unscrew the plastic bottle of pinot noir and pour a cup of the fruity, pale red wine.

He took the cup from d'Arbaud. "Thanks," he said, with a polite smile.

Marie hunched her shoulders. She pressed her thin lips together and turned back to the microwave.

The wine added to Jaeger's relaxed feeling. Conversation turned to recapping everyone's shift. As d'Arbaud spoke about her shift studying local bacteria for heat- and drought-adaptations, Jaeger lost track of details. But her animated demeanor made clear her mood. First time she'd seemed upbeat in a long time. Seeing his teammate productive and happy warmed Jaeger's belly.

McIlroy shot up his hand. A grin pried apart his beard and mustache. "Pardon the interruption. We have mapping results."

The drowsy edge to Jaeger's warm feeling vanished. Eyes wide, he leaned forward. "Show us," he said. The others echoed his sentiment.

"Sending to everyone now."

Jaeger's wearable projected a 3d image into the air above the table. A cube, mostly gray emptiness, about a yard on a side. Inside the emptiness, blue-white lines marked out chambers and corridors. Red lines ran along them like arteries in an anatomical model.

He craned his neck, trying to see more. Two levels, maybe three?

Ingvarsson angled her head, exposing her long throat. Feng lifted his baseball cap by the bill and ran his fingers through his hair while he looked from a different angle.

"I'll set it to rotate around the vertical axis," McIlroy said. "Tell me what you see."

The image spun slowly. Jaeger's gaze danced from point to point. The highest level had one huge rectangular area, fifty yards by thirty according to a scale projected at the bottom of the image, and edged with sharp lines. In its interior, though, fifteen or twenty streaks of bluish fuzz ran parallel to one another across the entire width.

"Are those streaks in the big upper room real, or a glitch in the algorithm's output?" Jaeger asked.

"That's not a typical error pattern," McIlroy said.

"You mean, those streaks are real?" d'Arbaud said.

"That's my first guess."

Ulanovas brushed a lank lock of hair from his eyes. "Of course they're real. They're spaced apart like the timber platforms in the pit at Oak Island."

McIlroy scratched his beard and gave the Lithuanian a jaundiced look. "They might be internal walls that partially collapsed. I'll crunch the raw data with a better but slower algorithm over our sleep shift. That way we don't have to talk through our hats."

The highest level of the alien facility included a corridor running from near one corner of the rectangular area. The corridor, six yards wide, branched into narrower hallways. Small chambers budded off the hallways. The red lines split apart like capillaries going to cells, one going to each of the small chambers.

"If you're wondering," McIlroy said, "the red lines are metal of high purity, compared to the rock they run through."

"Cables?" asked Feng in his accented, nasal voice.

McIlroy nodded. "The red lines trace back to a nexus near the surface. From there, more red lines branch out to connect each of the energy-absorbing formations."

Ulanovas said, "That's how they power their base."

"Or powered. Past tense," Jaeger said.

"Keep looking," McIlroy said, like a teacher reasserting control of his class.

The virtual cube rotated a new feature toward Jaeger. In the corner of the rectangular area nearest the corridor, white and blue jumbled a patch of floor about fifteen feet across. The distortion might be the top of a rubble plug about ten yards high.

Below the distortion plug, the lines blurred. Did a shaft run straight down? Did another run horizontally? And how many hallways and chambers branched off that horizontal shaft?

"Will your better algorithm resolve the lower parts?" Jaeger asked.

"It will improve, but don't expect perfect."

Ingvarsson rubbed the side of her nose. "Might the lower level be natural features?"

Jaeger's eyes widened. He cracked his knuckles, one finger at a time, his pent-up energy going to ground. "No."

She raised an eyebrow at him—maybe she learned that expression of silent admonishment at psych school—then turned her brown eyes to McIlroy. "What does a *geologist* think?"

"I think Jaeger noticed *this*." McIlroy shoved his palm at the air. The rotation stopped. Then he traced a veiny hand along a thick red bundle. It branched off the main trunk near the large rectangular area, then ran down past the distortion plug. It spread out from there. The ends got lost in the area of blurry lines.

"Oh, cables," Ingvarsson said.

"Not just cables." Feng grabbed the bill and rotated his ball cap back and forth. The Chinese characters on the cap changed color from green to blue as he fidgeted. Lenticular, was that the word? "Thick cables."

Much thicker than the ones to the rooms on the upper level. The thicker the cable, the more current it could carry.

Whatever lay below the distortion plug used a hell of a lot of power.

Whatever lay below the distortion plug could benefit all mankind.

Or whichever faction could seize it for itself.

He stole a glance at McIlroy. The Humanist absently ran his fingers through his beard under his lower jaw, which made his chin more prominent than usual. His face showed no guile.

McIlroy didn't show guile before he overthrew your control of a dominant empire and won an UltraHistory game, either.

"Keep looking, y'all," McIlroy said. He gestured in the air. The virtual cube rotated.

Jaeger's gaze roved the lower level smear. An alien structure, full of wonders.

The warmth of wine and hot food spread from his belly up his chest. Wonders, a boon for all mankind. Ready to explore....

If they could get in.

From the rectangular area, he looked up. Obvious, now. A helical shaft spiraled from one end of the rectangular area, like a wide spring with a gentle pitch. Easy enough to walk down. Maybe even drive, if Ulanovas would ride the brake most of the way down.

The helical shaft rose from the end opposite both the corridor to the small rooms and the cylindrical plug in the floor. From the bottom of the shaft, the streaks of distortion across the rectangular area might block their progress, like the rows of blocks in a brick-buster video game.

But that wasn't the only thing blocking their progress.

Where was the top of the shaft?

"That shaft must be the way in," Ulanovas said. "But where's the top?"

"I'll zoom in." McIlroy gestured at the air.

The view enlarged the helical shaft. The bottom scrolled out of the cube. The top slid into view and down about halfway. An upright mass of solid red covered the mouth of the shaft. Blank and mostly transparent gray surrounded the shaft and rose up with the vertical red area. Above the shaft, the color turned fainter and grainy.

The bite of plant protein in Jaeger's mouth turned chalky. "That grainy area isn't air, is it?"

"Sand," McIlroy said. "About sixty meters of it."

Dammit. Jaeger swallowed his food around a groan, part of a chorus coming from the others. Two hundred feet of sand? How could they dig down far enough to reach the entrance?

A chill crept up his legs. Two hundred feet of sand.

"How long would it take that much sand to pile up?" he asked.

McIlroy scratched his beard. His face scrunched around his eyes. "We don't know enough about Bravo Charlie's atmospheric and geologic processes for me to give y'all a good answer."

"We'll take a wild-ass guess."

"A hundred thousand years? Ten million? Somewhere in that range."

Ulanovas whistled. Marie d'Arbaud's eyebrows arched.

Jaeger sagged back in his chair. He sluffed out a breath.

A million years, give or take. Around the time his ancestors mastered fire, aliens dug this base out of rock. Maybe after traveling light-years from their native world.

Why?

Jaeger's mouth fell open in a rapt grin. Varanathan's schemes, and all the plots of the Coalition leadership in St. Petersburg, didn't mean a damn right then.

The greatest discovery in the history of mankind. His team would explore it.

After they figured out a way to get in.

CHAPTER 6

16 APRIL 2127 (EARTH REFERENCE FRAME) | 17 JUNE 2125
(CONCORDIA REFERENCE FRAME)

THEY CALLED in a one-way pod from *Concordia* with a second fabricator. Warning chimes through their earbuds and flashing red lights in their vision heralded its descent through the atmosphere. One of the pod's maneuvering rotors crapped out.

Everyone's stomach flopped like a fish in a boat as it streaked down the deep blue sky. They exhaled gasping breaths when the droge chute opened, a tiny cup of circus pinwheel colors... then muttered mild curses as the pod drifted the wrong way on a stiff wind.

Jaeger rode as Feng drove eight miles beyond the target zone to the pod's landing place, halfway to the anomalous lava bed McIlroy mentioned from time to time. Half Jaeger's height, the pod had a teardrop shape, half-buried in the sand. Despite scorching, the pod's heat shield held up. Through thick, heatproof gloves, under Alpha

Centauri B's afternoon rays, the two men wrangled the pod out of its landing place.

McIlroy, watching remotely through their head-mounted cameras, said over the radio, "That's a job for Paul Bunyan's sand wedge."

Feng pulled his ball cap down toward his eyes, but made no comment. Maybe Humanists didn't hate golf as much as Coalition propaganda said they did? Or else Feng wouldn't criticize others to avoid getting tarred with the crimes of the old Chinese regime. On the Trad side, Tsai had held his tongue dozens of times on the trip out....

Jaeger stood tall to stretch his back. Sweat trickled down his neck. A rocky ridge, too steep to drive up, plus jumbled with boulders, rose half a mile away. "At least it didn't land up there."

They heaved the pod into the trailer behind their off-roader. They drove back, saying little. Jaeger's breath roared in his ears. Ulanovas, listening in, made a crack over the radio. "You should play basketball with me on the sports court." A zone of packed and congealed sand at the edge of the station, just past the latrine. "Get your wind up."

"You promise to spare me any hot air about ancient aliens? Thought not."

Jaeger watched Feng in profile. He breathed hard too and had done his share of sweating—salt splotched the side of his baseball cap —and hadn't complained.

He never complained. Not about the work. Not about the wary looks he sometimes got, or the whispers behind his back. All for crimes committed by a handful of Chinese men of his grandfather's generation who believed themselves fit to remake the world. Three broken eggs are an omelet. A million broken eggs are a statistic.

"Thanks for helping," Jaeger said. "Driving, too."

"I do my job." One-handed, Feng scratched his scalp through the crown of his cap. "What do you think we'll find?"

A sand grain rolled against Jaeger's front teeth. He shoved it with his tongue and puffed air out of his mouth to expel it. "You don't mean in the pod?"

"No, underground."

Jaeger squinted. Of course Feng must be curious about the alien facility. Like the other five of them. But did Feng ask for himself, or for Sandford?

"No idea," Jaeger said. "I'm trying to keep an open mind."

As soon as the words left his mouth, a nugget of guilt lodged in his gut. He never viewed McIlroy or Ingvarsson with distrust when they speculated about the alien facility.

This wasn't an UltraHistory game. Treat everyone as a friend until they show themselves to be an enemy.

Their off-roader topped a low rocky slope. Atop the next rise, a quarter of a mile away, the tent showed taut plastic and the dark gray of solar film across its low-pitched roof. Behind it stood the legion of support equipment. A shimmering column of deep blue sky marked waste heat from the polywell reactor.

They drove up the slope and around the tent. Feng slowed more than Ulanovas would have when they drove over the rigid slabs of black-and-yellow plastic covering the power cables. The heavy equipment lay in neat rows across the desolate ground. Automated machinery hummed and chugged. The antenna transmitting telemetry from their wearables and data from their discoveries pointed a few degrees south of the zenith, toward the nearest of *Concordia*'s comsats riding in synchronous orbit.

The fracking sites his grandfather had worked on as a young man might have looked like this.

Feng parked next to a canopy, where McIlroy and Ulanovas waited. They left the pod on the trailer and popped off the cargo lid. The alloy sheet wobbled in Jaeger's hands, astonishingly thin for something dropped out of orbit and surviving atmospheric entry.

The cargo inside looked intact at first glance. A pouch the size of a military backpack held a bundle bound together by hook-and-loop fabric straps. McIlroy carried the bundle to a patch of bare dirt in front of the off-roader. He opened the straps, *scritch scritch scritch.*

The bundle popped open, into a ring ten feet across. When looked at from up close, the ring had a D-shaped cross-section.

McIlroy squinted at an ultrafine mesh on the flat, inward face of the ring. "Looks intact," he said.

Ulanovas brushed sandy-blond hair from his eyes, then reached into the pouch for a collapsible fluid line. Even after it expanded, the outer diameter would only reach a quarter of an inch, but the line's length was over five hundred yards.

The Lithuanian set the collapsed line on a worktable under the canopy. He next pulled out a twin line. After that, he drew from the pouch the field fabricator. He moved it with easy flexes of his ropy arms. A hard plastic shell the size of a briefcase.

So small an object to cause such huge arguments in the crew forum. Amundsen and leaders of the other teams protested the xenologists' proposed use of nanotech. Earth biology couldn't outcompete life evolved for Bravo Charlie, but a nano core built to turn atmospheric CO_2 into an alloy of carbon nanotubes and diamondoid could do a hell of a lot of damage, if ten things failed in a particular cascade.

But there was no other way for the xenologists to reach the buried facility. Sandford and Varanathan agreed. They rejected Amundsen's arguments with high-minded words about the importance of exploring the buried base.

For the good of all mankind, of course.

The vast majority of the crew, good scientists all, believed them.

Jaeger peered at McIlroy, standing in sunlight, running his fingernails through his brown beard while his gaze slowly tracked the ring at his feet. Unease gnawed at Jaeger's stomach.

Did McIlroy work for the good of all mankind?

Even if he did now, what alien discovery might make him change his mind?

For the next month, they tunneled their way to the alien facility, sixteen inches per hour.

First, they laid the ring on the sand over three hundred yards from the buried entrance. Next, they hooked up the collapsed lines, one end of each to the ring, the other to the field fabricator. They deployed every solar panel and spare battery they could scrounge from the camp site and *Gagarin*'s cargo hold to power the fabricator.

The nano core synthesized a slurry of nanotubes and diamondoid, then pumped them down one line. The ring's CPU, so small it made no bulge on the ring body, channeled the slurry out the mesh to crystallize into the final alloy. The result was a rigid tube, growing and pushing the ring into the sand, like the open mouth of a snake made of solidified gray smoke. The CPU adjusted the flow to be higher or lower out different parts of the ring to steer it toward the alien facility's entrance.

Nano formed the wall of the tunnel. But it couldn't do anything about the tons of sand inside it.

For that, the main fab at the camp site spat out a collapsible dumpster and shovels.

A low-friction material coated the dumpster's bottom, a wired remote allowed the driver of the off-roader to open the back gate, and acclimation to the atmosphere's low O_2 content along with the planet's point-eight g made each shovel load a little lighter than Jaeger had first dreaded. Still, Jaeger and McIlroy spent most of their daylight shifts flinging sand into the dumpster. They got only five minutes at a time to guzzle water and suck wind in the off-roader's passenger seats, each time Feng or Ulanovas towed the dumpster to the dump site, ease up the loose sand slope, open the rear gate, and return.

Jaeger savored every second of each ride, until the machinery around the tunnel mouth came into view.

The driver turned the off-roader around and backed into the tunnel. One last glimpse of their campsite on its higher ground, and the top of the tin-can shape of *Gagarin* shimmering in the desert heat a half mile beyond that. Then the tunnel mouth cut the intense desert sunlight like a knife, plunging his elbow into a shadow that made his eyes clamor for light.

The bright glow from the tunnel's mouth shrank every second. Jaeger looked away, or else the tunnel would seem to be constricting between them and the surface. He tried not to think about the thousands of tons of sand above his head, held back only by a quarter-inch thickness of alloyed diamondoid and nanotube.

Occasionally, one of them would hop out with a backpack-sized tank of fixative and spray the sand remaining on the tunnel floor to maintain a flat, packed surface for the knobby tires. But even the maintenance work provided scant respite. Mostly, they descended, deeper and deeper, on a straight line into darkness. The work lights mounted on the back corners of the dumpster failed to widen the vista. If anything, they emphasized the claustrophobia of the tunnel.

Jaeger's shoulders hunched more and more, until the driver braked at the working face of the tunnel, and their labor crowded out everything else. Scoop, fling, repeat, despite the growing ache in his arms.

"At least we can skip our weight training this month," McIlroy said.

Thirty-three Earth-standard days, actually, passed before, on their eighteenth shift in the tunnel, Jaeger scraped his plastic shovel into the sand and hit something hard.

"The front door," McIlroy said. "Right where we mapped it."

Jaeger's heart slammed. After working so hard for so long, it seemed impossible the tunnel excavation could be over. "I'll believe it when I see it."

They shoveled harder, with help from Ulanovas. Even Ingvarsson managed to get a couple of shovelfuls out of the way without spilling much.

Sand slumped down from the tunnel ceiling, exposing a shadowed surface that became more and more clear with each toss into the dumpster.

A few minutes later, Jaeger believed.

A metallic wall stood before them. It filled the view granted by the ring and expanded beyond it on all sides. Gray metal, dull despite the glow of the work lights. Three seams lined out the top and sides of a square about five feet by five. The sand and nanotube wall at the bottom of the tunnel obscured the bottom of the square. Other than that, no features were apparent.

An inscrutable slab of metal. Put in place by hands—by *appendages*—unknown and buried by the desert for millennia. Or megayears.

McIlroy rapped his knuckles on it. A *bong* sounded so low Jaeger barely heard it. "Not too thick. And there's an atmosphere behind it."

"Whether we can breathe it, we don't know," Jaeger said.

A nod. McIlroy traced his fingertips across the metal. "Rough surface. How long has it gotten a slow-motion sandblasting?"

"Is that the important question?" Ingvarsson asked. "Is that a door?"

McIlroy ran his fingers down one of the seams. "I'm sure it is." He turned to them with a raised eyebrow. "Anyone got any idea how to open it?"

They spent the rest of that shift and all of the next studying the metallic wall. X-rays, ultrasound, reflection, refraction. McIlroy worked a rotary tool with a diamond-tipped coring attachment like a jeweler. The tool's motor whined for long minutes to give him three samples of about a gram each.

Jaeger wedged a knife into a side seam. Wiggling the knife snapped the blade into two jagged pieces, one jutting out. "Sorry, guys," he said. To McIlroy, he added, "Do you have a grinding tip for your rotary tool?"

He did. He swapped tips and handed the tool to Jaeger. "Careful with it."

"I will." Jaeger held the rotary tool and touched the grinding tip to the wedged chunk of the knife blade sticking out of the wall. Steel dust, orange and hot, streamed away. The broken knife blade barely resisted the tool. The proverbial hot knife through butter—

The grinding tip touched the metallic wall. The tool kicked back and almost flew from his grip.

"Need me to finish up?" McIlroy asked around a grin.

"I got it," Jaeger said. "What's this wall made of?"

"We'll find out later."

Jaeger finished blunting the broken knife edge. Ingvarsson's long fingers pressed the surface for hidden buttons or sensors, and found none. Meanwhile, Ulanovas brushed his dirty-blond hair from his eyes and took high-magnification photos of every square inch of the wall. The floodlight on his camera reflected off his broad face and the Swedish woman's high cheekbones.

Back at the tent, late that wake shift, dinner tasted better than it had in a month. Not just because Jaeger decided he'd never lift a shovel again in his life. Marie d'Arbaud coaxed extra flavor from a sous vide bag of carrot-, onion-, and beef-like extruded food, thanks to chives and basil snipped from an herb garden set up near the science tent. She also revealed her latest culinary experiment, a baguette of glutinous starch baked on the waste heat radiator of the polywell reactor. "When you radioed you had finished the tunnel, I thought we deserved a special meal."

Feng adjusted his baseball cap by the brim. "She thinks I can't run the microwave well."

Everyone laughed, Marie included. She even gave Feng a smile that squeezed the usual sadness out of her soft eyes.

"Every expedition should have a French person," McIlroy said with a smile.

She raised her chin, a teasing mirror of his common expression. "That's *Provençal* to you, *cavaller*."

The warm mood persisted over red wine and hot fresh bread. They worked through dinner, under photographs and pages of data projected over the table. Jaeger couldn't think of the time as work. They played a cooperative game, like some UltraHistory variant where all the peoples of Earth won or lost together as a team.

A challenging game, with a simple goal.

Open the door.

A door with no lock. No key. No instructions for entry.

If the builders had printed any message on the metallic wall, the slow grind of sand particles erased them. A lot of erosion could happen in one-point-four million years—McIlroy's estimate from the hardness of the alloy, the thickness of its skim of rust, and extrapolations from terrestrial geology. Even laser lines etched into the slab couldn't survive that long.

"We could transmit a message," Ulanovas said. "The first hundred octal digits of *pi*. Or *e*. If there are multiple receivers down there, we are close enough they can triangulate our signal source and discover we have landed. Then they will open up."

"Possibly," Jaeger said, "but there's a catch. There's no power to the door." He called up the 3d map. The lines suggestive of power cables, as red as the tart wine he sipped, did not reach the metallic slab.

"Hydraulics?" asked Feng. "Pneumatics?"

"We would see machinery for those as well, wouldn't we?" said Ingvarsson.

Marie d'Arbaud frowned. "Could the door be simply set into place? After all, the ancient Egyptians placed the stones of the Pyramids together as precisely as the aliens sealed up this door."

"Of course!" Ulanovas nodded, mouth open in a grin. "The ancient Egyptians had help from the aliens' levitation beams." He grinned preemptively at the ensuing chorus of groans.

McIlroy waved his baguette like a conductor's baton at Ulanovas. "Setting aside foolish speculation, there's a practical problem, Dr. d'Arbaud. From our subsurface mapping, the door is the only way in. If the aliens set it in place, that means they shut themselves in. They buried themselves in their own tomb. There's no reason intelligent beings would commit suicide."

A bleak look came to d'Arbaud's soft eyes. "Isn't there?"

The mood around the table chilled. Jaeger peered at d'Arbaud.

Her next words sounded matter-of-fact, but brittle. "Perhaps they ran out of reasons to live."

CHAPTER 7

ALPHA CENTAURI B SYSTEM | BRAVO CHARLIE | GAGARIN STATION

22 MAY 2127 (EARTH REFERENCE FRAME) | 23 JULY 2125
(CONCORDIA REFERENCE FRAME)

IN THE TUNNEL the next daylight work shift, Marie d'Arbaud's eyes had the same look. Though it might be a trick of the off-roader headlights' reflections and the plastic covering her face. She wore safety goggles over her soft brown eyes. An oxygen mask covered her mouth and nose. The ear loops trapped wisps of gray-streaked brown hair escaping from her bun. A rippled tube ran over her cheek to the combo O_2 tank and CO_2 scrubber strapped on her back.

They sat in the off-roader, not moving, Feng's hands loose on the wheel.

Next to Feng, Jaeger's breaths echoed in his own mask. "Ready?" he asked.

The Chinese man tugged his ball cap a little farther down his face. "Ready." His mask muffled his voice. He tightened his grip on the steering wheel.

The off-roader eased forward. A rubbery bumper the size of a round ottoman jutted from the front. Feng and Ulanovas had fabbed the bumper and mounted it during the previous shift, working by stand lights in Bravo Charlie's long night. Overhearing them work together, Jaeger learned new obscenities in Lithuanian and Chinese.

While they worked, a gentle bonging sound in Jaeger's right ear told him he'd gotten a text message. Then he saw who sent it and his chest tightened. Varanathan.

Steps into the chill desert night. He read. *I have enjoyed the chance to educate you about the Hindu faith. Do you have a better understanding of the concept of* dharma* yet?*

Jaeger clamped his lips together. Plain what Varanathan meant. Have you learned anything about the aliens' legacy?

His fingers tapped a reply on the thighs of his cargo pants. His wearable interpreted the motions as touch typing on a virtual keyboard.

I know little, and no more than anyone else.

He told his wearable to send the message. It should buy him some days free of the co-commander's nagging. Still, he hurried off to the others, eager to lose himself in work.

Of which there was plenty, fabbing airtight plastic walls and an oxygen-removal pump, to create a bubble of nitrogenous ambient at the working face of the tunnel. Inert. The bubble served a double purpose: to dilute any airborne contaminants behind the door, and to protect the contents of the alien facility from oxygen, if need be.

The headlight reflections on the dull alloy narrowed, focused. The bumper touched the door. The reverberation brought Jaeger fully back to the present.

Feng fed power to the wheels. They tossed up chunks of sand. Adhered sand clumps clunked inside the wheel wells. The off-roader's electric motor whined.

Feng pushed the pedal down harder. The motor keened. The wheels spattered sand up the tunnel.

Jaeger's chest tightened. A month's labor, for nothing?

A shriek came from the metallic slab.

"We push it!" Feng said. "Two millimeters!"

"Good job!" Marie d'Arbaud sounded pleased.

McIlroy fidgeted with the straps on his mask. "It's a far sight thicker than that," he said.

Indeed. A digital readout, projected into the top of Jaeger's vision, claimed the off-roader had pushed the door two millimeters and change, climbing a fraction every second. But the seams looked as tight as ever, from his seat in the vehicle.

Feng clutched the steering wheel in his hands. The wheels kept spinning. Metal groaned and roared. Alloy surfaces scraping over each other that loudly should be generating sparks, but none went flying.

Another push. Almost a centimeter, now. Shadows widened along the door frame. Gas detectors, mounted on the wall before they pushed the door in, extended their mechanical noses over the growing space.

The plan, though brute force, worked.

So far. Murphy's Law could kick in any moment—

The off-roader lurched forward. The metallic wall rushed at Jaeger's head. He ducked. Late. The wall above the opening would've brained him, if not for the front of the roll cage clanking against the wall. The rear wheels kicked up. Feng jammed the brake pedal. The headlights played crazily, over growing darkness, angling, tilting metal—

WHOOM. The door slab thundered like a single note plucked on an electric bass turned up to eleven. The sound died out quickly, swallowed by the vast facility ahead and below.

Jaeger slid down in his seat and bent to his left. The slab lay on a flat area of the spiral ramp, surrounded by motes of dust dancing for the first time in a million years. Beyond the slab, the floor slanted down and curled to the left.

Air from inside the tunnel pushed on his cheeks. His face broke into a wide smile. "We're in," he said. "We're in!"

"What's the air like in there?" McIlroy said.

Feng nodded. "Can we take off these masks?"

Jaeger called up the feed from the gas detectors. "Slight overpressure relative to Bravo Charlie ambient. One-point-one atmospheres. Nothing poisonous. Nitrogen 99.34%. Traces of CO_2, argon, helium. Water, oxygen, too low to detect." Their recent dinner conversation came back to him. "If they were life as we know it, they didn't survive in there."

"They could have left robots," Feng said. His voice grew even more nasal than usual. "They could *be* robots. Without water and oxygen, metal could not rust. But now that we are in, the metal will not rust in the months we have to explore. Let us pump in air and take off our masks."

"No," said d'Arbaud. "I agree the masks are uncomfortable, but we must keep them on. For now."

"Why?" McIlroy asked the question with a tone that he already knew the answer.

"Metal may not rust much in a year. But biological samples could rot to uselessness long before."

"Biological samples." McIlroy jutted his chin at her. "Anaerobic life forms? Alien corpses? Could they survive one-point-four megayears?"

"I don't know. The air is dry and inert, like the deserts of ancient Egypt that preserved mummies for millennia."

"A thousandth of the time the slab sealed this space," McIlroy said.

"If there is no light, especially not ultraviolet, another source of sample damage is removed. Perhaps it is enough for samples to survive." Marie d'Arbaud shrugged.

Jaeger cleared his throat. "Even if none have survived, we can't take the chance of contaminating or damaging any samples until we know. What could samples tell us, Marie?"

"First, whether the builders came from Bravo Charlie, or elsewhere."

And if they came from elsewhere, their technology had been at least as advanced as Earth's. If not more so.

Jaeger stole a glance over his headrest at McIlroy on the back seat. The Humanist geologist gave him a friendly look. Like he had a dozen times at the UltraHistory table before playing the card to steal control of a mighty empire from someone else.

"Looks like we're agreed," McIlroy said.

"Agreed?"

"We preserve the nitrogen atmosphere down here and work with masks."

"Yes, yes." Guilt needled Jaeger. Just because McIlroy back-stabbed in the game didn't mean he hid a real-life knife. "Exactly."

Feng lowered his large eyes to gaze at his feet. "You are right, sirs. We leave on our masks."

Jaeger checked the O_2 levels telemetered from their tanks. The off-roader couldn't fit through the opening, but they carried enough air to walk in.

Wheeled robots and small drones would do most of the exploring. Safer. More sensible. But damn right men and women were going to tread and touch surfaces sealed up for over a million years.

"Back us up," he said.

Feng eased the off-roader back ten feet. The airtight plastic sheet behind them looked tight, its last wrinkles flattened by the overpressure from within.

Jaeger reached for the top of the door frame. "I read that we can breathe thirty-three minutes of air before we have to turn around. Who wants to take a look?" He climbed out before anyone could reply.

The rest followed. Marie retrieved from the off-roader's cargo bed four shape-memory hardhats, packed mostly flat. Battery pack, headlamp, camera, microphone, hours of recording time.

Recordings that would go straight upstairs. Nothing they found here could be kept secret from the Humanists, no matter how many of the people now gathered here Jaeger could kill.

He couldn't be expected to keep any facts secret. That would be his defense if Varanathan called him on the carpet. Then he suddenly realized, with a chill across his shoulders, only a physicist might recognize some things as being valuable.

He was the only physicist here.

Jaeger snapped open his hardhat and put it on. He turned the cinch knob until the hardhat squeezed his forehead. Feng took off his ball cap with a sigh and put on his hardhat in its place. Everyone synced to wearables, tested recordings.

Four pale beams danced over the fallen slab and the walls of the shaft.

Twenty-nine minutes to go.

The opening was barely five feet wide. Though technically a square, the rutted mass of sand at the bottom of the tunnel made it even shorter than that.

Jaeger beckoned for McIlroy to go first. He crouched and went second. A clump of cross-linked sand flaked onto the bottom of the opening and into the shaft. Behind him came d'Arbaud, then Feng.

The shaft maintained the square cross-section, five feet by five. Impossible to stand up. Jaeger bent his neck forward to avoid the low ceiling. McIlroy bent at the knees.

"Looks like they were short," Jaeger said.

The stone walls gave McIlroy's voice a harsh echo. "Or they saved energy by excavating a tunnel just big enough for their needs." He trudged forward.

"They might have had the energy sources to travel light-years, but they saved on their electric bills after they got here?" Halfway through the words, Jaeger cursed himself. He forced a light tone into his voice.

You can keep high-energy physics a secret if you don't talk about it.

Marie d'Arbaud spoke. "We don't yet know where they came from. And energy always costs, even if the cost is minimal."

"And we don't know how they think," said McIlroy over his shoulder.

Jaeger swallowed around a dry throat. True. People barely knew how one another thought. Brains evolved for a different planet?

He straightened his back until his hardhat scraped on the tunnel ceiling. Pah. They didn't know how the aliens thought *yet*.

They spiraled down into the rock. Their headlamps cast bright reflections on the smooth ceiling inches in front of them. Though gentle, the slope would make them breathe harder on the way up. "We should budget more air for the return."

McIlroy's fingers trailed over the rock wall. He muttered something to himself before turning. "More air? Oh, turn around earlier than we planned? Good idea."

"I should have guessed rock would catch a geologist's attention."

"Old habits." With a sheepish grin through his beard, McIlroy pulled his hand back to his side.

After a few more turns, the spiral straightened and leveled off. The bright reflections off the ceiling faded. Their headlamp beams passed into an opening into the large rectangular area expected from the mapping.

Expected, but not like this.

Jaeger's heart hammered. He dropped to both knees on the stone floor just outside the opening. To get a better view, yes, but struck with awe.

"We know what those smears on the seismic scan are now," he said.

McIlroy nodded. Feng and d'Arbaud came closer and squatted behind Jaeger. No one spoke. All eyes tracked over the sight in front of them.

A solid wall, about five feet high and no telling how thick, rose about seven or eight feet in from the opening. The wall didn't quite reach the ceiling. Glances into the space, side to side, showed it went from one side of the rectangular area, about five yards to their left, most of the way to a shadowed end twenty-five yards to the right.

The wall was not stone. In their headlamp beams glimmered a deep gray, polished alloy. Thick vertical lines separated the wall into about fifty panels. Short etched lines, some straight, some curved, all of uniform width and depth, marched down the panels like columns of dutiful soldiers, broken up by artful shapes rich with textured edges and internal shadows.

Jaeger rose on his tiptoes. Visible through the narrow gap between the top panel and the low stone ceiling, more alloy walls glimmered until the depths of the stone chamber smothered his beam.

A hunch came to him. He drew in a deep oxygenated breath while blood roared in his ears. He rose to his feet, then went to the alloy panel in front of him.

His fingertips traced the lines in the cold metallic surface. In that moment, he *knew*. Words. Images. Ordered in metal by unknown appendages over a million years before.

"They didn't build this for themselves," he said. "They built it for us."

CHAPTER 8

26 MAY 2127 (EARTH REFERENCE FRAME) | 27 JULY 2125
(CONCORDIA REFERENCE FRAME)

THEY NEEDED three shifts to map out the rectangular area, the rooms off the far corridor, and the top of the rubble plug. Battery-powered robots did most of the work, blithely ignoring the unbreathable air inside the facility, while Jaeger and McIlroy monitored from the seats of an off-roader parked on the surface. Both the sweltering brightness of the desert day and the chilly, cloudless night spangled with distant stars and the tiny ball of Alpha Centauri A seemed less real than the data streaming up from the alien facility.

Nineteen alloy walls ran across the rectangular area. Each wall contained a gap near one end. The gaps through successive walls alternated. Robots could pass the first wall at the right end, the second wall at the left end, and so on. Not like a brick-breaking video game. More like a game Jaeger played as a kid, where the player built a maze of antipersonnel weapons to block the computer's cannon fodder soldiers from making it across the battlefield.

The metaphor quickly fell apart in Jaeger's mind. No weapons here. No hostility to visitors. Instead, 893 panels carved on both sides with many hundreds, in some cases well over a thousand, symbols. Data. Messages, sent by the builders to minds unknown that might find this site someday.

The rectangular area wasn't a maze. It was a library.

He cracked his knuckles and wished the regs allowed the station fabricators to make chewing gum. The frustrated urge to decode the messages made him grind his teeth. The delay made sense, though. Gather all the data they could, then piece it together. He and McIlroy had agreed. Holographic avatars of Varanathan and Sandford, participating in a virtual meeting with the two men, each narrowed their eyes but accepted the decision. At least publicly.

Good job keeping your focus on the mission, Varanathan texted him an hour later. The sarcasm came across without any trouble.

Jaeger frowned, then left the main room to avoid the others. He needed time to think. A few minutes outside, in baking heat, taking deep breaths to pull enough oxygen into his lungs, gave it to him.

If I understand correctly, many can see the signs of dharma, *but very few can see* dharma* itself.*

He hit send. By the time he got back into air conditioning and hyperoxic air, his wearable chimed in his ear. Varanathan's reply was a single emoji, hands pressed together in a prayer or *namaste* gesture.

Tension bled from Jaeger's shoulders. He'd bought some more time to avoid Varanathan's pressure.

He needed more time, in the face of the flood of data. Like an explosion at a jigsaw puzzle factory. The robots imaged each panel at wavelengths ranging from radio to X-ray. If the expedition needed to do further analysis of the alloy panels to read the full messages, they had time. The alloy panels weren't going anywhere.

Neither were the mummified remains they found in a small room off the side corridor.

Two bodies, curled up on a low, misshapen lump of brittle yellowish material. Tiny creatures, maybe two feet tall, with dull green skin free of feathers and hair. Four arms, much longer in proportion than a human's, each ended in two long, triple-jointed fingers.

Back in the tent, amid warm smells of microwaved tortillas and sous vide taco filling, Ulanovas brushed his sandy-blond hair from his ear. "Four arms times two fingers. None of us had that in the betting pool."

Marie d'Arbaud crossed her arms and scowled. "Did you bet on that?" Her scowl swept across the other three men. "Any of you?"

The Lithuanian idly waved his hand. "It is, how is it said in English, a figure of speech?"

Her arms slid a few inches open. "It is still rude," said d'Arbaud. "They were sapient creatures. And they cared for each other, at the end."

The two aliens lay with their arms and tails intertwined and their heads turned to one another. They could have looked into each other's eyes—their front eyes—as they died.

Jaeger lowered his head to his beer glass. Better than how he would probably end up going, he mused.

And maybe the same now held true for d'Arbaud, after her husband moved out of their cabin. Feeling sentimental about the eight-fingered aliens? Better than hating the Humanists after one of their hussies stole her man.

He lifted his gaze. Peered at d'Arbaud, then Ingvarsson and the two Humanist men. No sign she held a grudge against them. But worth keeping an eye on.

"Were they friends or mates?" Ingvarsson said. She took a bite of taco, then opened her mouth and waved at it while her other hand groped for her margarita glass.

"I do not know yet," d'Arbaud said. The video shot by the drone showed both wore matching pants of some crinkly fabric. The material would probably flake apart if touched. "Tissue samples should contain genetic differences, like our X and Y chromosomes. A physical examination would reveal their genitalia and reproductive organs."

Feng, ball cap off for dinner, ran his palm over his slicked, black hair. "How did they die?"

"Suicide." Jaeger said the word quickly and with certitude. He sipped his beer, malty and hoppy, and eyed the others over the rim of the glass.

Ingvarsson sipped her sweet, tart margarita and blinked in surprise. "You Texans have contributed at least one thing to civilization. But what makes you say the aliens committed suicide?" Her cheeks around her birthmark still looked red, hot from her spicy bite.

"They died together." He called up a photo of the alien corpses, zoomed in, pushed it into their shared data space. "If one had died of natural causes and the other crawled into bed when it knew it was dying, the last survivor couldn't pull the other's arms as tightly around it as it did."

Ingvarsson fixed her brown eyes on him. "You assume their limbs are jointed like ours."

Jaeger said, "They have bones." X-rays showed mineral deposits in their limbs, torso, and head.

Ingvarsson tossed her head enough to make her blond ponytail sway into view. "You also assume rigor mortis and other decay proceeded for them like terrestrial life."

"No," said d'Arbaud. "They died together. Mutual suicide best explains it. I feel it in my heart."

With a roll of her brown eyes, Ingvarsson picked up her drink. Ice rattled in her glass.

"Suicide, yes," said Feng. "But how did they suicide?"

McIlroy set down his fork next to his dwindling serving of refried beans. "The answer to that is in the air."

Feng frowned. "I do not know what you mean."

"The air around them. Over 99% nitrogen. If they metabolized carbon compounds to release energy, they required oxygen. Just like a fossil fuel car engine back in the day. Nitrogen is too inert to react with oxygen. If they breathed an oxygenated atmosphere, when they decided to end their lives, they pumped out the O_2 and suffocated themselves."

"Perhaps," d'Arbaud said. "We will find out in time."

Jaeger nodded and leaned forward. "Forget how they committed suicide. The real question is *why?*"

Not from lack of comforts, they guessed. The lumpy pallet the aliens lay upon crumbled when a robot snipped a sample, sending yellowed motes into the thick air. But the material might have been plush memory foam a million years before.

Other rooms off the side corridor held boxes of chrome-like metal and a brittle material, somewhere between plastic and ceramic, in color a mottled light gray. Age might have leached brighter pigment from it. The boxes were proportioned to the aliens' short stature and had arrays of control buttons, knobs, and sliders that might have taken all eight of their thumbs to operate.

Yellowed bedding material lay in most rooms, perhaps used as couches or chairs. Most ceilings had at least one disc mounted in them. The discs, each about three feet wide, sandwiched a cloudy goo above a sheet of a soft material that deformed under gentle pressure and sprung back instead of cracking.

"Those ceiling discs are where we'd put lights," Ingvarsson said.

"According to the subsurface radar robot," McIlroy said, "those discs are wired." He scratched his brown beard. "Though damfino what light-emitting material would degrade into that goop inside them."

Marie d'Arbaud angled her head. "There are photophoric biological molecules on Earth."

Jaeger made a blank face at *photophoric.*

She hurried on. "Like the tail of a firefly."

Jaeger imagined making a ceiling light made from firefly tails and gave up. He shivered, and not from the air conditioning. Just how *alien* were the thoughts once flowing through the builders' brains?

In one chamber, instead of one or two of the discs, the ceiling near the door held nineteen of them, butted together in two concentric circles, the outer of twelve and the inner of six, around one disc in the center. At the back of the room, a metallic pole mounted in both floor and ceiling bore twenty-three jutting beams, from which dangled sheets and strips of plastic and the same fabric as the aliens' clothing. The mild wash of the drone's motors crumbled the edges. Flakes rained like yellow dandruff onto the smooth stone floor and brittle couches ringing the pole.

"What did they do in that room?" Ulanovas picked up a churro from the dessert plate, snapped off a half-inch length, and chewed it. He made a *pah* sound. "Cinnamon." He dropped the rest of the churro on his plate.

Ingvarsson idly rubbed her nose on the side away from the mole on her cheek. "Don't you know?" Her accent was too precise for Jaeger to tell how much she mocked the Lithuanian.

"Whoever these aliens are," Ulanovas said without any sign of offense, "they did not lead humankind from the Stone Age to the Bronze."

"How can you tell?" McIlroy asked. He then mashed his lips together, visible between his beard and mustache. Regretting he engaged with the other's ancient astronaut theories, Jaeger guessed.

"I've studied all the known clues about alien visitors to ancient Earth. None of them had four arms with two fingers each."

"Otherwise you would have won the betting pool," Jaeger said.

Marie d'Arbaud focused an arched eyebrow on him. He laughed. He couldn't help it.

Ulanovas grinned. "Absolutely correct."

McIlroy cleared his throat. "Back to your question. What did the octal aliens do in that chamber? Lots of light, lots of couches, a sculpture like a tree...?"

"A fitness chamber." Jaeger reached for the plate of churros on the table, under the cloud of virtual displays. Scents of hot dough, sugar, and cinnamon danced in his nose.

He drew his hand back, empty. A fitness chamber? Now that he was done shoveling, he needed to resume regular kettlebell workouts and cut back on empty calories.

"A gathering place," said Ingvarsson.

McIlroy rubbed at his beard. "A temple?"

The corners of Jaeger's mouth curled up. He eased back and said, "I didn't know y'all believed in temples."

McIlroy's face turned into a wall as inscrutable as the doorway to the spiraling shaft. "We have about as much, or as little, faith in higher powers as you Trads do. But it's not about what we believe. It's what the Octaliens believed that counts."

Jaeger flashed his palm. "Just making a joke."

Marie d'Arbaud spoke up, her tone one of peacemaking. "Why would two aliens need a temple?"

Feng blinked his large eyes. "And couches in every room?"

"There were obviously more than two Octaliens," said McIlroy.

"Absolutely," Jaeger added.

Marie brushed cinnamon and sugar dust off her fingers with dainty motions of her other hand while her gaze challenged the two men. "Where are the remains of the others?"

"They recycled them," said Ulanovas. "There is no garbage about, okay? No robots, no heavy machinery to dig out the tunnels and put up the message panels? They recycled all those things. They disposed of their dead the same way."

Marie shrank back. Her hands came together palms-up on her lap. Her soft eyes looked aghast. "Beings who loved each other as much as they did, why, they could not be so callous with the remains of their dead."

Ingvarsson's voice carried like a teacher's. "Human cultures have a spectrum of funerary customs. There are two extremes. Some cultures aspire to preserve their corpses for eternity. The ancient Egyptians did so with their mummies. Moderns use embalming fluids and airtight steel caskets. Other cultures strive to return their dead to ashes and dust as quickly as possible. The Romans, the Vikings, and many moderns cremate. The Parsis expose their dead to vultures. A Siberian tribe before Russian dominance fed its dead to their sled dogs, as a gesture of respect to both."

Marie d'Arbaud pressed her lips together in a sour expression. "Those are *human* cultures."

"But if there is such variety in what humans do, should we be surprised by what the octal aliens might have done?"

Her mouth softened. "I see your point," d'Arbaud said.

Jaeger cracked his knuckles. "We've done a lot of speculating. Time to decode their messages and learn some facts."

Nods and mumbled yesses answered him. Except from Feng. "We have limited time on the planet. We can decode the messages when we go back to Earth. Now we should dig out the rocks and explore the lower level."

"It won't be that simple." McIlroy looked thoughtful and scratched the underside of his chin. "The robots confirmed what the detailed analysis of the seismic and ground-penetrating radar data indicated. The rubble plug lies on a metal plate. Maybe the same alloy as the front door and the library panels, and about a meter thick. Digging out the rubble would only face us with a massive cutting job."

"We have the energy to laser through any material," said Feng. "no matter how strong and thick."

"Here's the real reason we don't want to do that," Jaeger said. "It's a test." He called up a 3d virtual of the rubble plug and its surroundings. It hung in the air over the dwindling pile of churros and empty dinner plates. "See the corridor into the lower level?" He flicked his finger from the vertical shaft below the rubble plug toward the large rooms wired for high power.

A shudder rippled down his upper back. Rooms which might hold secrets Varanathan wanted him to kill for.

He hurried on. "The empty volume of the vertical shaft, from below the corridor floor to the bottom, is the same as the volume of the rubble plug."

"The Octaliens expected their visitors to drop the rubble into the bottom of the shaft," McIlroy said.

A snort from Ulanovas. "How? By teleporting it through the metal plate?"

Both Ingvarsson and d'Arbaud raised their eyebrows at him. The Swedish woman spoke. "You are skeptical of *that*?"

He gave her a disbelieving look from beneath his bangs. "The ancient astronauts levitated the stones of the Egyptian pyramids following the laws of nature, not by magically beaming them into place."

"Forget teleportation," Jaeger said. "There's a puzzle to solve, up here." He circled his finger at the top of the rubble plug. The plug lay in the corner of the great upper room, the Library. The nearest walls held flush-mounted and recessed objects. Three on one wall, five on the other. Metallic rectangles and squares ranging from a few inches to a couple of feet across, and eighteen inches above the stone floor.

"What could those be?" Feng asked.

"The locks to a puzzle. The metal would probably conduct electricity and definitely conduct heat. They're wired to the solar absorbers on the surface."

McIlroy spoke, voice softer than usual. A sign his mind raced. "The metal plate holding up the rubble is wired, too."

"You're saying, if we do something to the metal objects—" began d'Arbaud.

"In the proper order." Ingvarsson raised her graceful fingers in apology. "Pardon me."

"—in the proper order," d'Arbaud went on, "the metal plate will open somehow, drop the rubble, and we will be able to explore below?"

Jaeger cracked his knuckles. "You follow me," he said with a grin.

Ulanovas scrunched up his face. "If those metal objects in the walls are locks, where are the keys?"

With motions of his thumb and forefinger on his thigh, read by his wearable, Jaeger zoomed out and panned over until the entire Library came into view. All 893 panels showed, but the writing on them remained invisibly small.

Jaeger could almost taste his excitement. "There."

CHAPTER 9

ALPHA CENTAURI B SYSTEM | BRAVO CHARLIE | GAGARIN STATION

26 MAY 2127 (EARTH REFERENCE FRAME) | 27 JULY 2125 (CONCORDIA REFERENCE FRAME)

AFTER JAEGER CLEARED the dinner dishes and Feng and d'Arbaud finished their assigned washing and drying duty, all six of them settled in to the seating area. With only a minute of discussion, most of them agreed the place to begin deciphering the Octalien messages was near the bottom of the spiral shaft, near the entrance to the Library. "They would start with how their numerals tie in with numbers," Jaeger said.

Ingvarsson pulled her fist around her ponytail. "That's what we would do if we tried to leave a message across deep time. Can we assume that about them?"

Jaeger vigorously shook his head. "They lived differently than us. They thought differently than us. But if they didn't understand math, how could they have built all this?"

"We have to start somewhere," McIlroy added. "If math isn't universal, we'll be shooting blind."

"Everyone, review a panel," said Jaeger. He let the others reach for the virtual pile of images floating in air above the coffee table, then grabbed one for himself.

They fell silent, save for the grunts and mumbles of thought and the occasional rustle of fingertips over blue jeans or plastic chair arms, work notes scrawled on virtual scratch pads. The tent roof and walls darkened and a string of LED bulbs clipped to the ceiling slowly grew brighter. A breeze outside rippled the tent's outer wall, and the air conditioner chugged like a slow but dogged marathoner. Almost 320K outside, over 110°F, late in the local morning of a long hot day.

Looking at the images would be a marathon, too. Jaeger pored over columns of squiggles. Aligned a couple of millimeters at the top of the panel, the columns had ragged ends at the bottom. A line of text from top to bottom? Probably, but how could he tell the difference between a *c* with a serif curling up from the top of the curve, and one with a serif in the same place curling down?

It's all Greek to me didn't capture it. The Greeks had minds like his. He could tell one letter of theirs from another, look up the sounds their letters made, and match that against common suffixes and prefixes in scientific and technical English to get a handle on their concepts. But this?

His jaw ached. How long had he ground his teeth?

He shut his eyes and drew in a deep breath until his mouth relaxed.

"Aha!" Ulanovas exclaimed.

Jaeger's heart raced. He swiped the columns of squiggles down and out of his augmented vision. "What do you have?"

"Their numerals. Enough to tell one number from another. Here." The Lithuanian shared an image.

A column began with a symbol, then a dot, followed by a symbol. Below that, two dots side by side, then a third symbol.

Jaeger squinted. Yes, all three symbols were different.

The procession continued, with a unique symbol for each set of dots up to seven.

At eight dots, the pattern changed. The second symbol, then the first. For nine dots, the symbol that followed the single dot appeared again. Twice. An odd arrangement, rotated a quarter-turn from multi-digit Arabic numerals, but the pattern was unmistakeable.

"These symbols—" Ulanovas said, finger jabbing the air above and below the single dot at the top, "—are their numerals for 0 and 1, okay? The two symbols together in this order—" He gestured again, below the eight dots. "—represent eight, which in base-eight is written 10."

McIlroy jutted his chin forward. "And their numeral for nine is a double of their numeral for one. Nine in octal being 11."

Jaeger's eye ran down the column. 1-2, 1-3, … 1-7, 2-0, 2-1. Those last the base-eight notation for 15, 16, and 17.

Warmth rushed up his chest and into his face. He grinned. Thinking in octal would stretch his brain. But they had an entry point, now, into the alien library. Mathematics, the universal language.

His grin faded. Congrats. You know as much of the Octalien number system as a kindergartener. They didn't yet know the symbols for basic operations, add and subtract, never mind trigonometry and calculus. And reading numbers gave him no help in decoding squiggles into words on the image he'd swiped out of view.

Or the hundreds more panel images waiting for them.

Despite the LED bulbs, the main room of the tent suddenly seemed dim. The walls and ceiling had opaqued heavily, preparing them for a sleep shift in the middle of Bravo Charlie's long daylight hours. Deep in thought, he hadn't noticed.

Ingvarsson squinted at the dark ceiling. Her birthmark stood in contrast against her pale pink cheek. "What time is it?"

"Time for the bell to ring," Jaeger said. The non-Americans frowned at the idiom. "A good first day of school. Class dismissed."

CHAPTER 10

ALPHA CENTAURI B SYSTEM | BRAVO CHARLIE | GAGARIN STATION

25 JULY 2127 (EARTH REFERENCE FRAME) | 25 SEPTEMBER 2125
(CONCORDIA REFERENCE FRAME)

THE RIGHT METAPHOR for the Library wasn't a brick-breaking video game. Nor a tower defense maze-builder. The next two months reminded Jaeger of the levels of a shoot-'em-up, with each boss they defeated giving them a weapon to use against the next one.

The action, though, took place between their ears, and the bosses were concepts guessed at from new symbols and their growing bank of knowledge. Addition and subtraction came quickly—there were only three ways to combine two numbers and an operator symbol. The Octaliens used reverse Polish. Multiplication and division soon followed.

The panel of c-shaped squiggles came next. Jaeger woke up early for a nighttime shift and lay listening to the wind trickle sand over the stony surface outside. Eyes closed, the squiggles danced and spun across his mind's eye, taunting him.... then two with the upswept serifs drifted near one with the serif pointing downward, and the trio rolled together against the gray backdrop of his eyelids.

He sat up, making his cot creak. Ulanovas shifted and mumbled something. Jaeger noticed, briefly, and felt glad he hadn't woken the pilot. Then his attention raced back to his insight.

Two ups, one down. The quarks that made up the proton.

He spent the first half of the shift under the artificial lights in the tent's main room, ignoring the others, occasionally sipping coffee that cooled without him noticing, or taking bites of a breakfast wrap with fake sausage, cheese, and egg. It cooled too, only half-eaten. Jaeger didn't care.

He raced through the images of the panels, taking notes. New info that didn't fit made him revise the framework growing in his mind. Take the symbols that had come to him when half-asleep. Actually two down quarks and one up, a neutron.

More associations fell into place. Rather than write out all three quarks every time, Jaeger assumed they had symbols for protons and neutrons. Electrons, too. He searched until he found them, and grinned.

Another panel. One proton, one electron. Two protons, two neutrons, two electrons. Hydrogen and helium. Isotopes, too. Deuterium, tritium, helium-3. Numbers next to the isotopes... He spoke a few words to Ulanovas. "Look there. Probably percentages and decimals."

Ulanovas pushed back his bangs with his hand. "Good guess. I'll get on it."

Jaeger kept going. Another panel showed a spiraling pattern of circles, parallelograms, and squares, each with a set of symbols inside. Amid the other symbols in each shape stood the proton symbol and numbers, with one in the middle of the spiral and the numbers increasing outward. The spiral made eight lines of shapes radiating from the center. Three loops of shapes jutted outward like giant prominences from a flaring star, bringing the total to over a hundred and fifty.

A periodic table with hydrogen in the middle.

When he showed the others shortly before lunch, Ingvarsson's brown eyes widened. "This may give us a path into their writing system and language."

"How can that be?" McIlroy asked over his pointed, bearded chin.

She drew loops in the air, each one around a group of symbols inside one of the circles. Jaeger noted the proton numbers. Hydrogen, nitrogen, oxygen, the innermost halogens, and the slice of the spiral starting from helium.

"These elements," said Ingvarsson, "are all gases at pressures and temperatures comparable to Earth. Look at the symbols I marked."

Jaeger wanted to smack his forehead. Obvious after she pointed it out. "There's the same one in each." Grouped with a variety of symbols, usually five to nine below it, but the top one was always the same.

"A fair assumption is that symbol is their word for *gas*. And the symbols grouped with it are adjectives describing the element." The Swedish woman rubbed the side of her nose. "I'll see where this leads."

They slowly progressed through the Library over the next standard weeks. Ingvarsson found fifty-four different symbols on the periodic table. Too few to be ideograms like Chinese characters or Egyptian hieroglyphics, where one symbol stood for one word. But how could the word for *gas* be a single letter?

She went out one afternoon shift to sit on a rock and tap the hot, thin air. Jaeger looked up from a panel describing what might be the ideal gas law when she ran in, brown eyes bright. "It's a syllabary," she said. "Each symbol stands for one syllable. We can't know what spoken sounds they represented, and I'm guessing at some of the meanings...."

Ingvarsson showed a table of symbols with arbitrary sounds and possible translations. Hydrogen was *gas-burned-make-water*. Nitrogen, *gas-no-breathe*. Technetium, the first element humans had

synthesized before discovering, had the same history for the Octaliens: *metal-born-of-fingers-and-tool.*

Some of the team's results were also born of hands and tools.
Marie d'Arbaud mounted all the non-invasive scanners that fit onto
the drone. It hovered over the Octalien corpses, sliding an inch per
second, streaming data for d'Arbaud to made guesses at their internal
organs.

She didn't stop there. Backed by both McIlroy and Jaeger, she
pitched to the mission co-commanders a plan to perform autopsies
and take tissue samples for biochemical studies.

"Is that needful?" asked Varanathan. The co-commanders stood
next to each other in virtual projection in the tent's main room. "I
haven't had a chance to review all the data you've already uploaded. I
don't see what more we can learn from invasive studies." He sipped
from a coffee mug.

Jaeger cleared his throat. "Those tissue samples might tell us if the
Octaliens originated on Bravo Charlie." He looked at the eyes of the
virtual projection.

The software managing the conversation on Varanathan's end
lined up their gazes. Varanathan put on a bland mask and nodded at
Jaeger.

"Bloody hell," Sandford said. She rolled her eyes, sending a ripple
of scorn down her shoulder-length white hair. "'Is it needful?'"

On the other side of d'Arbaud, McIlroy pulled in a heavy breath
and studied the plastic floor. Embarrassed by his commander's crass
communication style? Or remembering a conversation with her like
Jaeger's with Varanathan, about where the aliens might be from, and
what that might mean?

Varanathan went on as if she'd never mocked him. "You. All of
you—" He gave McIlroy a small bow. "—have shown to my satisfaction the results of tissue testing could be quite valuable. I approve."

"Agreed." Sandford raised her eyebrow at d'Arbaud. "Don't
bugger it up."

Marie goggled with fear. "Of course, I'll follow every protocol—"

"We know you will," Varanathan said, voice buttery. "Marie, you have always been dedicated to the mission. I see that has not changed."

Her soft eyes turned to his projection. "Thank you, sir."

"We're all clear, then?" Sandford asked. "*Concordia* command signing off." She moved her hand and their projections winked out.

With approval from the co-commanders, d'Arbaud spent three weeks of standard time, almost six local days, running experiments. She performed the autopsies in a mostly-empty chamber off the Library, near the fitness center-slash-temple. Preserving the Octalien remains under nitrogen outweighed the discomfort of wearing an oxygen mask. She sterilized her tools in a makeshift autoclave at the camp, using waste heat from the reactor near the tent.

Parallel evolution with humankind showed itself in two sexes. The female lay eggs, judging by the similarities to the reproductive organs of terrestrial birds. More parallels: the Octaliens had a four-chambered heart, with two chambers pumping deoxygenated blood to the lung and the other two sending oxygenated blood to the rest of the body. A skeleton of calcium with rubbery biopolymer binding it together. Sharp teeth in the front of the mouth for tearing meat, heavy grinding ones farther back for cracking bones for marrow.

Evolutionary parallels eventually ran out. A dessicated green powder filled the heart.

"Fourteen grams of what I presume is dried blood," she said over the radio. Excitement brightened her next words. "That alone should be enough to tell us their origins."

Taking a break from analyzing lava samples from the anomalous field, McIlroy handled the comms to her from the station. "How so?"

Octalien physics suddenly paled in importance. Jaeger lifted his head to virtual projections of d'Arbaud and her camera feed.

She rolled her wrist in the air, a sign she switched mental gears to teaching mode. "Hemoglobin is conserved among the species of Earth. Though variations exist, everything from soybeans to people have proteins with similar amino acid sequences, similar three-dimensional structure, and an iron atom in a heme group that binds oxygen. Once nature had the basic structure of hemoglobin, evolution tweaked it in particular organisms, rather than start anew."

"Jaeger here. I get that. But I'm not following how that tells us where the Octaliens come from."

"Work by Amundsen and Smalley at Glenn Station has found proteins in native life that transport oxygen. They use iron but have little else in common with Earth hemoglobin."

The next shift, all of them followed d'Arbaud to the chemical sciences tent. The cloudless desert night, and Bravo Charlie's approach to aphelion, the farthest point in its orbit from Alpha Centauri B, made Jaeger hunch his shoulders against the cold and hurry his footsteps crunching the rocky ground.

They soon traded the chill glitter of the stars for the stark LED ceiling panels of the science tent. Bulky equipment—Jaeger remembered manhandling it with Ulanovas out of *Gagarin's* cargo hold, three months ago—lined the back and side walls. Wires and cables snaked around the equipment. The tent's thick plastic walls trapped the team's body heat.

Their excitement soon became restless. Not much to see as d'Arbaud worked. She flicked switches and ran diagnostics on the equipment, before opening the lids of metal hoppers, dropping in samples, pressing keys. Motors, pumps, and cooling fans mumbled inside a plain plastic housing and data trickled down shared virtual displays.

At first glance, the data made as much sense to Jaeger as the Octalien symbols. Maybe less, after his study of their messages so far.

The others mostly chatted as they waited for results. Jaeger tuned out the conversation. The next stage of decoding the Octalien's messages filled his mind. He had a guess, based on panels full of symbols for isotopes and numbers, and wanted to flesh it out with more examples. What it meant bubbled in his chest, making him grin. With luck, he could share his findings with the others today.

Not to steal d'Arbaud's thunder, when she reported biological evidence of the Octalien's origins. To add to it.

In a corner of the tent near the zip-up door, Ingvarsson worked too. She stared at the gray wall, her brown eyes focused on what he could tell were virtual object visible only to her. Her slender fingers pinched and slid through the air.

A mechanical hum died down. A virtual ping sounded from the mass spectrometer.

Marie leaned closer. Hair whisped out of her bun, reminding Jaeger of the static balls at a children's science museum. Her soft eyes looked brighter than he'd ever seen them. "As I suspected," she said, while a grin showed on her thin lips.

"Do not tease us," Feng said, tone playful.

Playful? But the question fled Jaeger's mind, crowded out by Marie d'Arbaud's next words.

"They are from another world."

Everyone leaned forward. Ingvarsson gasped. Ulanovas muttered something in Lithuanian.

"Wait." McIlroy pointed at the hulking machine. "That's not the protein sequencer. The mass spec only tells you what elements are in your sample."

"This is a sample from inside the heart. We assume it is dried solids from their blood, yes?"

"Yes."

"All the native life uses iron to help carry oxygen in its blood. Amundsen and the others reported that."

McIlroy said, "I'll take your word for it."

"Look at the metal content of this sample." She zoomed in on the data display.

Copper. Over 98% of the metal content in the Octalien blood sample came from it. Iron was a tiny fraction, comparable to zinc and manganese.

Marie's grin remained. "I suspected from the green tint of the sample. This makes it clear to me. They are not from this world."

She worked the rest of the shift to confirm her conclusion. She dropped more samples into the mass spectrometer. Jaeger only turned away from his calculations and lookups of the isotope panels when she announced results. Copper, not iron, was the most likely candidate for the metal that carried oxygen in Octalien blood.

The protein sequencer added to the mound of evidence. In his physics training, Jaeger had rarely considered molecules larger than hydrogen, H_2. But more complex molecules, Marie explained, come in two mirror images. She held up her left and right hands until everyone nodded.

The amino acids chained together to make the proteins of Earth life were all, in chemistry lingo, left-handed. The native life on Bravo Charlie used right-handed amino acids.

The Octalien's? Proteins from blood, from internal organs, from both bodies: all left-handed, like Earth life's.

Marie d'Arbaud raised her shoulders and her voice. Her tone showed she knew this moment would echo through history. "All the biological evidence points to them coming from another world."

McIlroy and Jaeger led a round of applause. Feng looked thoughtful, then a grin spread across his face. Ingvarsson came closer to the group, late to join the clapping. Happy for d'Arbaud, yes, but the look on her face showed she had something else to say.

After the applause for d'Arbaud died down, Jaeger asked her, "What do you have?"

"I know where they are from," Ingvarsson said.

After a moment, her words sank in. More cheer bubbled up from the others. Jaeger gave both her and d'Arbaud a wide, lazy smile.

Ingvarsson's brown eyes squinted at him. "Marie and I bring good news, and you are the one who looks like the cat that ate the canary?"

"You two did great work. Thanks to you, we know where they came from."

His smile broadened. "I can tell us *when.*"

CHAPTER 11

ALPHA CENTAURI B SYSTEM | BRAVO CHARLIE | GAGARIN STATION

25 JULY 2127 (EARTH REFERENCE FRAME) | 25 SEPTEMBER 2125 (CONCORDIA REFERENCE FRAME)

How DO you communicate time to an alien race you've never met? The orbital and rotation periods of your planet come from astrodynamic chance, not universal law. The divisions of those periods, months, weeks, hours, minutes, and seconds, were created when your species did not distinguish magic and science.

"Radioisotope decay," Jaeger explained in the main tent, over a dinner of microwaved sandwiches and bags of veggie chips. The half-lives of uranium-238 and uranium-235 are the same regardless the units of time you use to measure them.

McIlroy set down his beer glass, then tugged on his mustache with his lower teeth. "That gets you ratios of relative time, but you only get absolute time if you know they used half-life and not, say, time for one-eighth or seven-eighths of the starting sample to decay."

"They gave us a key." Jaeger showed a graphic of some symbols.

Second nature to him, but the puzzled and glazed looks he got from the pilots and d'Arbaud the biologist led him to explain. "Those are the symbols for the isotope hydrogen-7. In our terms, its half-life is about two times ten to the negative twenty-three seconds. 2E-23 seconds, if you think of it more easily that way. Ulanovas, what's the number next to the symbols?"

The Lithuanian brushed a lock of his dusky-blond hair off his forehead. "It's in their equivalent of scientific notation... very small...." He used his forefinger as a stylus and his other palm as a slate. "Rounded off, 1.28E21."

"I got that too. Thanks for checking my work." Jaeger turned to all of them. "I played with the numbers. The number they wrote down is three half-lives—call it the eighth-life, I guess—of hydrogen-7, in units of the Planck time. A fundamental constant. The shortest length of time that can exist."

McIlroy's head lolled back. His mouth hung open. "Which gives you absolute time."

A gust buffeted the tent wall for a moment. The cold night outside was no match for the bubble of warm companionship in here. "I found another panel with radioisotope decay times correlated with the Octalien's day-to-day time units. Remember the periodicity in the original signal? 3.2454 seconds? That's their equivalent to a second in our units. Looks like they divided their days into eight parts, and those into eight parts, and so on. Their day is 32,768 seconds. Eight to the fifth power."

Feng smoothed down his black hair. Eyes larger than usual, he said, "Well done."

Jaeger gave a brief nod to show he heard. "Their day is 29.54 standard hours. Their year, 173.86 standard days. Five and a half months. They have another time unit, it might be called an *about-half-day?*" He showed them the symbols and turned to Ingvarsson. "Did I read your translation dictionary correctly?"

"*Half* and *day,* yes. What makes you say *about?*"

"The duration is around 15.3 standard hours. Close to but not exactly half an Octalien day."

"I'll add that to the list of possible vocabulary words." Her brown-eyed gaze met his and her lips parted, showing slivers of polished white teeth.

Jaeger returned a lazy grin. After three months on the planet, was she now showing an interest him? Or had the bubbly mood of the day's discoveries put her in the mood for something more frisky?

Then her expression returned to its usual cool aloofness. Half-dejected, half-relieved at not having to navigate a tryst in the isolated quarters of Gagarin Station, he went on. "We can access their calendar now. And you know where they came from?"

Ingvarsson set down her sandwich. "We have talked they might have evolved on Alfa Echo, in orbit around Alpha Centauri A, before it became inhospitable like Venus."

Jaeger clamped his facial features down on a spike of guilt. Had someone overheard his conversation with Varanathan in the chapel? He put on a stern face. "I don't recall any discussion of that." When put on the spot, flip the script and put them on the defensive.

"Weren't you part of those conversations? Marie and I have talked about it, I remember, and I think it's come up with all of us. But the textual evidence is clear. They traveled *fast-to-them-slow-us* and *speed-no-faster*. Indicators of relativistic speeds."

Jaeger sluffed out a breath. "You can't get that fast crossing the 20 AU from Alfa Echo to here. The acceleration to reach relativistic speeds would smear anything other than diamonds across the deck. Unless...."

McIlroy peered at him. "Unless?"

Thinking out loud will get you in trouble. Jaeger's mind groped for ideas, until he noticed Ulanovas crunching chips between his jaws. "Unless you've got artificial gravity inside your ship. Like the ancient aliens did."

Everyone laughed. Including McIlroy.

Jaeger reached for his beer. He'd recovered from the slip. "So we can only conclude they're from another star."

"There is more evidence in support," said Ingvarsson. "I found numerals grouped with the symbols *water-hard* and *water-gas*. The proportions between those numbers represent absolute temperatures, degrees Kelvin. They reported their home star's effective temperature was the equivalent of 5531 K. I looked it up and that gives a spectral type of G8."

"Cooler than Alpha Centauri A and hotter than B," piped up Ulanovas.

Ingvarsson flourished one hand to Jaeger. "Boosted by your decoding of their time units, I filled in another blank. They traveled about six Octalien years, in the reference frame of their home world, to get here. About five and a half on their ship."

Jaeger did rough math in his head. "Their homeworld was about three light-years from Alpha Centauri, when they left."

A frown creased d'Arbaud's eyebrows. "There's no star that close."

"Not now," Jaeger said. "Stars orbit the galactic core, each on its own trajectory. Their home star happened to make a close approach. It could be hundreds of light-years away by now. There are hundreds, maybe thousands, of G8 stars within range. We'll never be able to find it. Let alone travel there."

"From all we have learned today, we could reconstruct much about their home star and world," Ingvarsson said. "But isn't doing so less important than learning why they built the base?"

Jaeger and the others shared glances. Agreement was plain on every face.

"Tell us," said McIlroy.

In broad strokes, Octalien history resembled humankind's. Fueled by a growing rate of technological development, tribes gradually formed states of greater and greater military power.

Feng's large eyes crinkled. "They fought among themselves?"

"That's no surprise," said d'Arbaud, in a tone of a teacher eager to get through to a student falling short of his potential.

"Because they are carnivores?" Ulanovas asked.

Marie turned her soft eyes to him. A shake of her head loosed another strand of gray-streaked hair from her bun. "The bitterest rivals are those sharing the same evolutionary niche." She pronounced it *neesh*.

Jaeger frowned to himself. Had he pronounced *nitch* wrong his whole life?

"An example. Bucks do not grow antlers to fight wolves. They grow them to fight one another. The victor claims a harem of females. Male lions do the same, but are even more brutal. If a newcomer ousts another male from a pride, the newcomer kills the cubs sired by the other."

"The Octaliens warred among themselves." McIlroy stroked his beard, looking thoughtful.

Jaeger pictured it. Individual states rose and fell, like the kingdoms and empires of an UltraHistory game.

He let out a sigh. Maybe on the journey home he and McIlroy would find time for another game.

Ingvarsson went on. Her crisp voice and cool blond beauty recapture his attention. "On the Octalien homeworld, individual states rose and fell, but the overall trend raised up states of increasing wealth, population, technology, and military force. Until a few superpowers backed with weapons of great destructive power divided up their world."

"Sounds familiar," Jaeger muttered. Loudly enough to get a sidelong glance from d'Arbaud.

"Did they unify to send their mission?" Ulanovas waved in the direction of the buried alien base.

"No. One of those superpowers did."

"'We come in peace for all mankind,'" McIlroy muttered into his beer glass. Jaeger threw a questioning glance his way, but the geologist tilted back his head and drained the glass without meeting Jaeger's gaze.

A question came to Jaeger. A question that might force him to decide to follow or reject his orders from Varanathan once and for all.

"How did their ship fly?" asked Ulanovas.

Jaeger opened his mouth. Relief washed through his gut that Ulanovas asked the question, not him.

Though why had Ulanovas asked it?

"They refer to it as *new-way*," said Ingvarsson. "A scientific break-through of some sort, releasing immense energies."

Jaeger's heart thudded. He kept his voice nonchalant. "Send the relevant Library entries my way. I'll see what I can figure out."

A creak came from McIlroy's chair. He shifted his weight, and no longer scratched his beard. His hands lay on the chair arms. His gaze studied Jaeger.

"I will," Ingvarsson said. She rubbed the side her nose, then pulled her hand away. Her face grew solemn. "The scientific break-through also provided immense energies for weapons. The secret did not stay long with the base builders' home society. Soon, all the Octalien superpowers learned it, and built weapons based on it."

Warmth drained from her voice. Her eyes glistened with mois-ture. "The mission was in transit when the superpowers fought a war with weapons of mass destruction. A war that melted the land, boiled off the oceans, and created an asteroid stream trailing in the planet's wake."

Jaeger slouched in his chair. McIlroy's face sank closer to his beer glass, as if he'd forgotten it was empty. Marie d'Arbaud's hand trem-bled up to cover her mouth.

A frown formed around Feng's large eyes. "That is a... way of saying?"

McIlroy nodded. "A simile. A metaphor?"

Ingvarsson's voice shrank. "Their exact words."

The wind picked up in the cold desert night. Jaeger slouched further. Imagine the idiots back home, as inept or corrupt as

Varanathan and Sandford, and wielding ten thousand times the power. Shrink them and turn their skin green. Or don't. Either way, there's your answer.

They blew it up. God damn them all to hell.

"What kind of weapon could do that much damage?" McIlroy said.

It took Jaeger a moment to realize the Humanist spoke to him. "I don't know. Ten thousand fusion bombs couldn't do it."

Did that power lie dormant under the rubble plug?

If it did, leave it there. Don't bring it back to an Earth whose superpowers already stockpiled enough weapons of mass destruction.

"The mission crew suffered a crisis of consciousness. Conscience?" Ingvarsson said. "Conscience. What was the purpose of their mission now? Deaths happened on board, though whether murders or suicides I cannot tell. Perhaps some of both. Until they found an answer."

"Build the base?" Ulanovas asked.

Feng said, "I don't understand."

"Building the base gave them a purpose," Ingvarsson said. "Though not to occupy their hands while their minds drifted into madness. To teach any other intelligent species that might find this planet to learn from their mistake and save itself from self-destruction."

The overhead LEDs now seemed weak, like guttering candles soon to blow out. Solemn faces surrounded Jaeger. Save the human race from itself? They all wanted to. But what good could the six of them in this tent, or even most of the 150 people on or orbiting the planet, do to change the destiny of billions over four light-years away?

Silence settled deeper in the main room. Outside, the wind skittered sand along the edges of the tent, like dust blowing over the funeral cairn of a desert traveler long since dead.

Intuitions aligned inside Jaeger. He ground his teeth, noticing only when he relaxed his jaw to speak. "There's something I have to confess." He swiveled his gaze to McIlroy. "So do you."

McIlroy lurched, sitting up straight. "I'm not sure what you mean."

Jaeger gave a slow, exaggerated shake of his head. No fence sitting, no dual loyalty, no serving two masters. "Sandford summoned you to a secret meeting just before we came down in *Gagarin*, didn't she? I know, because Varanathan did the same to me."

Ingvarsson rubbed the side of her nose. Ulanovas swiveled his head between the expedition's co-leaders.

McIlroy held his chin up. A wry grin formed inside his beard. "She did."

"What about?" asked Ulanovas.

McIlroy said, "About what advanced technology might lie inside the base—"

"—and how each of us should steal it for our faction back home." Jaeger glanced at McIlroy.

The Humanist gave a single nod. From his face, Jaeger read that she'd told him to kill for it if he had to.

Ulanovas jittered his head to sweep his bangs away from his puzzled eyes. "How could either of you steal technology? With three from the other faction here? And many more on *Concordia*?"

Ingvarsson frowned and muttered something in agreement.

Jaeger spoke. "He gave me a code word. And a pistol. I was to send him the code word. He would take control of command, control, and comms. Then I was supposed to kill the Humanists. And Ulanovas and d'Arbaud if they stood in the way."

The Swedish woman's fair face turned pallid. Feng returned an unreadable look. Confusion still showed on Ulanovas's face. The soft-eyed gaze of Marie d'Arbaud fell to the floor and stayed there.

McIlroy inclined his head toward Jaeger. "She gave me the same orders."

"I told Varanathan I'd follow them," Jaeger said. Pressure built up behind his eyes. His voice hung up on his next words. "God help me, sometimes I even thought I would. But from what Ingvarsson decoded, I can't. None of you are my enemy.

Varanathan. Sandford. The people above them on Earth. They're my enemy. Yours too."

He went on. "If there's a technology down there that can wreck a planet, do you trust Alliance or Coalition leadership to use it responsibly? I don't. So I'm telling you I will never turn against you. I refuse to follow Varanathan's orders." He drew in a breath, then turned to McIlroy. "What about you?"

McIlroy spoke slowly. "I grew up fifty miles from the inner Texan border. I did my national service year reviewing video from our cameras on our fence. Looking for FSNA forces doing something that escaped the notice of our video analysis algorithms. But all I saw was countryside that wasn't different from where I was, and guys my age running patrols who weren't much different from me. And it broke my heart like two hundred years of sad country and western songs all rolled into one."

Jaeger thickly swallowed. "I was one of those guys running patrols on the other side."

"Naw. You must have been out of national service by the time I started, old man." McIlroy's grin dried up. "Sandford knew how to get to me." He waggled a finger at Ingvarsson. "What did you give her out of my psych file?" he asked, tone light enough to make his words teasing.

She replied, face solemn. "What you said. Though not as metaphorical."

"I'm joking." He looked to the others. "Like I said, Sandford knew the right things to say." He mimicked her accent. "If the aliens buried powerful technology with military applications, and both factions get it, it shall be two minutes to bloody midnight forever." The British accent fell apart. "A stalemate. The borders would never change. Texas would be split forever."

McIlroy's eyes turned shrewd. Jaeger knew that look from negotiations over the UltraHistory table. "But if I could make sure powerful Octalien tech only ended up with us Humanists, then we could do what the Americans failed to do after the Second German War. Use our monopoly on advanced weapons to defeat the Trads. And unite Texas under the Humanist Alliance."

A grim look hardened his brown beard. "She almost fooled me."

Jaeger blew out a breath.

"What do you mean?" asked Ingvarsson.

"Took a while," McIlroy said, "but I realized what defeating the Trads would really mean. A hundred cities around the world burned up in firestorms. A hundred million dead. What good would unification be, if it required us to kill a bunch of my people on the other side of the border? A unification, on paper, but it would make the survivors hate us a hundred times more than they do now."

Jaeger studied the man. He'd read McIlroy's expressions over the UltraHistory table a thousand times.

McIlroy had never looked as sincere.

Jaeger asked. "What do you say?"

"I say, to hell with her orders." He extended his hand to Jaeger.

Jaeger took it. "What we learn from the Octaliens, we use for the good of all humanity."

"Agreed." They pumped hands. Their grips were solid.

Jaeger knew what he'd just promised. Texans had made deals that way for three hundred years. God willing, they would for three hundred more.

A chill thought ran across his back. He broke the handshake, then turned to Ulanovas and d'Arbaud. "Which one of you is Varanathan's backup plan?"

A small gasp escaped from d'Arbaud. Ulanovas squinted. "Backup plan?"

Jaeger's eyebrow rose. "Maybe Marie can explain."

Her soft eyes looked trapped. Her lower lip trembled. "How did you know?"

"A good guess. I'm sure Varanathan worried my friendship with McIlroy would interfere with his plans. He seems the type to always have a second scheme working."

She closed her eyes. Pain crinkled their corners.

"You sided with your leader instead of the mission?" asked Feng. Anger clung to his nasal voice.

Marie's wince intensified. "He came to my sleeping closet late the night before we descended. He brought up the possibility of advanced alien weapons, then asked me to watch Jaeger." She squared her hunched shoulders to him. "Varanathan feared you would betray us and help McIlroy and the Humanists gain the Octalien weapons. You can't trust the Humanists, he said. They can seduce away the loyalty of anyone." Her head sank, her brow coming to rest in her palm. "He knew exactly what to say."

"It's okay," Jaeger said. "We've all bought into the us versus them story. Tough not to." He smiled while his thoughts raced. Had Varanathan handed her a pistol like his? He asked, "Anything else?"

"I was to watch, then send a coded message if it looked like you were betraying us. I don't know what he would do then."

"What are you going to do now?" asked Jaeger.

"I joined the mission for the good of all mankind. I am with you. I will not follow his orders." She kept her gaze on Jaeger for a time, but soon it drifted toward Feng.

"Me too," piped up Ulanovas.

Jaeger nodded, not really hearing the Lithuanian. He looked from d'Arbaud to Feng. There seemed to be little to Chinese man, other than introversion and lenticular ball caps. Little, to Jaeger's eye. "Since everyone's coming clean...."

"Yes," d'Arbaud said. She lifted her chin. "Feng and I are having an affair. We didn't plan it. But we've been around each other every daylight shift for months now. Things grew, until...." A little shrug, then she turned her soft eyes to the Chinese man, in his chair on the other side of the sitting area.

Ulanovas put on a lazy grin, then leaned toward Ingvarsson. "The same is true for us. What do you say?"

She turned an icy stare on him until he laughed.

"We had an affair," Feng said, voice cool. "Not anymore."

Her brows crinkled together. "What?"

"You do this thing for Varanathan. You never tell anyone. I cannot trust you."

"Do? I didn't *do* anything. He asked me to do something—"

"You did not say no." Feng crossed his arms and scowled.

Marie licked her thin lips, then pressed them together. "And what would you have done if Sandford asked you to spy on McIlroy?"

He flinched. A moment later, he leaned forward. "I would tell her no. Like you should have done. All this time you lie to me—"

"What secrets have you kept from me?"

He forced his eyes wide and unblinking. "No secrets."

McIlroy cleared his throat. "You mean to say, you aren't Sandford's backup plan?"

Feng's gaze jolted to McIlroy. "No. She did not ask me spy on you."

"Reckon she didn't. Ingvarsson?"

The Swedish woman slowly reared back her head, as if a snake slithered in McIlroy's brown beard. "No."

"Guess she isn't as conniving as Varanathan."

"Or she trusted you more than he trusted me," Jaeger said. "Her mistake for never playing UltraHistory against you."

McIlroy chuckled. Tension escaped from the room, save for d'Arbaud's stiff neck, pivoted far enough away from Feng to make a tendon stand out, and his crossed arms and scowl turned even deeper.

"I'm glad we've brought all this out into the open," said Jaeger.

"Me too," McIlroy said. "But now what?"

Ulanovas spread his arms as if the answer was obvious. "We keep exploring."

"I share the sentiment. There's something in the vault under the rubble plug. It could be the biggest boon our species could imagine. But what happens when we find it? All our raw data gets sent to *Concordia* for backup. All our analysis too. Even if they don't read about the fate of the Octalien homeworld in Ingvarsson's files, someone in orbit is going to figure it out soon enough."

Jaeger continued the train of thought. "And assume the breakthrough technology is in the vault."

"Maybe that's Sandford's Plan B," McIlroy said. "She'll know about the breakthrough tech, if any, a few hours after we find it. If I don't try to take control of it, she will."

The tendon in d'Arbaud's neck remained rigid. "How?"

"Prepare a team of armed, loyal Humanists. Kill or capture the Trad leadership team on *Concordia*. Send her team down here to do the same to us."

Jaeger drew in a long breath. "Unless Varanathan beats her to the punch."

"Or that." McIlroy swept his hand, palm up, in Jaeger's direction.

The wind sighed through the vast desert night. Still sixteen hours before Alpha Centauri B would rise. Their bubble of warmth and light and oxygen-rich air suddenly seemed tiny.

Jaeger's heart beat a little faster. Sunlight. What was the old phrase? "There's another option," he said, hope in his voice.

The others turned to him. Except for Feng, their faces showed they heard the emotion. "What is it?" Ingvarsson asked, as doubt lurked around the corners of her brown eyes.

The old phrase came to him. "Sunlight is the best disinfectant."

CHAPTER 12

27 JULY 2127 (EARTH REFERENCE FRAME) | 27 SEPTEMBER 2125 (CONCORDIA REFERENCE FRAME)

THOUGH THE CEILING panels emitted the same stark white glow, the control room felt chill to Varanathan. The climate control worked as normal, blowing the prescribed rate of air out the vents for the room's cramped volume and normal complement of workers. Instead, the chill came from the glances over cold shoulders, the sullen looks in eyes, the mouths clamped tight.

Jaeger and McIlroy's message blast. Damn them. They'd revealed everything, to everyone, on the planet and on the ship. Secret orders to steal any valuable alien tech. They even showed the pistol he'd fabbed for Jaeger and a comparable handgun given to the geologist. A civil war between the factions on the ship. A world war when the victorious faction returned to Earth.

They made those sound like bad things.

Most of the crew responded in their favor, and turned against the co-commanders in petty ways. A side screen on the front wall showed Octalien script and Ingvarsson's translation. Boiled oceans. Rocks propelled into orbit. Echoes of a common refrain in the crew forums in the past two days. Even spoken to his face in the cafeteria by one bold Traditionalist, a bioinformaticist named Wycuff. *What you tried to do would have destroyed Earth just like it destroyed the Octalien homeworld.*

He'd plastered a confident smile on his face, then spoken of the need to prevent Sandford from stealing any Octalien tech. He held his ground long enough for Wycuff's steely expression to waver and the man to take his leave.

He'd added Wycuff's name to the list of those to be dealt with someday.

Not merely for opposing him. For misreading Ingvarsson's translated history.

The Octaliens destroyed their homeworld because multiple factions deployed the superweapons.

If only one had monopolized it, their world would still exist.

Under that one faction's control.

Common crew didn't recognize that. Instead, they worked together, his people and the Humanists, to annoy him. The air came out of the vents in his quarters a good five or ten degrees too hot. Maintenance kept losing his service requests. Anonymous notes slipped under the door spoke of betrayal, of treason. No overt threats, but the blocky handwriting exuded menace. Worse, the Trad psychologist, Stevens, refused to share her files on Wycuff or anyone else, citing patient-client privilege. For the first time in four years.

Her Humanist counterpart was even less helpful, of course. Ingvarsson had opened her records on Sandford and the rest of the Alliance leadership team, along with her notes on him and his staff.

Here, now, the chill reception from the control room staff added to the social pressure.

At least his shift officer, broad-shouldered and crew-cut Kuzmich, and reserve shift officer, O'Daniel with lean arms but a paunch, had greeted him with respectful nods and tones of voice. Good men, both, especially O'Daniel, who could always be relied on to take care of things a leader of Varanathan's station couldn't be seen doing. Right now, O'Daniel studied something in a private virtual. Probably censoring outbound messages, to keep word of the Octaliens from reaching Earth as part of someone's weekly message to family or friends.

Or word of disagreement with Varanathan's leadership.

A bustle came from the door in the back center of the room, to his left. A straight fall of white hair reached the corner of his eye.

Most shoulders around the room stiffened. A few department heads, Traditionalist and Humanist alike, scowled over their shoulders.

Warmth trickled into Varanathan's gut.

At least Sandford faced the same pressure he did.

It meant she might heed his request.

She shuffled sideways, between the back wall and the Humanist co-command panel. Her officer of the watch, Quesada, black hair and narrow jaw, planted his heels on the floor and pulled his chair forward on its cantilevered arm to give her some extra room to pass.

Before she moved behind Quesada's bony elbows, Varanathan said, "I would have a talk with you."

She arched her eyebrow. "I have my bloody job to do."

"For the sake of the smooth operation of the ship," he said. "Quesada can keep the watch for a time." He was good at least for that. The other man at the Humanist panel, Lavin, sitting in the corner with deep lines running down past his mouth and a thick shock of coarse brown hair, was her aide he always kept an eye on.

A sigh and an eye-roll later, she made her way past Quesada. He hunched forward, like someone trying to put meter-long pipes in an eighty-centimeter box. After her passage, he moved his chair back and extended his long arms to rest on the controls.

She stood tall, the effect heightened by the padding under the shoulders of her pantsuit. "Reports," she said, voice imperious as ever. "Life Support."

Yokogawa, a Trad from North America, had the watch. His station was two rows down and directly in front of her, and at enough of an angle for Varanathan to see he folded his arms and turned his Japanese features to the video wall.

"Life Support." Fraying patience sounded in Sandford's voice.

Yokogawa kept his silence, like a scene from silly film, about samurai swords and prattle about honor.

Varanathan angled his head. Should the man go on the list? No, not for defying Sandford. She'd plotted murder and mayhem against the Traditionalists, after all.

Sandford slammed her flat palm on the panel in front of her. "Life Support, you will give me a report or I'll lodge a demerit on your record."

Arms still folded, Yokogawa drew in a breath that lifted his shoulders and head. His chin rose. Still his mouth stayed shut.

"Damn you, you will get another demerit. Don't think I can't make your life a hell, you miserable little—"

Varanathan cleared his throat like a chain saw working through a log fallen across a road.

Sandford swung her head. The ends of her white hair whipped around. "Don't you defend your people getting insubordinate with me."

"I would never condone insubordination," Varanathan said smoothly. "But perhaps it would be best for you and I, and perhaps O'Daniel and Lavin—" He looked past her to the man in the far corner. "—to discuss some things privately."

If her eyes were lasers, his retinas would have been scarred for life. "My personnel are..." Finally the words sank in. She knew O'Daniel worked for him the way Lavin worked for her. "A sound suggestion. Quesada, the watch is yours. Lavin, come with me."

O'Daniel pivoted his chair. His round face showed no expression, but a questioning look showed in his hazel eyes when his gaze met his co-commander's.

Varanathan replied with the barest of nods.

In the corridor outside the control room, Varanathan led the way to the row of conference rooms. To distinguish them from one another, and from every conference room he'd ever sat in from New Delhi to St. Petersburg, they were named after famous artists throughout history. Reproductions of famous paintings hung on the plain white walls. He passed the Picasso room and a copy of *Guernica*, all drab colors and cartoonish figures. The Humanist planners had chosen it, of course.

A scene one could understand at sight decorated the Friedrichs conference room. A man on a promontory, back to the viewer, looked over a fog bank to mountains rising above it. The art did not come from India, but otherwise, it pleased him.

More importantly, the Friedrichs room had the tightest security on the ship.

He nodded at O'Daniel, who opened the door and held it for Sandford. She peered down her narrow nose at him. Varanathan could see the metaphorical gears turning behind her eyes. Anger that a man acted patriarchal toward her, or satisfaction that someone served her the way she deserved?

She went past O'Daniel without a word. Satisfaction, then.

Varanathan made patting motions toward O'Daniel's shoulder to steer him into the room. He followed his subordinate in as the door swung shut behind them. Varanathan himself turned the paddle knob of the deadbolt.

Bog standard on the inside as well. A video display filling the wall to the left, behind the head of the table. A thin tabletop of vinyl made to look like a lustrous brown wood with a tight grain. Eight chairs like stainless steel barrels cut in half, polished, padded, on single legs mounted to machinery hidden under bunched plastic, like the gear levers in manually-driven automobiles seen in old films. Other than the residual odor of lemony cleaning product squirted by the janitor robots, the air felt comfortable. Almost chill on the backs of Varanathan's hands. No one in climate control realized the co-commanders had taken the room.

His wearable popped up a notice of successful connection with the monitor even before Sandford took a seat. Middle of the table's far, long side. She tossed her head to ripple her white hair as Lavin sat next to her. He interdigitated his hands on the tabletop, turning them into one giant fist.

Varanathan sat opposite Sandford. O'Daniel, Lavin. "Verify we're secure," Varanathan said to O'Daniel, at the same time Sandford gave a similar command to her subordinate.

Both men stared at private virtuals for a moment. O'Daniel nodded. Lavin mumbled something in Spanish.

"We're here," Sandford said to Varanathan. "Spit it out."

"Firstly," Varanathan said with a twinkle in his eye, "bearing in mind we are off the record, as Traditionalist co-commander, I must protest your scheme of arming one of your men and plotting crimes against the mission and the Traditionalist Coalition."

"Look in the mirror, Mr. Pot."

Varanathan spread his hands. "I'll interpret that as the same protest made by you against me and those loyal to me." He rolled his wrist in O'Daniel's direction.

"Don't waste my time with bloody nonsense."

"I'm pointing out the elephant in the room, to allow us to shoot it before it rampages. I don't fault you for trying the same thing I tried. In fact, I welcome it. It proves we are cut of the same cloth, with the only difference being the color with which it is dyed."

Sandford squinted at him. She'd get no clue from his expression. "Cut to the chase."

"We both realized there might be Octalien technology worth seizing. Rightly so, given what Ingvarsson said about how they journeyed here."

"You wouldn't put it past her to lie?"

Varanathan kept his face still. Had the Swedish woman spun a fiction out of the raw data? Had the people at Gagarin Station made up a story to discredit his leadership? Sandford's also.

He kept his gaze on her while turning his head to O'Daniel. "You've looked at the data and Ingvarsson's interpretation more than I have...." A knot formed in his stomach. Would O'Daniel read that he bluffed, and cover for him?

"Her work checks." O'Daniel's voice came quietly, as if he'd worked late nights deciphering the raw data on his own. He rubbed the purplish bags under his eyes for emphasis.

Good man with a good play. Or perhaps he'd actually burned the midnight oil to verify the Swedish woman's work?

A loyalist and a hard worker? Varanathan's assessment of O'Daniel climbed.

Not time for that now. Varanathan said to Sandford, "We both misjudged the men—and in my case, also the woman—we tasked to do so."

Her squint eased. For a moment, she rolled her lips together.

"And now the crew are united in antipathy for the actions we plotted."

Shoulders stiff, she said, "I know damned well how the crew feel." She glowered at him.

Varanathan raised his palm to mollify her. She was not an underling, who could only listen until he came to the point. She was a peer and could not be dominated that way. Especially if he wanted any chance of her to agree with his proposal. "Here then is my point. We have both lost our chances of seizing Octalien technology for ourselves. What is the next best thing? For each of us to return to our factions with as much of it as possible."

She regarded him for a moment, then smiled for perhaps the first time since they'd left Sol System. "What's your angle?"

The research park. The corner office, looking out on hundreds of underlings scurrying beneath the red bowers of cotton trees. "The same as yours, I should think. Position. Influence. Power. And all the other benefits flowing from those." He glossed over bribes, kickbacks, insider trading, and mistresses with a tight-lipped smile.

She peered down her nose. "I do not aspire to base things."

Varanathan threw back his head and chortled. "If you lie to yourself, that is your choice. But you are too much like me. I will see through any lie you may tell."

Her eyes widened. She dropped her gaze to the table in front of Lavin. After a time, she raised her head. A faint smile played on her lips, like that of the Italian woman in the painting copied down the hall at the Leonardo room. "You are a blunt little social climber. Continue."

"I propose we work together to maximize the Octalien technology we carry with us back to Earth. You take half, I take half. Both our leaderships will be delighted with what we bring. But they'll need so much help, understanding it, deciding what to keep classified and what to share with the public. If anything. We will each rise through our ranks as our faction's expert on Octalien technology."

She eyed him but said nothing.

"And what will happen," Varanathan said, "if we unlock superior propulsion technology down on the planet? Our factions won't have to pool their resources to build a solitary ship. A fleet for you, a fleet for me. There are a hundred stars within twenty light-years of Earth. I would be satisfied directing the exploration and colonization of fifty of them."

Her face masked her emotions, but her torso rose and fell with heavy breaths. "You offer an intriguing vision of the future." Her breath caught. "Assuming we each could claim the role of our factions' experts."

"A fair assumption, I should think."

"Six people at Gagarin Station might say otherwise."

Varanathan gave a close-lipped smile. "Six people might suffer a tragic accident."

Sandford looked thoughtful for a moment. She shared the barest glance with Lavin. The man inclined his head. Shadows thickened in the lines down his face.

"Space travel is dangerous, even today," she said. "But what are we to do about crew, like your Life Support man?"

"We shall speak publicly, you and me both, to all crew and science personnel on *Concordia* or on the planet. We will, how do the Americans say it? Throw London and St. Petersburg under the bus."

"Go on," Sandford said.

"Both our leaderships on Earth gave each of us conditional orders. If we found powerful alien technology, we were to seize it. A mistake, but we did so, out of loyalty to the people who gave us this opportunity, out of mistrust of each other, and out of fear the crew and scientists would not support us if it seemed we betrayed our factions."

Sandford sniffed out a breath. "We'll need more than a bloody—" She shifted to a mocking American accent. "—'my bad.'"

"We will be contrite," Varanathan said. "Through their resistance, the crew and scientists have shown us we had no need to fear. In the face of their common purpose, we spoke frankly, and overcame our mutual mistrust." He lifted a hand and turned it in a lazy circle, indicating their current conversation. "And through our frank talk, we realized the bureaucrats in Alliance and Coalition headquarters weren't the ones who gave us this opportunity. Billions of common citizens hoping for peace and discovery gave it to us."

"You expect that to work?"

"If it gets us to Earth, it worked well enough. And if, after we four and our alien cargo are offloaded, a tragic accident were to strike the ship and all still on her, how did you put it? Space travel is dangerous?"

She turned to Lavin. The other shifted his seat over, moving his mouth close to her ear. They didn't whisper, but at that range, their wearables could communicate directly, at low power, and encrypted, without needing to send packets through the ship's network, where IT workers from either faction could decipher them.

Sandford squared her padded shoulders to Varanathan. "I take it you've drafted some remarks?"

"I'll share them with you after the meeting."

"Please do. Lavin, I'll leave the control room to you and Quesada." To Varanathan, she said, "Gentlemen, good day."

Varanathan stood up and extended a hand to his counterpart across the table. O'Daniel did likewise. After the handshakes, the Humanists left.

O'Daniel stood with an uncertain look in his baggy eyes. Varanathan raised his finger to his lips. Certainly possible one of the Humanists had stuck a bug onto a chair cushion or the underside of the table. "Come, we could use some coffee."

"Sure," O'Daniel said. "Late night last night."

They stepped into the corridor. Empty, though it wouldn't matter. Varanathan ambled toward the nearest kitchenette. He made come-here motions with his fingers until O'Daniel flanked him and matched his pace. The American kept a couple of inches between their arms. Good man. Always careful to avoid debasing a superior with physical contact.

O'Daniel reached for his chest. He pushed the flat nubbin of his wearable to his left, toward Varanathan.

Peer-to-peer contact requested popped into Varanathan's view of the stippled black non-slip decking.

Varanathan thought words. Patches on the sides of his throat picked up the faint electrical of words he thought about speaking but did not voice. *Accept.*

O'Daniel's words sounded in Varanathan's auditory nerves. No one else would hear them. *How much of that did you mean?*

I've prepared the speech to the entire expedition.

Puzzlement came through the link. *So you'd split the nearby stars with her?*

I'd be content to oversee fifty expeditions. I didn't say I wanted her to oversee another fifty. Varanathan gave himself a satisfied smile. *I didn't even say I'd share the nearby stars with the Humanist Alliance.*

CHAPTER 13

28 JULY 2127 (EARTH REFERENCE FRAME) | 28 SEPTEMBER 2125
(CONCORDIA REFERENCE FRAME)

FROM THE GARAGE TENT, Ulanovas's whoop carried across the sun-baked equipment yard. Louder than the rustle of wind and the hum of d'Arbaud and McIlroy's equipment in the science tent, it reached Jaeger near the water condensator's towering half-funnel on his way back from the latrine. The excitement in the shout made Jaeger's heart beat a little faster.

Bloops chimed. A trio of red exclamation marks popped into the lower right corner of his vision, and blinked. A priority video call. He answered.

A window appeared over his view toward the garage. Ulanovas, tousled hair and teeth bright in a laughing smile. "We did it!"

The others came on the call, in windows in line with their locations. From the main room of the tent, Feng said, "Do what?"

"Varanathan and Sandford gave in! I'll share it."

Another window popped up. It slid over the background, and the windows showing the others at Gagarin Station, to stay in the center of Jaeger's vision as he went into the main tent. Varanathan and Sandford, side by side in one of the conference rooms off the control room.

The window seemed to brighten in the shaded light inside the tent. The cool and rich air filled his lungs.

Varanathan made a little half bow and said, "...We plotted against one another, and against all of you, out of fear."

"We feared our superiors, Coalition and Alliance, would punish us if we came home without following their secret orders." Sandford looked more humble than Jaeger could ever remember.

"We feared one another." Varanathan glanced at Sandford. "Or rather, we feared the labels we each assigned to the other."

"Above all," said Sandford, "we feared you would consider us traitors, to Alliance or Coalition, if we worked for the common good."

Jaeger sat with Feng and Ingvarsson, each in their habitual spot in the sitting area. The Swedish woman parted her lips with a puff of breath. "She's done a skilled job with eye makeup."

From the science tent, an aha moment lit up d'Arbaud's face. "That's it. Something looked off about her that I couldn't put it into words."

"Sounds like she wants to sell it," Jaeger said.

"Sell what?" McIlroy jutted out his chin. "I hear a lot of talk but no substance."

Jaeger listened for the substance, but none came. Just more lofty words, about a meeting of the minds between them, about mutual assurances they both sought the common good, about humbly accepting the revealed will of the crew and the scientists, about realizing their highest loyalty was to all the people of Earth. An act? Almost certainly. But they both looked and sounded sincere....

Too sincere. "They don't mean it," Jaeger said.

McIlroy's fingers paused from scratching his beard under his jaw. "I reckon so too."

Silence filled the group video call, broken by Feng. "What are we to do?"

"Call them out." Jaeger cracked his knuckles.

Ulanovas looked to the side. His mouth scrunched up. "Most posts in the crew forum are taking their word for it."

"If that's so," McIlroy said, "and since we don't have any proof they're still plotting something, I think we have to let it go. For now."

Jaeger asked, "For how long?"

"When the time comes, I reckon we'll know."

The time didn't come in the next few shifts. Varanathan and Sandford approved a plan for an Octalien memorial service, including a broadcast to the ship and the other two ground stations.

They sealed off the rec room/temple with a triple layer of gas-tight plastic and laid the alien corpses together on a couch under the low beams at the base of the pole. Limbs not enmeshed, but side-by-side, with hands clasped together as much as d'Arbaud could manage without tearing the dried-out skin.

McIlroy said a few words, then Jaeger, followed by the other four. All were solemn in the face of mortality. As Jaeger spoke, the words coming out of his mouth felt hollow. The usual funeral vagaries from modern people who believed in God, but not very much.

Ingvarsson showed the most emotion. A tear ran down her cheek and trickled over the O_2 mask shielding her birthmark. Even through the mask, her voice choked up. "You did not live in vain and you did not die in vain. We hear your warning. We will not use our powers or yours for destruction. I vow it. We all vow it."

Jaeger's gaze studied the grain of the polished stone floor. Funeral rituals were never about the dead. They were about the living.

After the prayerful words, d'Arbaud placed a sheet over the deceased aliens. She was the smallest person, best able to crawl in, and continually apologized to living person and dead alien alike about the autopsy scars she'd covered as best she could with synthsilk thread and green paint. The others handed to her small rocks from the desert outside, and she laid them in a ring to hold the sheet in place.

Outside the chamber, they zipped up the three plastic doors and sprayed airtight sealant over the teeth. Finally, they bolted to the wall two sheets of aluminum, with words laser-etched in English and pidgin Octalien.

In this room lie two explorers from an unknown world, laid to rest by explorers from Earth.

Next daylight shift, they put up more gas-tight plastic across the mouth of the side corridor, then finally took out the plastic airlock in the tunnel. On a trailer behind the off-roader that brought them there, a box fan rattled to life. Oxygenated atmosphere trickled into the Library for the first time in over a million years.

Faces free, and wearing jackets in the dry, cavernous cool of the Library, they kept exploring.

There were things you couldn't see through video. The fine differences in how the same character from the Octalien syllabary showed up on different panels. Most visible as tiny shadows cast by the beams of their headlamps. Wear and tear in the Octaliens' laser etcher? Or had they carved these by hand, with different individuals leaving their unique marks across a million years?

Close consideration of a row of panels revealed something else they hadn't seen in the tent. A thousand images of blobby shapes of various sizes joined by wavy lines, from half an inch to three inches long. The blobs held symbols from the periodic table.

"Wait a moment," d'Arbaud said. "Is it? Yes. Those are deeper...."

"What did you find?" Jaeger asked. His voice echoed.

"Three-dimensional molecular structures. The blobs are atoms. The wavy lines between the are bonds. The Octaliens showed depth-of-view by etching some atomic symbols smaller and deeper into the panel. Now that I know what to look for...."

From the symbols and accompanying notation, she figured out the Octalien's chemical knowledge within three shifts. They were no more advanced than humankind in chemistry. Ingvarsson updated the English-Octalien dictionary with new terms and revised meanings. At d'Arbaud's request, McIlroy worked with her on metallurgical data. They figured out how the Octaliens alloyed the metals to form the entry slab and the Library panels. Another metal—one that changed shape, though it wasn't clear how—formed the bottom of the rubble plug.

McIlroy and Jaeger sat on the rock outside the tent just before dinner that shift. Everyone called it the front porch, now. Alpha Centauri B squatted near the horizon like an egg yolk about to break. Behind them, the blower motors roared to cool the polywell reactor.

The tent flap opened. Out came d'Arbaud. Ice rattled in an insulated cup.

"Water?" Jaeger asked.

"I was in the mood for a white, but I didn't have a bottle chilled." She gestured to the rock next to Jaeger, on his side away from McIlroy. "May I?"

He shifted his rump to give her more room, than patted the rock. "What kind of mood calls for white wine?"

A gleam came to her soft brown eyes. "I found the key to one of the locks."

Jaeger's eyebrows jumped up. "Keep going."

She sat and twisted forward, to make eye contact with either of them. "You recall there is a niche in the corner of the Library near the rubble plug?"

"The one with the clear cover?" Jaeger asked. She nodded and he asked, "Glass or plastic?"

"Glass, though I don't know it matters. If we're reading the Octalien instructions right, the floor of the niche is made of some sort of organic polymer—"

"Like a protein or their equivalent to DNA? That doesn't make sense. That stuff in their bodies didn't keep its structure for a million years. We know they built to last—"

McIlroy gave quick head-shakes. "I think Dr. d'Arbaud is using *organic* like a chemist. It doesn't mean biological. It means compounds containing carbon."

"Precisely," d'Arbaud said. "The organic polymer we're talking about is some sort of plastic with an extremely long shelf-life."

"I follow you so far," Jaeger said.

"Another panel of Octalien instructions includes the recipe for making another compound which will react with the plastic. The plastic will depolymerize. Fall apart at the chemical level. The bottom of the niche will collapse and expose something. A button, a pressure-sensitive switch? It's not in the dictionary and it didn't come to Ingvarsson's mind when she first looked at it."

McIlroy went on. "Seems unlikely. The Octaliens would expect mechanical switches to break down over time."

Marie smiled over the lip of her cup. "Even if they made them from their fancy alloys?"

"I see what you mean...." McIlroy's gaze drifted over the black fractal shapes of the energy absorbers scattered across the desert below. "But from what we know about the Octaliens, I don't think they'd leave it to chance. They couldn't assume we'd find the base so soon after they built it."

Jaeger took a pull of his beer. "Give me the instructions, please."

"Gladly," said d'Arbaud. In Jaeger's augmented reality vision, the file appeared in the air in front of her. He reached for it. With a squeeze of his fingers, it popped open and unfurled before him.

His gaze ran over alien symbols and their translations. Associations with other Octalien messages, glanced at but not yet decoded, tickled at the back of his mind.

"Who's cooking dinner?" he asked. "Feng, or—"

He didn't break off quickly enough to keep a weary scowl off d'Arbaud's face. Their argument several shifts prior hadn't been resolved. At least not happily.

"Ulanovas," said McIlroy.

"Gee, be a shame if I was late for dinner," Jaeger said. McIlroy chuckled. A wry smile tightened d'Arbaud's cheeks. "Let me check some things."

He opened up other files. Skimmed, read a paragraph, followed an annotated hyperlink, repeated the process. The ice in d'Arbaud's cup clinked as she sipped. Sweat trickled lazily down his back.

After a while, a smile crossed Jaeger's face. "Got it. It's a piezo-electric material. Physical contact will generate a current. No moving parts."

McIlroy and d'Arbaud sat in silence in the long late afternoon. After a time, the geologist said, "That lock still works."

Marie's soft eyes crinkled. "You wish it didn't?"

"Not saying that. Just thinking."

Jaeger peered at his fellow Texan. "About...?"

"Let's assume we put the fear of God into Sandford and Varanathan. Let's assume everything we find in the Vault gets put on the table and shared in full between the Coalition and the Alliance. And let's assume one more thing, that we find down there data on propulsion systems better than Bussard ramjets and superweapons that can wreck planets."

Jaeger read his expression. "Or working models?"

"That's even worse. Because if we find all that, and it gets shared alike back on Earth, have we removed the chance of it being used for mass destruction?"

Silence fell. All three of them studied the liquid left in their cups.

Jaeger considered around another swallow of beer. "Earth has survived almost two centuries of superpowers standing off with H-bombs. Maybe we're intrinsically more peaceful than the Octaliens were. They were carnivores, right? Marie?"

"As best we can tell."

"That might make the difference."

"Maybe." McIlroy fell silent.

Jaeger's voice grew firmer. "And there's another advantage we have the Octaliens don't."

Marie angled her head toward him. "What is it?"

"Mac knows the flavor text of *The Iron Chancellor*."

"The what?" asked d'Arbaud.

"An UltraHistory event card."

McIlroy looked wistfully down the slope, toward the off-roader track winding through the field of energy absorbers. "'Fools learn from their mistakes. Wise people learn from others' mistakes.'"

"When we get back to Earth," said Jaeger, "we'll shout about the Octaliens's mistake from the rooftops, at the top of our lungs."

"Yes, indeed we will," d'Arbaud said. "But will our warning be enough?"

"It'll be more than if we kept our mouths shut." McIlroy drank more beer.

Jaeger ran his thumbnail over a seam in his plastic bottle and mulled. You can't do everything. You can't solve all the world's problems. You do what you can and hope it's enough.

The three of them nursed their nearly-empty drinks, while the elongated shadows of the energy absorbers crept across the rust-colored desert toward their vantage point.

CHAPTER 14

ALPHA CENTAURI B SYSTEM | CONCORDIA | BRAVO CHARLIE ORBIT

13 AUGUST 2127 (EARTH REFERENCE FRAME) | 14 OCTOBER 2125 (CONCORDIA REFERENCE FRAME)

VARANATHAN CUSTOMARILY WORKED IN SECRECY, with only O'Daniel getting a close look at his work. A small price to pay to ensure the success of his mission. Now, though, secrecy felt a burden, to be endured with a stiff upper lip. In part because more than the usual number of pieces had to be moved on the chessboard. In part because he played two opponents simultaneously.

He and Sandford could cooperate on many things against the crew. Vile as she was, crass tongue and the vanity to call her white hair platinum blond, she said something perceptive in the Friedrichs room after they cut the broadcast to everyone on the expedition. *Ruthless people can't imagine how nice nice people are. Nice people can't understand how ruthless ruthless people are.*

He'd stiffened his back at her implication he was ruthless. He merely did what needed doing. And from time to time in his cabin, alone and late at night, his past triumphs would come back to him but feel less triumphant than they had. He'd outplayed all those he'd climbed over, for admission to the best university, for hiring and advancement in national government, in the Traditionalist international bureaucracy. Hadn't he? Or had all those he defeated been too nice to contemplate what exactly he'd been capable of, and prepare against it?

The thoughts would linger, like feral dogs near a trash heap, until he chased them away with a mix of lemon-lime soda and the smoothest Scotch whisky *Concordia*'s fabs could make.

Sandford's point proved itself regarding the *Yang* landing craft. After months on the planet at Yang Station, about two thousand miles inland, where bio teams examined grassland life and geologists studied a thrust fault for signs of ongoing plate tectonics, she and Varanathan called the landing craft back to *Concordia*. A few public words from the co-commanders about returning to the original mission plan, and most of the crew believed them. In a private call to the chief of Yang Station, a male American Traditionalist with a receding hairline and pendulous earlobes, Varanathan steered the conversation so expertly that the station chief sent the landing craft up with Sandford's most loyal pilot while making the American believe it was his idea.

Two days to refuel, then bullet-shaped *Yang* waited at its docking port off Module 6. Reserved for emergency use only, with Sandford's loyal pilot on call to fly to it down with a moment's notice.

Varanathan secretly assigned his most loyal landing craft pilot remaining on *Concordia* to be on call as well.

The mass of the crew were so nice, even the buildup of military forces escaped their notice. At the co-commander's orders, O'Daniel and Lavin put loyalists on the late night fab shift. The output hoppers extruded plastic rifles and ammunition, which disappeared by 0600 every morning. Also overnight, men hand-picked for loyalty to either faction held target practice in an empty cargo hold at the bottom of Module 4, and trained with low power lasers in mock combats against each other. O'Daniel and Lavin told the men they trained for defense, in case Gagarin Station awakened some dormant, hostile Octalien robots.

If the budding soldiers suspected they trained to kill the six explorers of the alien ruins, they kept their suspicions to themselves.

Doubly so, if they suspected they trained to fight their fellows from the opposing faction.

But even if they suspected, they shouldn't care. Their loyalty to the Traditionalist cause passed every test devised by the psych crews here and back home. A deuced shame that xenology had been considered so unimportant that a man as unreliable as Yeggs had got that assignment.

O'Daniel worked late, watching the Traditionalist men train, ensuring the location of their weapons caches remained hidden from Lavin and other Humanists, and doing his utmost to find where the Humanists hid theirs. With what remained of his free time, he pored over data from the Octalien Library, looking for clues as to what lay in the Vault and how the Traditionalists could seize it for themselves. When he dragged himself to Varanathan every morning to report, his eyes drooped more than usual, and his voice sounded ever more subdued. Loyal, like one of those comically sad American hunting dogs, the kind with jowls and long, floppy ears.

When Varanathan came into his proper station back on Earth, he'd let O'Daniel curl up at his feet.

Until then, his men trained, like a knife's edge honed ever sharper, while Varanathan tapped his fingertips together and waited for the right time to strike.

CHAPTER 15

16 AUGUST 2127 (EARTH REFERENCE FRAME) | 17 OCTOBER 2125 (CONCORDIA REFERENCE FRAME)

WHILE THE HOT desert wind billowed the walls of the crew tent, eight figures crowded the main room. The six physical inhabitants all sat in their usual seats, except that d'Arbaud switched with Jaeger to sit as far from Feng as possible. Virtual avatars of Varanathan and Sandford stood between the sitting area and the kitchenette. Although only the eight of them would speak, at a joint demand by McIlroy and Jaeger, the entire crew and science complement, on the ship or on the surface, could watch and listen.

Regina Smalley did Jaeger a favor and kept open a two-way, encrypted text stream proofed against man-in-the-middle attacks, providing live summaries of the transmission received at Glenn Station. McIlroy held a similar link open with a Humanist friend on board the orbiting ship. If the co-commanders tried to manipulate the feed in or out of *Concordia*'s control room, both Jaeger and McIlroy would know immediately.

"We understand you have a status report," Sandford said.

McIlroy took the lead. "We've mapped out solutions to the last two locks securing the Vault."

One of her eyebrows arched. "Continue," she said, while a smug smile formed on Varanathan's face.

"One of the niches near the rubble plug holds metal discs embedded in its walls," McIlroy said. "The Octaliens carved symbols under them. We now know enough to decode them."

McIlroy, Ingvarsson, d'Arbaud, and Jaeger each spoke to their areas of expertise. A few of the metal discs were the sides of piezoelectric blocks. If something continually pressed on several of those blocks simultaneously, the other metal discs would receive enough current to function. Those other metal discs were photoelectric sensors, coming in two types for different wavelengths common in the human-visible spectrum, to detect wavelengths pumped out by both Alpha Centauri B and the Octalien's unknown G8 home star.

The first type would look for an increase in infrared light at a wavelength around 1200 nanometers. The second type would sense decreases at ultraviolet wavelengths about 300 nanometers.

Marie d'Arbaud had figured it out, so she announced the niche's function. "It's a photosynthesis detector."

Varanathan gave her a pleased look. "How did you figure that out?"

"Plants grow by turning CO_2 and water into sugar. Oxygen is a waste product. As CO_2 goes down, it will absorb less infrared, and the first photodetector will give a positive signal. As oxygen goes up, it absorbs more ultraviolet light, and the second photodetector will give a positive signal."

"Why the piezoelectric blocks?" asked Sandford.

"If you put a plant in the receptacle but leave it free to the air we have let into the Library, the carbon dioxide it absorbs and the oxygen it emits will equilibrate with the atmosphere. The sensors won't detect any changes in light. The plant has to be in a closed system. A box of glass or some other material transparent at the required wavelengths would do the trick. The dimensions of the box must be chosen to contact the piezoelectric blocks."

"The Octaliens were carnivores," Sandford said. "Would carnivores test us about plants? And how could they assume plants would be the same for any species that finds the base?"

Marie held her chin up. "The Octaliens breathed oxygen, yes? Bravo Charlie has free oxygen in the atmosphere. These things only happen if photosynthesis continually occurs on a planet. Otherwise, oxygen combines with metals to form rust, and the planet ends up like Mars."

"They reckoned any species capable of traveling here would breathe oxygen too," said McIlroy.

"They also sculpted panels showing the photosynthetic reactions," Ingvarsson added. "Marie, I understand the pathway differs from Earth life?"

"Yes, but the end result is the same. Atmospheric oxygen and carbon dioxide absorption peaks occur at the same wavelengths regardless how those compounds are generated or consumed by photosynthesis."And to answer your first question, though the Octaliens didn't eat plants, their prey likely did."

Varanathan looked thoughtful. "If I understand correctly, you believe we can unlock this part of the puzzle by making an air-tight greenhouse?"

Marie's mouth hung open a moment. Jaeger understood completely. *Varanathan* and *understanding* of a scientific question rarely went together.

Silently, a green light blinked in the corner of his vision. A text from Regina Smalley. *Bet you a quid O'Daniel put the words in his mouth during the thoughtful look.*

I need better odds than that, Jaeger replied by virtual touch-typing on the sides of his thighs, where the arms of his chair hid his fingers from the stereocameras mounted on tripods near the co-comman-ders's avatars.

"Yes," d'Arbaud said.

Sandford squinted, like everyone around tried to trick her. "Why cobble together such a contraption? Just hack the damned thing."

"We thought of that," Jaeger said. Two lamps, one at each wave-length. Enough fiber optic light guides to cover each photodetector. Some tension rods to push on the piezoelectric blocks.

She swung her gaze on him, like the main gun on an armored vehicle's turret. "Why would you decide against such a thing?"

Jaeger held out a hand, palm-down, in McIlroy's direction. No need for the Humanist to get further on her bad side. "Our scheduled departure isn't for another six months. We're in no hurry to get to the Vault. Are you?"

Her nostrils flared with a sharp inhalation. The effort to keep her next words mild showed on her face. "Tell us about the third lock."

"I'd be glad to," Jaeger said.

Despite his physics degree, he hadn't studied the basics of elec-tricity since his undergraduate days. He flipped the switch and the lights came on, and he never thought about how they worked.

Still, he understood the Octalien's arcane notation for currents and circuits better than anyone else.

He opened up files and images and shared them with the co-commanders and the entire audience. Two ceramic plates stood on the Library walls near the rubble plug, at Octalien shoulder height, about the size of a woman's hand.

He pointed to one of the ceramic plates. "See these holes?" A cluster of rectilinear, metal-lined holes, from an eighth to a half an inch long. The holes stood in an asymmetric array, odd to his eyes.

"Reminds me of electric car charging ports in Britain," Sandford said.

"Exactly. Not for electric cars, of course, but power ports all the same. We have the material to fabricate plugs and wires, and Ulanovas will solder them together. And we'll need to condition the power. The amount of current has to be precise, down to accounting for the length and resistance of the wires and plugs."

"What happens if you fail to control it?" asked Varanathan.

"We don't know for certain...."

McIlroy spoke. "The alloy plate at the bottom of the rubble plug might go through a conformation change that we can't undo."

"Might?" Acid dripped from Sandford's single word.

"We don't know what kinds of booby traps the Octaliens might have set," said McIlroy. "Which is another reason we won't hack the photosynthesis detector. If something blows up, literally, it's our back-sides on the line."

"It would also put the contents of the Vault at risk," Varanathan said. "We can't risk a boon for all mankind because we are impatient."

What was that line from his one Shakespeare class in college? *He doth protest too much?* Jaeger nodded. "Completely agree."

Varanathan smiled, please with himself.

A text came in from Smalley. *He's a fair dinkum commander, now you took him to task.*

He's definitely changed. By being more cautious? Or was Jaeger seeing things?

Sandford's brows furrowed. "Just three things to open the Vault?"

McIlroy answered. "We've pored over all the Octalien writing in the Library. If we provide the current through the power plugs Jaeger just described, plus power trickles from the piezoelectric sensor under the chemistry niche and the photosynthesis photodetectors, the slab of shape-changing alloy at the bottom of the plug will dilate and corkscrew itself along the walls."

"From a disc to a spiral ramp?"

"You got it," McIlroy said. "The rubble will fall through or slide down the ramp, into the empty pit at the bottom."

"And the Vault will lie open," Varanathan said. There was as much greed in his voice as in Sandford's eyes.

"How much time?" the British woman asked.

"We'll fab, assemble, and test the photosynthesis box next shift.

Second shift from now, first thing in the local morning, we'll place it, then fab the electrical and chemical pieces. We'll monitor the photosynthesis box a couple of times each shift until it reaches the oxygen and CO_2 concentrations the Octaliens called for."

"A week?" Varanathan asked.

"Till we get in?" Jaeger gave a little nod. "About that."

A smirk flickered over Varanathan's swarthy face.

Sandford spoke. "Anything else of note?"

"I've deciphered some of the Octaliens history," Ingvarsson said, her English cool and articulated. "Rather formulaic. *Yellow vine pack rose in strength. Great tree pack and river rock pack united to defeat yellow vine pack. Great tree river rock tribe rose in strength. High cloud broad shoulders tribe and fourteen orphans tribe united to defeat great tree river rock tribe.* And on, and on."

"Small wonder they destroyed themselves," Sandford said. Jaeger knew her expressions well enough to tell she tried to hide boredom. Her avatar straightened, rippling the ends of her long white hair. "I have nothing more to ask. Varanathan?"

"We've taken enough of their time," the Traditionalist co-commander said. "Schedule our next meeting before you open the Vault. *Concordia* out."

The avatars blinked away, but persisted as afterimages on Jaeger's retinas. A shudder ran across his shoulders. They seemed to have yielded to the will of the crew and scientists, but had they truly changed?

While the others rose to go their other duties, a notification popped up in the corner of his vision. *Incoming group call request, Sandford to you and McIlroy, full virtual.*

He glanced at McIlroy. The geologist arched his eyebrows and shrugged. "Wonder what she has to say?"

Ingvarsson halted, half-unbent from sitting. "She? Ah."

"One way to find out," said Jaeger.

Sandford's avatar appeared over the table in front of the two men. Not a live hologram filmed by stereocameras, but a bit of CGI trickery generated by her wearable, with emotional displays based on her live biometric data. The effect fell somewhere in the uncanny valley. CGI avatars always reminded Jaeger of the animations when someone played an UltraHistory event card. And it didn't help that flesh-and-blood Ingvarsson, younger and prettier, waited behind Sandford's avatar.

At least instead of Sandford's usual arrogance, her avatar looked more personable. With a touch of worry. "Your pardons, gentlemen, I'm not in front of a camera and can't speak aloud." Her lips moved a hair out of sync with the words.

We understand, Jaeger said by touch-typing the words on his thighs.

Tiny muscles flexed in McIlroy's throat, near his subvocal pickup patches. *We reckon you're busy.* His fingers brushed over his beard.

"I thought it urgent to warn you both. About Varanathan. He hasn't given up his old schemes."

Unlike her? Jaeger kept the thought off his face as best he could.

You've got something specific? asked McIlroy.

"You heard him tell you to take all the time you need to open the Vault. The only reason he would do that is to misdirect you."

Jaeger replied. *For what purpose?*

"I wish I knew. He's locked down a brace of rooms in Mod 5. Says it's routine and authorized by protocol. Though the latter makes it permissible, it still seems suspicious, doesn't it?" Her avatar's eyebrows jumped in hammed-up, CGI surprise. "I have to break off. Please, remember, you shouldn't trust him. When one of his schemes ends, he hatches two more."

The avatar winked out. Only Ingvarsson remained in the room with the two men. She rubbed the side of her nose, then moved her finger away. "What did she have to say?"

"Don't trust Varanathan," Jaeger said. He twisted his upper body toward McIlroy. "Did you pick up anything more?"

"No. I'll ask my contacts upstairs if the Trad leadership is doing something in Mod 5." He aimed his chin at Ingvarsson. "Something funny?"

A rare smile curled up the Swedish woman's lips. A glint shone in her brown eyes. "If she tells us not to trust Varanathan, she's plotting something as bad as he. If not worse."

McIlroy chuckled. "They are two peas in a pod. Or two turds in a punchbowl."

Jaeger froze. An intuition flowed down his chest. An old ploy, to deflect suspicion off oneself by denouncing someone else. "Aren't they?"

"What's got into you?" McIlroy asked.

He gave Ingvarsson a moment's scrutiny. Her brown eyes stared back.

Probably not her. Jaeger palmed his forehead. "A twelve-ounce space in my gut." He heaved himself out of his chair and waved his hand toward the refrigerator. "Time for a beer?"

The geologist's eyes narrowed briefly. "Five o'clock somewhere."

Jaeger went to the fridge, pulled out two bottles, pried off the caps. He handed one to McIlroy, then led the way outside. Across the hot afternoon yard, past the sports court where a pickleball net separated the basketball goals like a border fence, to where they could turn their backs to the security cameras. Far enough for the skitter of pebbles on the desert wind to mask their voices as they planned.

CHAPTER 16

16 AUGUST 2127 (EARTH REFERENCE FRAME) | 17 OCTOBER 2125 (CONCORDIA *REFERENCE FRAME*)

AFTER DINNER, while McIlroy took plates flecked with marinara sauce and bits of proteinballs to the recycling hopper, Jaeger stood and stretched his arms toward the plastic ceiling. "Who's up for basketball?"

Ulanovas jumped up. "I'll get my shoes and my headband." He went to the men's quarters and left the door unzipped behind him.

"Basketball?" Ingvarsson patted her stomach. "We just ate."

"Nothing strenuous. Be good to get out of the tent for a while. Get away from them." He waved at the spot formerly occupied by the co-commanders's avatars. "Feng?" Jaeger sounded casual.

Feng looked hesitant, then lifted his shoulders. "I'll play." He turned his ball cap backwards, hiding its lenticular Chinese characters from view.

"Great! The pilots can pick teams. Ingvarsson, you in?"

"I've never played."

"You'll get the hang of it. What about you, d'Arbaud?"

Marie gave her head a little shake. "Someone must clean the cookware."

"I'll get it," said McIlroy. He bent a little, reached down, and rubbed through his cargo pants just above his kneecap. "My old football injury is acting up."

Part of the script. Jaeger said, "Come on, Mac. You aren't that old."

"I want to walk without a limp next shift. And you aren't young yourself. Make sure you stretch."

Ulanovas came out of the men's quarters. A pair of shorts hung below his knees. A white sweatband flattened his sandy blond bangs against his forehead. "McIlroy, the teams will be uneven if you don't play."

With a grin, Jaeger stretched his arms forward. "I'll be on one team, both ladies on the other."

Ingvarsson angled her face up, accentuating an arched eyebrow and the birthmark on her cheek. "You think we are twice the athlete as each of us?"

Jaeger laughed. "We'll find out."

Alpha Centauri B cast a long shadow of the goal post to the sideline and beyond. While the pickleball net wound itself up and its stanchions retracted, they tossed up shots from eight to ten feet. Ingvarsson dribbled like a beginner, too much movement of her hand. Marie d'Arbaud launched shots that brushed the bottom of the net. Jaeger's shots rattled the rim and fell with a thud to the packed, crosslinked sand.

"You're no better than we are," said d'Arbaud. Her breath came easily. They'd all adapted well to the under-oxygenated air.

"Fake it till you make it." Jaeger threw up another ball. It smacked the transparent backboard and rebounded straight at him.

"No no no, your shooting form is terrible," said Ulanovas. He came closer and slowly mimed a shooting motion. "Pancake to goose-neck, okay?"

"Thanks, coach," Jaeger said. He almost said *let's just play* but decided against it. No telling how much time McIlroy needed alone in the tent.

Warmups continued. Jaeger practiced his shooting form. Feng dribbled around, back and forth across the linear shadow cast by the top piece of the side fence, shot jumpers. He hit three out of five, then said, "I'm ready."

"Me too," Ulanovas said. "Full court, okay?" he asked with a grin.

Groans and headshakes outvoted him four to one.

They rolled excess balls toward the equipment hopper near center court. The hopper's gray plastic housing glowed orangey in the sunset. Robotic arms extended from the hopper and picked up most of them, with one straggler clinking to a stop a third of the way along the side fence. The scoreboard flashed, then showed red digits 0 - 0.

Ulanovas could have taken on the rest of them single-handedly. Too quick for Jaeger to guard, too tall for Jaeger to contest his shots. He broke double-teams by bounce passing through Jaeger and Feng's legs. Marie made a couple of shots, enough for Jaeger to cover her and leave Feng to guard the Lithuanian alone.

Offense was no easier. After Ulanovas jumped a pass he aimed at Feng and raced to the three-point line to reset the possession, McIlroy drawled through the fence, "I reckon his team's got the 14 and yours has the 4?"

The goal post rattled a little, followed by the swish of the ball through the net. "Make that 17," said Ulanovas.

"Sarcasm is the basest form of humor," Jaeger said. He glanced at his fellow Texan.

Beard ruddy in the sunset, eyes squinting under his shading hand, McIlroy dipped his chin, one solitary nod.

Jaeger raised his hand for the ball and jogged up to the three-point line. Stopping the game right after McIlroy arrived might look suspicious. After the teams traded baskets, and Ulanovas stole the ball from Feng's dribble and sank a long jumper, the Lithuanian said, "21-6. Call it a game?"

"Gladly," said Jaeger. Handshakes all around, though Feng pointedly avoided touching d'Arbaud's hand. He turned his ball cap around the right way and the six of them headed back to the tent.

Late in the ship's night, Varanathan waited in his office. The open door showed a slice of quiet and dark hallway outside. Most of the slideshow frames on his desk faced the doorway and the twin unpadded visitor chairs. In the frames, photos of him with a who's-who of politicians, both national and Coalition, dissolved in and out, like water dripping down the staggered leaves of a rain tree an hour after a downpour.

The only frame facing him showed a single image. A windswept field with wickets made from lengths of plastic pipe. The cricket oval of many long hours of his youth. Wistful in memory, despite the dust in his mouth and only a trickle of water from a rusty spigot to wash it away. Standing in the crease, bat in hand, striving to knock the ball for six. Taking aim at the clump of red cotton and jackfruit trees in the distance.

Knuckles rapped the door and brought him back to *Concordia* and his objective. From the thick hands and the sound of breathing in the hallway, O'Daniel.

"Enter."

The hinges creaked. The bags under the American's eyes looked like bruises. "I've got the latest personnel fitness reports."

Varanathan glanced at the time. 2125-Oct-23-23:43. "Just under the wire," he said, his tone a little cross for the sake of any microphones Sandford might have deployed in the corridor.

"I had to ride the department heads something fierce to get them on time. Like to go over them with you."

Varanathan gave an exaggerated sigh. "A leader's work is never done. Shut the door, if you would."

O'Daniel eased the door closed. The bolt sprang into the strike-plate, startlingly loud. From behind a potted cactus, he toed out a stuffed sock, about eighty centimeters long, and nudged it into place at the bottom of the door. It covered the gap with a few centimeters to spare.

He turned to face the desk, a question in his lidded eyes.

Varanathan's wearable reported no spy devices monitored the room, and the rattlers that set up subaudible vibrations in the walls, floor, and ceiling set up an interference pattern to prevent anyone converting the vibrations of their voices into intelligible speech. He beckoned O'Daniel closer. "We are secure," he murmured. A whisper would carry farther, maybe even through the stuffed sock and under the crack in the door.

With one hand, the American scooped up a chair by a gap in the backrest. He gently set it down and sat, so close to the desk his knees brushed the privacy panel. He leaned over the slideshows of Varanathan and politicians. "I did compile the personnel reports, if you want to review them."

"Anything change?"

"Nothing."

They knew who was loyal, and more important, who would follow orders. O'Daniel chief among the latter. "No need. Will Gagarin Station be ready?"

"The basil plant in their greenhouse box grew like they expected. Gas concentrations are in the go zone. That's one of the locks. They'll open the other two tomorrow."

"What will they find in the Vault?"

O'Daniel sucked in a breath through his teeth. "If I knew, I'd tell you."

Varanathan's face hardened. "This is a matter of human historical importance. If you botch it—"

"I won't." The American exaggerated his mouth around the words.

Varanathan peered at him. Copying a page from his playbook?

But the man held his gaze, and the bags under O'Daniel's eyes spoke of how much work he'd done. He didn't bluff.

"Tell me more," said Varanathan.

"I've gone over the raw data from the Library, Ingvarsson's translation, and intel leaked out by Lavin. No clue what's in the Vault. I'll watch Gagarin Station when they open the Vault and go over everything they send up."

"And if you find something?"

"The men we trust will be ready. Step one, neutralize the Humanist arsenal."

"You're certain you know where it is?" The words rushed out of his mouth. He noticed how far forward his shoulders hunched. He took a breath and leaned back. Calm and confident at all times. That's what leaders did.

A smile invigorated O'Daniel's face. "We got three sightings of them caching and retrieving weapons in locked storage low on Mod 2. I sneaked a pipe inspection robot in through the back. Its camera got pics of weapons and its sniffer caught propellant. Gunpowder."

"And our weapons cache is secure?"

Did annoyance flicker across the American's face? He hadn't reported on their counterintelligence operations against Sandford's ilk.... Wait, perhaps he had. Underlings sometimes imagined a leader should worry about all the details. They didn't realize how much a leader shouldn't be bothered. He had to focus on the big picture.

"Yes. Lavin bought our misdirection to Mod 5. Hook, line, and sinker."

"You misspoke, I should think. *Sandford* bought our misdirection."

"Sandford listens to whatever Lavin tells her, then takes sole credit for it." O'Daniel waved his thick hand. "We have the advantage on them."

Varanathan nudged a video frame on his desk. The magnetic base resisted his fingers. "I'll work on step two. I'll tell Earth we have to take the transmission antenna down for maintenance. Anomalous diagnostics. Then we remain silent until we return to Earth with our surprise." He gave O'Daniel a wan smile. "And the communique to the crew?"

"The draft I sent you yesterday is the latest one. Instead of saying 'she planned to betray all of us,' I went with 'she plotted treason against our mission and the peoples of Earth.'"

With the sides of his hands, Varanathan smoothed down his hair away from its center part. He practiced the solemn look he'd give the cameras, then smiled. "Treason, well said. And you went with 'preventative action' over 'preemptive strike'?"

"Just like you told me to."

He had? Varanathan didn't remember. "Very good. And after the ship is secure, are we ready to deal with Gagarin Station?"

O'Daniel shrugged. "They won't know what hit them."

CHAPTER 17

23 AUGUST 2127 (EARTH REFERENCE FRAME) | 24 OCTOBER 2125 (CONCORDIA REFERENCE FRAME)

THE OFF-ROADER ROLLED down the slope from the station and over the desert terrain. The low morning rays of Alpha Centauri B stretched the shadows of the vehicle and its trailers toward the energy absorbers poking out of the red sand.

Their own energy absorbers, solar panels laid flat on the reddish sand, came into view. Hardware modules—comms relay between the Octalien facility and camp, firefighting equipment, medkit, and a server controlling everything else—lay on a raised diamondoid platform under a canopy bearing a low sand drift.

At the tunnel mouth, more sand piled up along the lip of the nanotube alloy, but the structure inside remained rigid. The congealed sand floor, intact.

Feng swung the off-roader around and backed into the tunnel. Jaeger's eyes turned as they always did for a last, heat-hazed view of the campsite and a top sliver of *Gagarin* at its distant landing site. The constant beeping of the vehicle in reverse turned shrill as it echoed off the tunnel wall. Like miners in hard hats, descending into a working shaft on Earth.

Though instead of gems or precious metals, they sought veins of ancient knowledge worth incalculably more.

If there was anything more. Could it be a hoax? Or a further test sent by the Octaliens from beyond the grave? They might have decided any species curious enough to enter the Vault would be too dangerous to be trusted with their technology.

Marie d'Arbaud compressed her thin lips more than usual. She raised her voice over the backup beeps. "Can't we turn that sound off?"

Feng looked up from the hardwired back-up display long enough to meet her gaze in the rear view mirror. He dragged out his next word. "No."

McIlroy, fourth member of this crew, sat with his head down, finger as a stylus, tops of thighs as a slate. Jaeger knew him well enough to read his actions. Double-checking the protocols they'd worked out. Set up the fresh battery pack, cables, and sensors around the rubble plug, then retreat here. Detach the trailers from the off-roader. All four of them would board the off-roader, Feng at the wheel, before McIlroy sent the activation signal.

Jaeger would watch the sensors and tell Feng to drive like the devil chased them, if something bad came out of the Vault.

They unloaded the trailers, lashed cargo onto the flat tops of robots like magnetic pizza boxes on wheels, and descended the ramp. The robots' motors whined under their cargo. The robot carrying the new battery pack looked like an ant bearing a crumb of food three times its size.

The Library looked the same as ever. Low ceilings and serpentine path between the rows of panels. After months in the cool, echoing space, Jaeger belonged here more than any of the anonymous apartments he'd lived in during graduate school. The panels were like the walls of his childhood home, their etchings like the crayon lines he'd scrawled as a child to earn a fanny-swat from his mom.

Their headlamps glinted off symbols. He could read some as easily as English, now, the meanings coming to his mind without having to think about them.

Lessons in physics.

Lessons in history.

They rounded the final line of panels. The side corridor branched off. Its chambers held no interest now. They would return to gathering dust like the unused rooms at grandma's house. The last two Octaliens on their makeshift bier would continue their journey into eternity.

The interest lay in the other back corner of the Library, along the walls around the rubble plug. A side-facing bowl lamp stood on a spindly tripod. The lamp's bowl almost touched the airtight box wedged into the photosynthesis tester. A sunny glare rimmed the bowl. A cable, coerced into a nearly straight line by gray strips of duct tape, ran from the lamp along the floor to the old battery pack in the corner near the last panel.

Feng adjusted the brim of his cap as he read the old pack's power reading. "Down to 7%."

"I'll help you switch it out," Jaeger said. He gave orders to the robot carrying the new pack. It followed him around the jumbled pile of rocks in the floor. In the corner, Feng unplugged the lamp's power cable from the old pack.

The area dimmed. Jaeger's headlamp beam edged the symbols with sharp shadows.

He'd been reading up on Octalien history in what little spare time he had. His gaze stopped at a group of symbols. Their meanings came unbidden. *You grow stronger. We unite.*

Was that all the Octaliens had come to? A giant UltraHistory game, sound and fury, signifying nothing, until someone flipped over the board and sent pieces flying across the room?

Clammy air washed over his bare arms.

Is that all that humankind would come to?

He set aside his thoughts. They placed the new battery pack and plugged the lamp back in. The area grew brighter than before.

McIlroy and d'Arbaud squatted and peered in the photosynthesis niche. "Looks like it's growing," he said. His finger tapped the clear plastic box holding the leafy green basil.

"It would be delicious in a marinara sauce." She checked data her wearable must have projected onto her view of the wall next to the niche. "Local data agrees with telemetry. Carbon dioxide is down and oxygen is up enough to pass this test."

McIlroy stood up. "Means it's chemistry time."

She led the way to a niche on the adjacent wall. The robot porting the chemicals and related equipment followed at her heels.

The chemical reaction would be simple enough, but the fumes generated when the organic acid hit the Octalien plastic would sting their eyes and rasp their throats. McIlroy pulled out a rotary tool with a cutting wheel. Rough whining made Jaeger press his finger against his ear. Orange-hot shavings of the clear cover material spewed away from the niche.

Meanwhile, d'Arbaud set up a fume hood cobbled together by Feng and Ulanovas—wobbly aluminum flanges, intake fan, scrubber. Next, she laid out a safety kit. Squirt bottle of water for eye and skin wash, bags of absorbent powder for spills.

She put on safety goggles and thick rubber gloves, then held out another pair of goggles. "If you want to look over my shoulder, you'll have to wear these. You can get a better view tapping the camera feed from my wearable."

Feng said nothing. He leaned against the wall, arms crossed. The tails of his cargo shirt hang loose over his waist and the small of his back.

"I'll do that," Jaeger said. He borrowed the view from the cameras dabbed around d'Arbaud's eye sockets. He pinched and slid air to move the window out of his line-of-sight on Feng.

Not much to see as she worked. Marie pulled a flat-bottomed flask from a rack on the robot's back. She kneeled, corduroy fabric on the smooth stone floor, and reached into the niche with the flask. She brought the fume hood as close as she could, then worked loose a red rubber stopper from the flask's mouth.

She sniffed and coughed. Even Jaeger, standing eight feet away, squeezed shut his eyes, as if d'Arbaud had opened a door to an onion-slicing factory.

"Turn on the hood," she said. "McIlroy, the red switch. Yes."

The fan rattled up to speed. The chemical bite in Jaeger's eyes eased. He refocused on the camera feed.

With her gloved hand, d'Arbaud tilted the flask. The acrid liquid inside came out in a controlled pour, spreading across the Octalien plastic lining the bottom of the niche.

Black vapor curled up from the Octalien plastic. A rancid stench leaked past the fume hood. Jaeger scrunched up his nose.

"It should be only moments," d'Arbaud said, voice constricted. A faint hiss emerged from the niche. "Here it is."

She pinched her nose shut, then sank further on her haunches. Her cameras showed the floor of the niche had evaporated, save for a few stringy threads drooping down in the corners.

She stuck her head in and looked down.

Below the dissolved plastic stood the sheet of piezoelectric the Octalien messages had said lay within.

"Where's the stone?" she asked.

"Got it." McIlroy pulled it out of a robot's pack. A rock like any of the millions strewn about the square klicks of energy absorbers. Lumpy, gray, pitted by millennia of wind-blown sand. McIlroy prob-ably knew its name and how it formed, but for their purposes, it massed enough. The geologist needed both hands to cradle it. Marie d'Arbaud slipped out of his way.

McIlroy shoved it in the niche, then stood up. He wiped his hands on his pants, then looked around. "Did it trigger?"

"We won't know," Jaeger said, "until we wire up the main current."

More work, but not complicated. They ran cables from the fresh battery pack, through the control box and power conditioner, to the plugs in the ceramic wall plates. The plugs were asymmetrical and differed from each other, giving no room for confusion.

With deft movements, Feng helped him uncoil the cables. As eager as the rest of them to turn the key in the final lock.

Jaeger plugged in the last cable, then crouched over the control box. Ready lights green. Remote control ready to receive.

He looked over his shoulder. "Sensors ready?"

The other two had set up gas sniffers, thermometers, cameras, and accelerometers around the rubble plug. A drone rose from the floor near McIlroy's feet. It flew to the corner, motors buzzing when it banked around d'Arbaud.

McIlroy straightened up and leaned backward over his fists pressed to his lower back. "Everything checks."

"Time to get clear," Jaeger said.

Ten minutes later, the four of them sat in the off-roader. The tunnel entrance showed as a bright dot far up the matte black walls.

By mutual agreement between their wearables, the entrance disappeared from view. A virtual wall of camera views of the locks and the rubble plug crossed the entire bore of the tunnel five yards in front of the off-roader. Data feeds from the sensors filled in the curved slivers above and to the sides of the rectangular video windows. In the largest window, the jumbled tops of the rubble chunks lay like a scabrous growth on the Library's smooth stone floor.

Feng pressed the off-roader's start button. The vehicle rolled backward a few inches until he pushed harder on the brake pedal. "Ready."

Jaeger inhaled, chest tight. "Here we go."

His wearable projected a virtual button into the air in front of him. He lifted his hand and flipped open a virtual safety cover, then mashed the button.

On the video wall, nothing moved for a second. Another. A—

The rubble shifted, like sand slumping down in the upper lobe of an hourglass. A moment later, a metallic rumble thundered into their auditory nerves, like a truck full of steel drums had crashed. The rubble pile thundered down, out of sight.

By the time the sound echoed through the Library and up the ramp, only dust wisps trickled through air where rocks had lain undisturbed for over a million years.

"Hover over," McIlroy said. A command to the drone.

The biggest virtual window blinked over to the drone's stereo view. A spotlight on its undercarriage showed splotchy gray, out of focus in the distance. A curled and glinted reflection ringed the pit.

The focus shifted. The shape-changed alloy formed a thin but wide ribbon spiraling into the pit.

Downward flew the drone. Darkness swallowed most of the drone's spotlight. The camera gave glimpses of the deep gray rubble far below, veiled by motes of dust, focus wobbling, fumbling for a steady bearing the jumbled, uneven surface.

Someone shifted body weight. Someone else whispered an exclamation. Jaeger barely noticed.

McIlroy uttered a command. The camera pivoted to the pit wall. The alloy ribbon looked impossibly thin when seen from the side. The spiral ramp ended at a rectangular darkness in the pit wall.

It drew Jaeger's eye like a magnet. The entrance to the Vault. Exactly where McIlroy's seismics and ground-penetrating radars had mapped it months before.

A thrill ran along Jaeger's jaw. Alien secrets, hidden ages ago.

Secrets to benefit all humanity? Or damn them all to hell?

He shook his head like the thoughts were flies buzzing around him. First things first. He glanced at the data columns. "We didn't trigger an H-bomb."

"You reckon so?" McIlroy said, deadpan. He went on. "Gas composition changed a hair. More oxygen and less argon than Bravo Charlie ambient. My guess is they kept the Vault under atmospheric conditions of their homeworld."

"Temperature unchanged." Marie d'Arbaud glanced to McIlroy, to her left in the back seat. "Any movement?"

His fingers swiped at air. "The accelerometers spiked at the alloy shape change and fall of the rubble pile." His fingers pinched together and spread apart. He looked past his jutting chin at his private virtual. "A tremble here and there, probably the rocks settling in the pit. We didn't set anything else to moving."

Jaeger asked, "Send in the drone?"

"Send in the drone."

In the main window of the collective virtual display, the circle of darkness expanded, soon filling the view. The drone's light showed settling dust a few feet below it, but little beyond.Like a robotic submarine descending into sunless ocean depths.

The view tilted. Light glimmered off the alloy ramp.

The drone continued. Its flashlight showed the rough wall of native stone, then the dark rectangle came into view, grew, shifted its shape.

The dark area slid down the view. The drone's camera panned. The shape resolved into a square, height and width the same as the pathway between panel rows in the Library.

Nothing changed for a moment. Excitement edged McIlroy's voice. "In we go."

The temperature readouts vanished from the upper right corner of the public virtual display. In their place came a 3d wireframe map of the Vault. A moving yellow dot marked the drone's path. Down the main corridor. Into the first branch on the left. And on, through each sub-branch, then back to the main corridor for the next branch.

The drone floated peacefully through the air, mindless of the equipment it flew over and the messages lining the walls.

Jaeger's gaze raced to take in all the details speeding by the drone's cameras. It took high-res photos of everything, of course, that he could review in greater comfort back at the tent. But the urge to know what secrets the Octaliens left behind burned in his gut.

Glimpses tantalized him. Symbols from Octalien physics. Gravity, electromagnetism, the weak nuclear force, the strong. Boxy equipment made of their alloys and plastics. Cables snaked like roots from their lower corners and wrapped around thicker cables emerging from the floor.

Power cables, drawing energy from the absorbers poking above the desert sands. The sensors that picked up *Concordia*'s orbital insertion needed power. The computer generating the signal and the transmitter sending it did too.

Jaeger drew in heavy breaths. What other machines needed power?

The drone passed a history panel. Familiar symbols, mixed with unfamiliar ones, and all zipping by before he could make sense of them. *Unite you? Defeat us?*

After a while, d'Arbaud said, "It scanned every room."

A set of symbols in the feed caught Jaeger's attention, like a rock smacking the undercarriage of a car. His gaze roved the drone's camera feed but the symbols were already gone.

Had they really said—?

"Just in time," said McIlroy. A low-battery icon flashed red in the status bar at the bottom of the drone's camera view. "It's got enough juice to make it back to us. Time to head home. We've got plenty to look at back at camp."

Jaeger planted his feet on the floorboard and pushed himself taller in his seat. His short fingers tapped the air. A private virtual opened in front of him, hovering in front of the windshield. Scroll, scroll, where was it?

"I'll put it in power save mode. The camera feed will stop." McIlroy spoke with an amused edge.

Jaeger realized the Humanist talked to him. "Yeah, sure."

McIlroy peered at him from above his brown beard. "Anything worth seeing?"

Feng twisted in the driver's seat. The brim of his cap shaded the expression in his eyes. Marie d'Arbaud shifted in her seat to look around Jaeger's headrest.

All eyes on him, Jaeger said, "Maybe."

"We can talk about it at camp," McIlroy said. "Feng, take us home."

The wall-to-wall shared virtual blinked out, leaving only the monotony of the nanotube wall in the headlights, and the tiny circle of daylight far ahead. Feng put the off-roader into gear. It trudged upslope toward the daylight. The trailers rattled along behind.

Jaeger's attention returned to his private virtual. The color scheme jumped between dark and light as a sensor reacted to glimpses of daylight from the tunnel mouth growing larger in front of them. A scroll, a zoom. *There.*

The off-roader emerged into sunlight. Jaeger's private virtual settled on light mode. He squinted at it, and though the morning baked his skin, a coldness washed down his throat and pooled in his gut.

He didn't need Ingvarsson to tell him what the symbols meant.

Energy from nothing.

CHAPTER 18

Not literally nothing, of course. Jaeger knew that as the off-roader rolled back to camp over the dust-strewn terrain. He knew it when Ingvarsson hurried out of the main tent, hand pressing a broad sunhat against her blond hair. She jogged toward the garage and waited with wide brown eyes as they climbed out.

"What is it?" McIlroy asked.

"I started decoding the Octalien symbols in the Vault." Her voice sped up. "What I read, it seems to untrue, I double-checked my prior work, if it says what I think—"

"I bet it does," Jaeger said.

She swung her gaze his way, her birthmark on her cheek away from him. "You found it too?"

"I might not be a linguist, but I can read Octalien physics. Much of it."

Ingvarsson's nose crinkled. "I suppose there must be physics involved...."

Jaeger intoned his next words. "*Energy from nothing?*"

"No. *We hide ship for you.*"

Muffled gasps sounded around the garage. Wide eyes turned to one another. Jaeger sagged against the side of the off-roader. He thought he'd had the big news. "You go first."

McIlroy shuffled his foot over pebbly ground. Sweat trickled down his cheeks and got lost in his beard. "How about we talk inside."

Cool air, thick with oxygen. They talked over lunch. Ingvarsson's words held their attention so strongly Jaeger forgot to rib Ulanovas for running the microwave short and leaving cold spots inside their vegan shepherd's pies.

"I found this panel in the Vault," she said. Into a shared virtual, she projected an image. Two views, top and side, of a squat cylinder with the approximate proportions of a can of nicotine pouches distending the back pocket of a country boy's jeans. Then she zoomed in on a tiny blip next to the cylinder. The blip resolved into the shape of an Octalien body. "Based on the scale, the cylindrical object is about eleven hundred meters in diameter and three hundred meters tall. Comparable to the interior volume of all six of *Concordia*'s modules."

Marie d'Arbaud extended her neck toward the projection. Her soft eyes crinkled. "But can it be a ship? *Concordia* is long and graceful. This is a can of cat food."

"It's got a different propulsion system," Jaeger said, voice heavy. "Not a Bussard ramjet."

The other three men all eyed him. "What, then?" asked Ulanovas.

"We'll get to that. Ingvarsson, go ahead." He bowed to her.

"I do not know the propulsion system, but all their written description of it calls it a ship. Their ship, which they flew here."

"And they hid it?" McIlroy scrunched up his face. "Where?"

"Underground."

The geologist spread his hands and gave her a sour look. "The seismic survey and the ground-penetrating radar showed nothing that big anywhere near the Library or Vault."

"They didn't hide their ship under the energy absorber field," Ingvarsson said. "They hid it about thirty-five kilometers from the Library entrance."

"Thirty-five klicks," McIlroy muttered. "About twenty miles...." His mouth sagged open. Then his eyes glinted. "I will be damned. The lava field. The 'anomalous' lava field." He used his fingers to make air-quotes.

"Precisely. They made a controlled descent. Their exhaust was so hot it melted the native rock at their landing site. Somehow they created a bubble around their ship as it went through the molten rock."

"Which solidified above them," McIlroy said. "That rock cap has to be at least two hundred meters thick. Any less, and our wide area ground-penetrating radar scans would have detected their ship beneath."

"And we had no reason to do seismic scans." Ulanovas took a bite of his shepherd's pie. After a frown, he got out of his seat and took a step toward the microwave.

"We do now," said Feng.

Ingvarsson said, "They tunneled out of their ship and sealed the exit behind them. But the tunnel will open for a species that is measured for the ship."

"*Measured* for their ship?" Jaeger asked.

Ingvarsson pulled her hand along her blond ponytail. "That is the best translation I can make."

"Could it be a, how do you say it in English?" Ulanovas worked his hand like he reeled in a fishing line. "Semaphore? Metaphor."

McIlroy cleared his throat. "The Octaliens have alloys that can change from a thick slab to a spiral ribbon. I reckon they mean it literally."

Ingvarsson jutted out her hand. Jaeger and the others gave her their attention. "The machineries in the Vault will take our measure if we go to them. The tunnel will open for us and the ship will make itself ready."

Jaeger's heart hammered warmth through his chest. *Concordia* and the Octalien ship, flying in formation back to Earth. Talk about a boon for all mankind. "My god."

Clamminess stole over his neck and cheeks. If Varanathan or Sandford still harbored hopes of stealing Octalien tech, they had more reason now than ever.

Especially because of what he'd read.

"It is your turn now," Ingvarsson said to him.

Jaeger sipped water. Too much salt in the shepherd's pie. He put the glass down and met the gaze of each of the others in turn. "The Octaliens unlocked vacuum energy."

"Vacuum energy?" asked d'Arbaud.

He added a photo of the relevant Octalien symbols with his scrawled translation notes to the public virtual. "We've known this for a couple of centuries. Empty space isn't empty at all. Every instant, in every cubic nanometer—" He held up his thumb and index finger a hair's width apart, then flapped his hand. No way could gestures capture the minuscule scale he talked about. "Trillions upon trillions of paired particles and their antiparticles emerge from quantum fluctuations and release energy. We call them *virtual particles*, because, an infinitesimal moment later, almost all those particles recombine in matter-antimatter annihilation and reabsorb the same amount of energy they released."

"Like sham transactions by some stock market criminal?" Ulanovas said.

Jaeger frowned to himself, then nodded with wider eyes. "I suppose so. The energy balance goes unchanged on the ledger of the universe."

"This sounds philosophical," d'Arbaud said. "If all the released energy is reabsorbed, how could the Octaliens use it?"

"*Almost* all," Jaeger said. "In the twentieth century, Hawking postulated that near the event horizon of a black hole, one virtual particle can remain trapped in the black hole's gravity well while the other escapes, taking some of the black hole's mass and energy with it. Eventually, all black holes completely evaporate."

Feng stared at the virtual display of the Octalien ship. "There is a black hole on that?"

"Not necessarily. A more down-to-earth example of vacuum particles is the Casimir effect. Put two flat plates a nanometer apart in a vacuum." He used his palms this time, and didn't worry that they were a million times farther apart. "Vacuum energy fluctuations, distorted by the plates in the space between them, can pull the plates closer together. Some of the transistors in our wearables function that way. Don't ask me how, I don't do electrical engineering."

McIlroy stroked his beard. "The summary is, colossal amounts of energy exist in every cubic nanometer of space, and the Octaliens knew how to use it. You agree with that?" he asked Ingvarsson.

The Swedish woman looked back and forth between Jaeger's shared photo and what had to be a private virtual displayed on her knee. "Jaeger has the gist of it. *Energy from nothing.*"

"And we've barely scratched the surface of it," said Jaeger. "Like medieval Arabs or pre-Columbian Native Americans burning handfuls of petroleum seeping out of the ground."

Ingvarsson arched an eyebrow at him, but her lips curled up a little and her voice held a hint of playfulness. "Luckily we have some Texans who can pump out the black gold?"

Jaeger smiled, briefly. "To fly their ship interstellar distances, the Octaliens extracted more energy in ten seconds than the whole world got from oil in over a century."

Marie d'Arbaud shrank in on herself. "With enough left over to destroy their home planet."

Jaeger's gaze cycled between the Octalien ship and the physics symbols. Data that had already been backed up to *Concordia* in orbit.

Who would review that data? For the good of the mission or the good of a faction?

Had they reviewed it already?

He swallowed a last bite from the middle of the shepherd's pie. Chalky and cold. He dropped his fork to his plate. "We need to go to the Vault. All of us. Now."

Marie spoke through thin lips. "Why?"

"To get measured for the Octalien ship. So we can fly it home to Earth."

"Why us?"

Jaeger leaned forward. "Because I trust everyone in this tent to use the Octalien ship for the good of all mankind," he said, lying a little. "I don't trust Varanathan or Sandford."

ALPHA CENTAURI B SYSTEM | BRAVO CHARLIE | GAGARIN STATION

23 AUGUST 2127 (EARTH REFERENCE FRAME) | 24 OCTOBER 2125 (CONCORDIA REFERENCE FRAME)

An hour later, Ulanovas backed the off-roader down the tunnel to the Library. Despite the reverse warning beeps and Ulanovas' penchant for more speed than Feng, the descent into darkness felt more comfortable to Jaeger than the bouncing, broiling ride across the desert he and d'Arbaud shared in the lead trailer. He sat sideways, knees bent, one arm extended along the edge of the trailer's bed.

His gaze kept going back to Feng and McIlroy in the back seats of the off-roader. All normal. For now.

With a few commands through his wearable, he shut down the comms relay.

Ulanovas hit the brakes, jostling Jaeger and d'Arbaud against the trailer's nanotube alloy walls. "Careful there," he said to the Lithuanian.

"Sorry." Ulanovas jammed his foot on the parking brake, turned the key, hopped out. "I'm eager. I'm going to fly the Octalien ship!"

"Their ship waited over a million years," d'Arbaud said. "It can wait a few seconds more."

"You won't be the only pilot," Feng said, voice defensive.

Jaeger swung one leg over the side of the trailer and hopped down. He opened the rear gate and held out his hand for d'Arbaud while the others climbed out of the off-roader. They pulled on their hardhats. Headlamp beams bobbed over the curved tunnel wall. They unloaded their gear from the rear trailer. Robots too. Not expecting to need them, but unsure what items the Octaliens might have planned for their successors to carry from the Vault to the buried ship.

They descended the spiral ramp to the Library. The robots' motors whined and tracks clacked as they followed the people like loyal dogs.

Feng's nasal voice echoed off the low, sloped ceiling. "Why did the Octaliens hide a ship for another species?"

"I wondered that too," Ingvarsson said. "I do not know yet. The closest I have found is, let me open the file.... *We are too few to repro-duce. Our meta-nation made this concession to the other meta-nations during mission planning.*"

Jaeger inhaled a cool dry breath. "'Meta-nation' is a superpower or an alliance of great powers?"

"Like our two factions on Earth. There is more. *We will choose our time and way to die. We do this to preserve our knowledge without rust and rot. We preserve it for you. You are the nearest to kin we can ever have.*"

All fell silent. How long did it take one of the Octaliens to etch those sentences in the superhard alloy? What feelings went through its body as it slowly voiced those thoughts?

Jaeger shivered. That other intelligences had once lived, and cast a slender thread of hope into the future....

The ramp leveled out. They slipped into the Library's maze of panels. Only the robots and their footfalls made any noise.

After the final panel, a glance to the left dazzled Jaeger's beam over the aluminum memorial plaque. The final two Octalien corpses remained in their anoxic tomb beyond. *Thank you for your gift*, he mouthed, before he faced forward.

Their headlamps pushed back the shadows over the puzzle niches. The grow lamp still glowed, powering photosynthesis for the basil plant. The Octalien instructions didn't say they had to keep the plant reducing carbon dioxide to oxygen, but better safe than sorry. If their alloys could change shape one direction, they could easily change back.

The walls and low ceiling diffused the reflections of their headlamps. In the floor, the top of the alloy ribbon glimmered. When they approached and looked down to the end of the corkscrewing alloy, the glimmer off the alloy gave just enough light to make out the deep shadow of the Vault entrance, about thirty feet below.

The ribbon spiraled down to the right, about two feet wide and impossibly thin, like a sheet of paper made rigid. Ingvarsson stiffened. Her fingers clawed the air. Her voice came around rough breaths. "I don't know if I can do this."

"We've got a cable," McIlroy said gently. "And stick-on carabiners to mount it to. We'll make a handhold running all the way down."

While Ingvarsson hung back from the edge of the pit, Marie and the men went to work. Uncoil the cable, clip it into a carabiner. The *snicks* of carabiner latches closing on the cable echoed throughout the pit. A squelch of adhesive on the carabiner's transparent mounting plate and the blue-white glow of a UV penlight to cure it.

Jaeger tapped his foot every time the curing timer counted down. But they slowly spiraled down, pressed against the wall, holding on the unreeling cable, gazes away from the three-story drop to the jagged boulders below. One-handed, Marie adhered motion-activated puck lights on the wall above every fourth carabiner. Their wan glow gave a little ambience, like the spiral ramp led to some tourist cave on Earth.

Finally they got to the bottom of the spiral. More adhesive glued the loose end of the cable back on itself. Jaeger took two steps into the Vault, Feng and Ulanovas behind him. Their headlamp beams got lost in the darkness. Jaeger rocked his weight for the minutes McIlroy and d'Arbaud spent returning to Ingvarsson and guiding her down the spiral. Eventually their encouraging words to her and the shuffle of their feet down the ramp sounded just around the corner.

The Swedish woman entered the Vault, eyes squeezed shut, torso heaving like a bellows, her left hand groping in front of her to the right. Seeking the cable lifeline. Instead, she jabbed Ulanovas in the ribs.

Jaeger and Ulanovas each extended a hand to her. "You're safe now," Jaeger said. Her fingernails dug into his forearm as he and the Lithuanian tugged her closer.

Her eyes opened. Her anxiety and the glare of the headlamps made her eyes look like onyx against pallid marble. "Thank you," she said. She slipped out of Ulanovas' grip, then Jaeger's, and leaned against the nearest wall. "A moment, please."

Jaeger tapped his foot, once. No point getting angry. With a joking tone, he said, "How did you ever pass the phobia test?"

Her face had a touch more color. "I knew how to cheat." She straightened her shoulders. "I wanted to be part of our discoveries. Even before we discovered this." She extended her slender arm and graceful fingers toward the first side corridor on the right.

In they went. She took the lead, next to Jaeger. The rest trailed after, McIlroy in the back. Into the side corridor, then to the first room on the right.

"Stop here," Ingvarsson said. "One at a time."

"Why?" asked Feng.

"Because for this machine, taking our measure is meant literally. Jaeger, let us take care of you first."

He squatted and ducked his head to enter. Cautiously, he straightened into the lamp-slashed darkness, used to the low ceilings prevailing throughout the Library. Even with a hardhat on, hitting the stone at speed could cause a concussion.

At his full height, he glanced up, then stretched his hand toward the ceiling. "Ulanovas, you'd like this room. You could play basketball in here." Then he glanced around. A rectangle, door on one of the short sides. The six of them would feel crowded if all were inside. "At least practice your skills in the paint."

Ingvarsson went to the far wall. Octalien symbols ran down alloy panels. Backdrop to a machine on the floor. A ceramic housing, tall enough to bang a human's shins, the same mottled gray as the equipment in the Octalien living quarters. A power cord, presumably connected to the energy absorbers on the surface, formed a knotted mass in a corner made by the machine and the back wall. A gable a few inches high bulged from the center of the machine's top front edge.

Jaeger bent sideways to get a better look. Under the gable, three pairs of transparent beads stared back at him. "Are those—"

"Stereocameras. Tuned to visible, infrared, and ultraviolet wavelengths," she said. She pointed at the floor in the center of the room. Visible through a thin coat of dust lay a laser-sharp circle about five feet wide.

He went to the center of the circle. Dust motes drifted into the air around his feet.

When she spoke again, her words were muffled. She faced the wall, crouched, her fingers on a bright green oval on top of the machine near the back corner. "If I press here...."

Top center under the gable, a blue light came on.

Ingvarsson craned her long neck toward the Octalien symbols. "*Face the cameras. Stand full tall. All limbs not for standing out full sides.*"

He did as instructed. If this were a movie, a low-power laser beam would scan him head to toe. Instead, he faced the machine and studied the unblinking cameras, long enough for an ache to creep into his outstretched arms.

Finally, the blue light turned yellow.

"*Stand full short. All limbs not for standing in empty sides.*"

Ingvarsson quirked her mouth under the mole on her cheek. "Crouch and pull in your arms?"

"Sounds reasonable." He squatted, forearms touching in front of his chest.

She pressed the bright green oval to reset the light to blue.

The process repeated, standing and squatting, facing one side, the other side, the back wall. The other's headlamps made a constellation outside the chamber. Feng stood in the back, behind Ulanovas sitting cross-legged on the stone floor. McIlroy waited behind d'Arbaud. Not turning his back on anyone.

"You are done," Ingvarsson said.

Jaeger shook out his limbs. "Is one enough? Or does someone else need to go?"

"*Five good seven better.* I'll go next. What you must do is...."

Pressing buttons. Sounded like his first summer job in a snowcone hut at a waterpark. And about as monotonous.

Eventually, though, all six of them finished their time in the scanning circle.

Feng's hands flexed in and out of fists. "Are we done?"

"No," Ingvarsson said. "There is much more their machines want to know about us."

They proceeded through the Vault. In one chamber, a flat-topped machine covered most of the floor, except for neat stacks totalling about a hundred stone cubes in one corner, and enough space for an explorer to sidle between the machine and the walls. The cubes came in three sizes. The most plentiful were about four centimeters per side, with a couple dozen half that size, and the rarest, double it.

"Each doubling in edge length gives eight times the volume," Ulanovas said.

Marie d'Arbaud looked over the flat top. Vertical and horizontal lines marked off spaces, each occupied by a set of Octalien symbols. "Chemical compounds," she said. Her finger ticked off spaces. "Nitrogen, oxygen, argon, water, carbon dioxide... common atmospheric gases."

"The top is a set of weight scales?" Jaeger asked.

Ulanovas gave a broad grin. "The cubes are the base-eight equivalents of 0.1%, 1%, 10%!"

"Yes, to all of you," said Ingvarsson. "Here we give their machines a first approximation of our preferred atmosphere."

A simple matter, converting Earth atmospheric concentrations to base-eight and setting out cubes. They opted for one tiny cube for carbon dioxide. Too much, rather than too little. Ingvarsson read that the Octalien ship would allow its crew to further refine the proportions. The extra CO_2 might give them headaches until they dialed it down, but no chronic ill-effects.

Further chambers featured more scales and more stacked cubes to enter quantities. Preferred temperature on the Kelvin scale. Preferred day-night cycles in Octalien time units. Preferred g force. Each chamber had the same proportions as the first.

In one room, after rising from a crouch to stand with ten feet to spare, d'Arbaud asked, "Why so small an entryway for so large a room?"

Ulanovas mulled the question. "Their alloys must have limits in how far they change shape. If an intelligent life form cannot fit in this room, it cannot fit in their ship."

"But the entryway?"

The Lithuanian chuckled. "You have never done maintenance work on *Gagarin*, have you? Some maintenance tubes might be constrained by other equipment, and cannot be made any larger."

The last room held another flat-topped table and stacks of cubes, along with a rack about three feet high at floor level on the three sides away from the door. On one of the short walls, the rack held two tip-out bins full of inch-long alloy rods, one set rectangular in cross-section, the other, semicircular. The other two walls held a couple dozen smaller bins, each with Octalien symbols on the front. Jaeger could tell the names of most of the chemical elements by sight, and text overlaid by his wearable translated the rest. Hydrogen farthest to the right.

His breath caught. "Careful."

Marie went to the bin labeled *nitrogen* and kneeled on the stone floor. She tipped the bin open. Something clinked inside.

She reached in and pulled out an alloy token. Her thumb and forefinger pinched the edge. The symbol for nitrogen showed on both the token's sides. "These appear to be only markers," she said. "We don't risk a flash-burn when we open the hydrogen bin."

Still, she extended her arm and leaned her head away when she opened it. She leaned closer and pulled out another token, labeled *hydrogen*. She hefted it in one hand and the nitrogen token in her other, then switched hands. "They might differ in weight, but I cannot tell."

"Chemical elements..." McIlroy said.

She pointed across the room, to the two large bins of rods. "Those represent chemical bonds. Remember, bonds are in three dimensions, and molecules can have handedness?"

Jaeger gestured at the flat tabletop. "We get to design molecules. But why?"

"And why numbers for quantities?" Ulanovas nudged the stacks of cubes with his toe.

Ingvarsson ran her fingers down columns of text on the long back wall above the rack. "For their molecular fabricator to prepare our first meal on board."

Marie scooped up heaps of carbon and nitrogen tokens and dumped them at one end of the table. At her instruction, McIlroy brought oxygen. Ulanovas, hydrogen. Jaeger took two trips to bring the rods representing bonds. Ingvarsson read the Octalien instructions. The women spent a minute confirming what orientations the different shapes of bonds meant.

"If we get this wrong, the molecules in the food will be the wrong handedness," Marie explained to the others. "Our bodies would be unable to digest them."

Inside his beard, McIlroy grinned. "Take your time."

Though d'Arbaud did not ask Feng for help, even he chipped in.

Unasked, he listened to her talking to herself as she worked, and grabbed the handful of tokens needed to represent iron, phosphorous, and other uncommon elements.

Why did that surprise Jaeger? Feng wanted the Octalien ship as much as anyone else.

For a time, the only sound came from the magnetic snick of tokens and rods she pushed together. Occasionally, later in the process, she told Ulanovas how many of the number cubes to lay out. How long? Minutes? Over an hour, according to the clock in the corner of his vision.

Finally, d'Arbaud stepped away from the table. One of her knees crackled as she rose to her full height. She leaned back over hands planted on her hipbones. "It's ready."

Jaeger eyed her work. Chains of tokens and rods, mostly carbon and hydrogen, but enough of the other elements that his knowledge, vaguely recalled from chemistry 101, soon gave out.

"I have instructed the Octalien ship to make for us a balanced diet," said d'Arbaud. "Forty percent of calories from protein, including the essential amino acids our bodies cannot produce. Thirty percent of calories from complex carbohydrates. Thirty percent from monounsaturated fats. Necessary vitamins and minerals mixed in. It will not taste good, but it will provide three thousand calories a day for each of us, until we can transfer our molecular fabricator from camp to the Octalien ship."

She gestured at small heaps of unused tokens and rods. "Clear these, please."

Jaeger and the others did. Feng dropped tokens, then slipped toward a position blocking the way out.

Marie turned her soft eyes to Ingvarsson. "You may activate it."

The Swedish woman crouched and pressed a bright green oval on the side. She held it for what seemed like forever but was only about five human seconds. A spaced-out line of yellow lights flashed once under the edge of the tabletop. "Food specifications sent," she said.

Jaeger's heart thudded. "We're done?" His hand drifted toward the tail of his untucked khaki shirt.

"Yes." Ingvarsson stood to her full height, then turned to the Octalien symbols on the wall like a teacher to a smartboard.

Jaeger looked in her general direction, but his peripheral vision took in the entire chamber.

"Every measurement room repeats this checklist. And this note. *Do all these. Ship makes itself ready for you. Entryway opens for you.* Followed by coordinates in the lava field."

Ulanovas gave a toss of his sandy blond bangs. His grin sounded in his voice. "We get to fly an Octalien ship!"

Motion blurred near the door. A plasticky *cher-runk* sounded. "No," said Feng. "*I* do."

Both his hands clutched a 3d printed handgun. Though Feng's grip shook, the muzzle stayed pointed at the center of Jaeger's chest.

CHAPTER 20

23 AUGUST 2127 (EARTH REFERENCE FRAME) | 24 OCTOBER 2125
(CONCORDIA REFERENCE FRAME)

JAEGER LAUGHED.

A question crept into Feng's eyes. Then he tightened his grip. "I take the Octalien ship for the Humanist Alliance." His tighter grip made the handgun wobble more.

Most of the others froze. Ingvarsson pressed her upper arms against her sides and splayed her long fingers, palms out. Marie stared at the handgun like a mouse at a snake. Ulanovas bent his knees and roved his gaze over the handgun and Feng's arms.

McIlroy gave an exaggerated shake of his head. "Not with that."

"I do not joke!" Feng steadied his aim at Jaeger's chest. "This is no toy."

Jaeger's heart slammed. Had Feng outplanned them? No. No way. Assuming he could trust—

He glanced at McIlroy. The other met his gaze and dipped his chin once.

Both men reached under the tails of their untucked shirts and drew weapons from the backs of their waistbands.

Feng's finger squeezed the trigger.

A single faint snap sounded.

A frown flickered through Feng's eyes. He pulled the trigger, harder, again, again. Only more snaps.

Jaeger let out a breath. He held his pistol in front of his torso, aimed at the floor, safety on. "We realized Sandford must have had a backup plan, just like Varanathan did with d'Arbaud. The way you overreacted when she admitted it got us suspicious."

McIlroy pointed his sidearm at the floor. "While the rest of you played basketball, I broke into your locker, found the handgun you're holding now, and removed all the cartridges from the magazine."

Large dark eyes turned between them. Then Feng flung his handgun end-over-end at Jaeger and bolted from the room.

Jaeger dodged. Plastic clattered against the stone wall behind him, then tumbled down and off one of the bins of model bonds.

"We've got to stop him," McIlroy said. He ducked his head and left the room, sidearm pointed at the ceiling.

Jaeger hustled past the shocked faces of the others. The corridor seemed narrower as he followed McIlroy. From around a corner came the stomp of Feng's boots on stone.

He would have tried to contact Sandford by now. And undoubtedly guessed Jaeger or McIlroy had turned off the relay to the campsite, and from there, to *Concordia.*

But if he got to the surface, within radio range of the ground-to-orbit transmitter, one word to Sandford could trigger a civil war on the ship, with the victor to try seizing the Octalien vessel.

Jaeger sprinted. The stone walls blurred by. His headlamp beam joined McIlroy's bobbing across the narrow passageway.

Shoulder to shoulder, they rounded the corner into the Vault's main corridor.

A glimmer of light from the Vault entrance showed Feng climbed the spiral ribbon.

Jaeger slowed his pace to enter the pit. Jagged shadows danced over the rocks near his feet. His left arm, jittery with adrenaline, groped for the safety cable. His second grab secured it.

He quick-stepped up the spiral, ratcheting his left hand along the cable. McIlroy's breaths rustled behind him.

The ribbon vibrated from Feng's feet pounding above. The man's headlamp beam jerked over the pit walls and the Library ceiling. Light and shadow raced over Jaeger and McIlroy when their quarry glanced down at them.

His beam suddenly gyrated. A Chinese curse, edged with fear, echoed through the pit.

Hand slipped off the cable? A twenty-five foot tumble to the rocks? But Feng recovered. The man's headlamp beam aimed upward.

A twenty-five foot tumble could befall them too. Jaeger clutched the cable tighter and did not look down to his right.

Feng reached the top. Nothing but flat floor from there to daylight. His boots slammed the stone toward the first gap in the Library panels.

Jaeger's last steps up the spiral seemed like he ran across tar. Finally, his hand left behind the last carabiner. He pressed against the remaining waist-high stretch of the pit wall. He kept his center of gravity away from the drop and rolled onto the Library floor.

He crouched, snapped his gaze toward the gap in the panels, brought up his pistol. Feng was halfway there.

Dead man can't give you intel—

Jaeger sprinted after Feng. The man slipped through the first gap. Reflected glimmer cast gray shadows through the gap.

A blob chilled in his gut. If Feng stopped and lurked, in an effort to wrestle the pistol from him—

—no, the backscatter of Feng's headlamp showed he kept running.

Jaeger grabbed the last panel's edge with his left hand and pulled himself through a semicircle. He sprinted. Chest heaving, legs burning. But he gained on Feng.

Near the far gap, the man turned, dazzling Jaeger with headlamp glare. Dark eyes, wide. Face livid with fear.

Jaeger lunged for Feng. Words from long-ago football coaches echoed through his mind. *Head up. Lead with your shoulder. Use your arms, wrap him up.*

He lunged at Feng. Shoulder to thigh, arms around legs. Twist the man off his feet. Hang on to that pistol.

They tumbled to the stone. Impact thumped Jaeger worse than he remembered from the gridiron. He scrambled away from Feng and brought up his pistol. A panel of Octalien history braced his back. His breath raced and limbs jangled. His aim wavered but stayed near the center of Feng's torso. He remembered to tell his wearable to record video and audio. "Stay down. Hands on the floor and away from your body."

McIlroy came up at a walk. He held his handgun with both hands. "We'd rather not kill you."

Feng lay on the cold stone. His hardhat teetered upside down. The beam whitewashed his face and made him squint. His hands slid across the floor. On the far side of his body, he touched a panel with some chemical symbols.

"Now talk," McIlroy said.

Feng's back rose and fell with his breaths. He gestured with his head toward his upside-down hardhat. His squint intensified. "It's too bright. Move it. Please."

Jaeger stood up. Eyes and pistol on Feng, he stepped closer. A sideways kick flipped it, rattled it into the corner of the next panel and the Library wall.

"You won't kill me?"

"Not if you talk," McIlroy said.

"Sandford knew you might betray us," Feng said. "You were too friendly with Jaeger. She gave me the handgun and told me what to do if we found something useful."

Jaeger spoke. "What did she have on you?"

"'Have on me'?"

"Figure of speech. Why did she think you would do what she wanted?"

Feng's breaths slowed. "If we found Octalien technology worth taking for the Alliance, we would be able to defeat the Humanists once and for all."

Footsteps sounded. Three discs of light came from the far end. "And destroy Earth in the process," Ingvarsson said, voice like a wind off a glacier.

"Both Octalien superpowers had vacuum energy weapons," said Feng. "The difference is that the Alliance alone would have them on Earth."

The other three drew closer. Over the shuffle of their feet, McIlroy's voice echoed off the alloy panels. "Sounds like defeating the Traditionalists matters a whole hell of a lot to you."

Sullenly, Feng said, "As it should have for you."

"How do you mean?"

"Your nation is divided. So is mine. Alliance victory in the final war would unify it. It would also unify mine. You knew these things, but believed the price was too high. You are soft. If your nation mattered to you the way you say it does, you would burn a hundred Coalition cities and a billion people. You would burn Dallas and its five million too."

"You would do the same to Shanghai?" Ulanovas sounded aghast.

"What is one city, against restoring my nation to its proper place in the world?"

Marie d'Arbaud folded her arms. Words slipped past her thin lips. "And the tryst we shared? It meant nothing to you?"

Feng spoke with a matter-of-fact voice. "The enemy's woman is to use as you wish."

"That isn't Sun Tzu," Jaeger said.

McIlroy nodded. "Sounds more like Genghis Khan."

Ulanovas sniffed in a breath of cool dry air. "What do we do with him?"

"Leave him here for Sandford to pick up," Jaeger said. "After we board the Octalien ship."

"You treat him too kindly," d'Arbaud said.

"The rest of the crew will judge him. And Sandford." Jaeger's gaze never left Feng. He went to the opening to the next sideways lane across the Library. "Get up. Slow and steady. Hands in sight."

Feng did as ordered.

"Hands on your head," McIlroy said.

Feng complied, fingers intertwined in his black hair. His head-lamp, still on the floor, cast upward shadows that couldn't hide his eyes shooting daggers at the geologist.

Be as angry as you want. Just don't do anything stupid.

Feng didn't as they switchbacked their way through the Library. Jaeger walked backwards, left hand brushing alloy and pistol in his right trained on Feng. Occasionally he glanced behind to make sure he didn't walk into the stone wall. McIlroy followed their captive, hugging the same wall to stay out of Jaeger's line of fire and return the same favor.

The angry look faded. Slumped shoulders and downturned eyes showed Feng resigned himself to his fate.

Or he lulled them, biding his time, waiting for an opportunity to wrest a weapon from Jaeger or McIlroy.

Jaeger tightened his grip on his pistol.

The procession spiraled up the ramp to the tunnel entrance. Ulanovas and the two women boarded the off-roader, then Jaeger and McIlroy ordered Feng into the rear trailer. McIlroy sat in the front trailer, facing backward. Jaeger twisted in the off-roader's rear seat. Their muzzles pointed at Feng and their headlamp beams pinned him. The man squirmed into the back corner, where the side of the trailer joined the locked gate.

"You can put your hands down," McIlroy said. "On the sides of the trailer. In sight."

Feng moved like an automaton. Like a POW whose war was over.

The off-roader's headlights scattered light down the walls. The vehicle lurched upslope. Seconds ticked by before wan light from the tunnel mouth showed on the walls. Then suddenly they burst into bright sunlight. Jaeger squinted at Feng as they zipped past the solar panels and machinery deployed around the tunnel mouth....

And coasted to a stop.

Jaeger kept his gaze on Feng and angled his head a fraction toward the driver's seat. "Why are we stopping?"

A nervous edge sounded in Ulanovas' voice. "I hoped you could tell me."

CHAPTER 21

23 AUGUST 2127 (EARTH REFERENCE FRAME) | 24 OCTOBER 2125 (CONCORDIA REFERENCE FRAME)

MURMURS, mutters behind him. Jaeger glanced at McIlroy, then Feng. "Got him?"

"He won't go anywhere." The geologist kept his handgun trained on Feng. "Figure out what Ulanovas needs."

Jaeger pivoted in his seat. "What is it?"

Ulanovas pointed into the distance. "Visitors."

Lines of dust plumed over the distant campsite. A tiny object barreled down the slope, heading their way. Another off-roader. Judging by the number of dust plumes, two others followed the same path.

The hell?

Jaeger put one foot on the running board and grabbed the roof frame with one hand. The vehicle leaned a little under his weight as he stood. He craned his neck and shaded his eyes against the bright day.

Near *Gagarin*, veiled by a cloud of dust, sat another of the landing craft. *Yang* or *Glenn?*

Did it matter?

The sweat trickling down his back turned chill. Intuition galvanized him. He jumped to the sand and turned to the front passenger seat. "Ingvarsson, give Ulanovas the coordinates to the Octalien ship."

"Why?"

"I'll explain on the way. Can we go faster if we ditch a trailer?"

Ulanovas swept sweaty hair away from his eyes. "Yes."

"Or two," Jaeger muttered. "Mac, squeeze into the off-roader with us." He raised his pistol toward Feng.

McIlroy stood up, flexing his knees to keep his balance. He faced the campsite and the second landing craft. "Are those Sandford's men or Varanathan's?" He shrugged. "Reckon it doesn't matter."

"The Octalien ship is too big a prize to share."

McIlroy climbed out, then took over guard duty. Jaeger went to the trailer hitch. Years since he'd ridden with his uncle to the boat ramp to go fishing at the lake. Ulanovas hopped out of the driver's seat and joined him.

By the time they disconnected the trailers, Feng turned nervous eyes between them and the campsite. "What are you doing?" He licked dry lips. "You can't abandon me in the desert!"

Jaeger rummaged through a cooler in the off-roader's cargo bin. He found a cold bottle of water and tossed it into Feng's trailer. "That'll keep you till your friends arrive."

"What if they are Varanathan's men?"

"Till your foes arrive, too."

Jaeger gave McIlroy the rear seat, next to d'Arbaud, then swung his legs over the side of the cargo bin. He squeezed between the hard plastic cooler and rough canvas, the emergency kit. More hard plastic, a toolbox, jabbed a corner into his calf.

The off-roader's motor whined. The rear wheels flung sand at the trailers. Ulanovas turned away from the campsite. The entryway to the Octalien ship lay almost the opposite direction.

Which gave Jaeger in the back a view of the dust plumes. Three off-roaders, at least.

Getting closer.

"How fast can you get us there?" Jaeger called to Ulanovas.

"I'll show you!"

The off-roader picked up speed. The rear wheels shimmied side-to-side on the sand until Ulanovas eased off the accelerator.

The two trailers receded from view. Feng remained in the rear one, looking forlorn, like a criminal sailor set adrift. His ego broken by getting outmaneuvered by Jaeger and McIlroy? Or did he assume Varanathan's men came his way?

A couple of minutes later, after multiple rocky outcroppings hid the tunnel mouth and the abandoned trailers, the answer came. In triple bursts of rifle fire.

Twisted in the rear seat, Marie d'Arbaud looked past Jaeger. Her eyelids fluttered and her thin lips parted to pull in hot desert air. "Varanathan's men?"

McIlroy reached over and patted her hand. "Sounds like it."

"How could he get a landing craft down with just his men? ...Oh."

"He and Sandford must have agreed to order it up," McIlroy said. Voice matter-of-fact, as if explaining an opponent's strategy to an ally in an UltraHistory game. "Probably lying to each other they'd work together to seize Octalien tech from the six—five —of us."

"'Gagarin Station grows in strength, Traditionalists and Humanists unify to defeat it.'" Gallows humor flavored Jaeger's voice.

"Except each planned to double-cross the other," McIlroy said. "Looks like Varanathan drew first."

The off-roader drove over rocky ground now. One rear wheel slammed over a bump. The toolbox poked harder into Jaeger's leg. He almost yelled at Ulanovas to slow down, but the three dust plumes had gained on them.

Ulanovas spoke over his shoulder. "How did he know there was tech to steal?"

Ingvarsson cast a gimlet eye at each of the Traditionalists. "Did someone alert him?"

"No," Jaeger said. "We're good little scientists. We upload all the data we get when we get it. Including data from the Vault. And the English-Octalien dictionary you put together."

"Varanathan realized the Octaliens gave us their ship?"

A shake of Jaeger's head. "Translating Octalien symbols is too much work for him. One of his loyalists. Probably O'Daniel."

"If that ship is going to benefit all mankind," McIlroy said, "we've got to get it first."

The off-roader sped up. Ulanovas settled himself deeper in the driver's seat. His arms wrestled the steering wheel over jumbled terrain. A moment later, the jumbles gave way to a flat expanse of black rock. The knobby tires whispered over the lava field.

From his awkward seat, Jaeger and watched their tail.

The dust plumes had gotten closer. Half a mile behind? Far out of range for a moving target of a 3d printed rifle, for even a skilled marksman.

Ulanovas put his foot down. The off-roader extended its lead on Varanathan's men.

A lead that would shrink when they stopped to enter the accessway to the Octalien ship.

"Even if we get to it first," said d'Arbaud in a quiet voice, "what then?"

"The Octaliens embedded the ship to push the lava above it out of the way," Ingvarsson said.

"With enough vacuum energy," Jaeger added, "that's easy."

Frustration pulled d'Arbaud's lips even thinner. "That isn't what I meant. Are we to go home with *Concordia* as if nothing happened? Even if we wish it, Varanathan couldn't permit it. If he seized control of *Concordia* in a coup d'etat, if we tell Earth the truth, we will destroy him. He would have to destroy us first."

Jaeger turned to look at the distant plumes of dust. Three off-roaders times four men each made a dozen rifles. Minimum. Did the specs for guided missiles exist in the database for *Concordia*'s fabs and 3d printers? "He's trying."

"Not here," d'Arbaud said. "Above the planet."

McIlroy spoke. "*Concordia* isn't armed, Marie."

She gestured in the direction of the abandoned trailers. "Neither were Varanathan's men."

Ulanovas veered the off-roader around a steep bulge in the lava. "*Concordia*'s fusion drive emits a superhot jet of plasma, okay? That is a weapon of itself. The Octalien ship's propulsion system is at least as powerful."

"*Deu mieu!* How many innocent crew and scientists are still aboard?"

"We would only fire if fired upon," McIlroy said. "We're doing this for all humanity."

"The Octalien ship may be able to fabricate precision weapons," said Ulanovas. His tone made it half a question.

No one spoke for a time. The off-roader raced up and down gentle swells in the resolidified rock. The rolling black plain ended a mile ahead. Just beyond the lava plain, dust trickled through the air above a truncated cone of a rock formation. Maybe twenty yards high and fifty across. Boulders lay scattered around the cone's base, spilling out a hundred yards or so in all directions. The formation's top looked sheared, as if Octalien tech had sliced through the rock with a laser.

Maybe they had.

"After taking our final measurement," Ingvarsson said, "the Octalien base sent a signal to blow off the top. The accessway is in the flat top."

Jaeger glanced back. The dust trails thinned out on the wind. Varanathan's three off-roaders showed as gray dots on the hard lava. Three-quarters of a mile behind.

Varanathan's men lacked guided missiles, he guessed. Or else they would fire them across the empty plain.

How much ground would their pursuers gain while they picked their way through boulders and up the slope? At least the giant rocks would provide some cover.

A sick feeling went through his stomach, as if he'd swallowed whole an icy fish. And if they made it to the ship? And launched? And got away from any weapons Varanathan might throw at them in orbit? Then what?

They would return to Earth in a moving treasure. Both factions would fight over it. The war they didn't want would break out anyway.

Hot dry air parched his mouth. At least that war would be fought with the devil everyone knew. Even worse would be if the factions didn't fight for control the Octalien ship. If they shared the Octalien legacy of vacuum energy extractors. Both sides would learn to build weapons of mass destruction that made all Earth's past and present arsenals look like firecrackers.

They couldn't go home.

His head fell back.

They couldn't go home as themselves.

Jaeger stared into the deep blue sky with a grin on his face. The plastic jabbing his leg, the armed men chasing them, all were forgotten.

He said, "I know why the Octaliens buried this ship for us."

The others turned in their seats. McIlroy raised an eyebrow. "Do you now."

"What did the Octaliens say over and over about their history? When one faction grew in strength, its new power scared two others to ally for mutual defense. Then the alliance shifted to offense, and they unified to defeat their common enemy. All the way up the chain, from clan to tribe, tribe to nation, nation to empire. Right?"

Ingvarsson nodded, bobbing her narrow nose and the cheek with the mole.

"A common occurrence in our history, too. Conflict against a mutual foe forges stronger bonds than anything else."

Marie frowned at him and McIlroy. "Is this the time for idle speculation based on that game you two play?"

Jaeger grinned at her. "The Octaliens are that new power. They will force Traditionalists and Humanists to ally for survival."

McIlroy scratched his beard. "You might not have heard, but the Octaliens went extinct a hell of a long time ago."

"Oh, I know it." Jaeger's grin widened, into holy fool territory. "But the faction leaderships on Earth don't."

From the looks on their faces, they all puzzled over his words. McIlroy responded first, with a smile that slitted his eyes. "You might could be right."

Ingvarsson's pale brow creased above her brown eyes. "Explain."

"We fly the Octalien ship to Earth. We destroy some military targets, maybe some political ones too. Trigger Earth to unify. Then we return here." He raised a hand in a *wait* gesture. "We can work out the details after we get the Octalien ship into orbit."

The rock formation loomed above them. The off-roader's wheels popped and crunched pebbles blasted off the formation's top. Ahead, scattered rocks gave way to a few boulders as tall as the off-roader's tires. Beyond those, veiled by shimmering heat, the boulders grew even taller and closer together.

Ulanovas eased his foot on the accelerator. "We'll have to stop."

Jaeger glanced over his shoulder. Still about three-quarters of a mile ahead of the hostiles. To the others, he said, "Everyone, grab your stuff."

Equipment rustled. McIlroy asked for water bottles from the cooler. Jaeger handed them over, then rummaged through the emergency supplies for the first-aid kit. "When we stop, run."

Ulanovas steered the off-roader around one boulder, threaded two more. A tire jolted over a rock. The rock thumped the undercarriage. The blow kicked Jaeger in the backside and made the steering wheel buck in the Lithuanian's hands.

The off-roader screeched to a halt next to a boulder with a jagged top higher than their heads. The boulder hid the oncoming hostiles from view. Hard cover against rifle fire.

Ulanovas scrambled out of the driver's seat. Pride shown on his face under his hardhat. Under the brim, sweat glued lanky hair to his forehead. "How'd I do?"

Nice cover, but useless. They needed to be out of here long before Varanathan's men got into rifle range. "Great," Jaeger said. He swung his legs over the side of the cargo bin. Hefted the first-aid kit with one hand. "Now move!"

The five of them ran up the hill. Ingvarsson led, followed by Marie and Ulanovas.

"Run from boulder to boulder!" McIlroy shouted. The water bottles bulged the pockets of his cargo pants. He and Jaeger brought up the rear.

The pursuing vehicles closed the gap. Half a mile now, and less with every second. If the hostiles were marksmen, they could lay down accurate fire from a quarter of a mile. Jaeger's pistol and McIlroy's sidearm had effective ranges maybe a tenth of that. And two against twelve?

They ran as hard as the others. Jaeger sucked wind through his gaping mouth. His heart knocked in his neck.

Ingvarsson's feet showered curlicues of alloy downslope. She slapped one hand on the flat stone and dove forward with a grunt.

Jaeger glanced downslope. The hostile off-roaders were a quarter of a mile away. The purr of their electric motors slowed.

"Stay low and away from the edge when you get up there!" he called.

Ulanovas and d'Arbaud reached the top of the slope, then disappeared from view.

Just five more yards. The steepest yards on the slope, slippery with pebbles and little bits of Octalien metal. The machine that cleared the top must have self-destructed.

The humming motors of the pursuing vehicles died away. Men shouted. Boots thumped the lava.

Jaeger leaned into the slope. His legs dug through the pebbles and metal particles for solid rock beneath. McIlroy lagged him a little more with each step. A wince distorted his beard and he reached for his knee.

"Stay strong!" Jaeger called.

McIlroy gritted his teeth and kept going.

Jaeger climbed the last yard. He stayed low and dove forward onto the formation's flat top. Like the Library's stone floor, the hard smooth surface hurt far worse than concrete under artificial turf ever had when he made a tackle in his high school football career. Hot in the sunlight, the surface burned the bare skin on the back of his hand.

His body could ache all it wanted tomorrow.

Now, he army-crawled back to the edge. McIlroy, almost within reach—

A hundred yards away, men in visored helmets, with oxygen tanks on their backs, lay prone, propped up on elbows, sighting their rifles through scopes.

Jaeger ducked his chin toward Varanathan's men. God willing the hardhat would deflect a plastic bullet. He reached for McIlroy.

The geologist grabbed his forearm.

Jaeger heaved.

A rifle barked, then another. Bullets thwacked the rocky slope.

Heart slamming, adrenaline surging, Jaeger rolled away from the edge. McIlroy's weight crashed over his knees. But both had made it. Unwounded.

Jaeger sucked in a breath. Heat seeped through the sweat-soaked back of his shirt. "No time to rest."

"I know," McIlroy said, short of wind.

"Come, now!" called Ingvarsson.

Their heads snapped around. A square alloy slab about four feet on a side stood erect on a pair of hinges bent like a strongman's arms. Two grab bars jutted out between the hinges. Next to the slab, Ingvarsson's body showed from the waist up. "Marie's already inside. Get in!"

Next to the opening, Ulanovas gestured like an impatient traffic cop.

Jaeger and McIlroy crouched and ran to her. She dropped out of sight with a rhythmic pinging. Her boots descended a ladder. Ulanovas followed.

The square slab stood above a shaft. A ladder ran down one side, rails narrow and rungs close together. Ulanovas wedged his toes between every fourth pair of rungs as he went down. Below him, two darting headlamps showed the women stood on a horizontal floor about twenty feet down.

"Go." Jaeger clapped McIlroy's shoulder.

The geologist stared into the shaft for a moment, face slack.

C'mon, Mac, head in the game. Don't freeze up.

McIlroy moved. His expression stayed the same but he moved. Grabbed the ladder. Down he went, ladder ringing under his first step. His second.

Another sound came to Jaeger. He looked over his shoulder to the edge. Their pursuers climbed. How close? He raised his pistol and scanned the edge for the first helmeted head.

"I'm clear," McIlroy said.

Jaeger let out a breath. No hostiles yet. He scampered to the ladder and down. His footsteps echoed off the narrow walls.

Waist-deep into the shaft, he reached for a grab bar. *Oh hell, I can close it, but—* "We can't lock it!" he called down, voice quick and high.

"Close the hatch, then pull the bar through!" shouted Ingvarsson.

He clutched the ladder tighter. Close it, yes, but he needed a free hand—

Focus. The pistol is no help now.

He shoved the pistol into a pants pocket, then tugged on the alloy slab. His headlamp came on automatically as the falling slab cut off daylight.

A metallic surface about five inches high lined the top of the shaft, all four sides. An alloy ingot jutted out. A solitary, miniature version of the grab bars on the underside of the hatch extended outward from the ingot's end, like the cabinet door pulls in a remodeled kitchen.

He hooked two fingers into the pull and tugged.

Metal groaned behind the surface. The ingot didn't move.

Killed by a million years of dust and rust. Somehow, his panic focused on the ingot's pull.

He heaved.

A metallic screech, but then the ingot moved. It rode on hidden rails, or something. It raced out of the wall. He barely yanked his fingers away before the pull passed through the first grab bar. That end of the ingot passed through the second, then toward a shadowed recess in the metallic lining. He extended his fingers to the sides of the ingot, then gave it a last shove.

The ingot's end slipped into the recess. Metal clanked inside and the bar stopped moving.

Above, footsteps pounded on stone.

"Your turn to move!" McIlroy called.

Jaeger went down the ladder, arms pressed against his sides, quick as he dared on the undersized rungs. Four headlamps bobbed below, welcoming him like friendly spirits in the darkness.

Muffled curses came from above. Quieter with each of his steps.

ALPHA CENTAURI B SYSTEM | BRAVO CHARLIE | GAGARIN STATION

23 AUGUST 2127 (EARTH REFERENCE FRAME) | 24 OCTOBER 2125
(CONCORDIA REFERENCE FRAME)

THE LADDER ENDED at the head of a spiral tunnel, twin to the one they first took down to the Library months before. This one was wider, taller, gentler in slope. Ulanovas cursed in Lithuanian, wishing for the off-roader.

Also in contrast to the Library entryway, this tunnel spiraled far deeper into the bedrock. Two hundred meters, McIlroy had guessed. But by the time it leveled out, they had descended closer to three hundred.

McIlroy paused and sipped from his water bottle. "I don't hear Varanathan's men behind us." He looked a question at d'Arbaud.

She cupped curved fingers around her ear and angled her head to the spiral. "Nor do I."

"We bought some time," Jaeger said. "But we have to spend it wisely."

They surveyed the tunnel ahead. Straight and flat to their head-lamps' limit.

A mile or more to the Octalien ship. They started off, Ingvarsson in the lead, Jaeger at the back.

The tunnel continued, monotonous as a West Texas two-lane highway. The only change came early, when McIlroy gestured at the wall. Brown striated rock gave way to grainy black. "We're entering into the melt zone."

The others looked back at him. None showed enthusiasm for a geology lesson.

Jaeger veered over to the wall. His hands traced the black rock. Despite its visible grain, his hand slid over the dark surface like ice. More testimony to the skill of the Octalien excavators.

He glanced over his shoulder, up the geometrically precise tunnel. If Varanathan's men could make it to the bottom of the spiral, the five of them would be sitting ducks despite the range. Plastic bullets could skip across the polished surfaces like flat rocks across a pond. They had no cover.

The adrenaline surge of their drive and climb faded, leaving a sickly residue, like the dregs in empty bottles left from last night's party. Time seemed to blur. Jaeger's wearable said twenty-two minutes since they left the spiral tunnel, but he didn't believe it. Twenty-two seconds? Twenty-two hours?

And if the Octaliens had lied to them? What if they'd built the galaxy's most gigantic practical joke? Just to see how greedy and back-stabbing other species might be? He'd consider laughing, if the prac-tical joke wouldn't get him and his friends lined up before Varanathan's firing squad.

He looked at the other four. Colleagues, yes. But friends?

They would have to be, to spend years of their lives staging a false flag attack on Earth.

Assuming there was an Octalien ship....

Something glinted ahead. His eyes widened.

Octalien alloy walled off the tunnel, filling more and more of their vision with each step. They stopped about ten feet away.

"The hull of the ship," Ingvarsson said. Her headlamp aimed at where the floor ended. She sucked in a breath. *"Herregud!"* She jerked her head away and groped for something to hold.

Marie d'Arbaud grasped her hand. "There, there. More heights," she explained to McIlroy and Jaeger.

Jaeger pressed forward and saw what she meant. About four feet separated the ship's hull from the tunnel floor. A sheet of alloy, a duplicate of the ribbon leading from the Library to the Vault, filled most of the gap. The alloy sheet sloped down to the left.

He turned to Ingvarsson. "We have to go down the ramp to enter the ship?"

She opened her brown eyes. "Yes." Then the gap pulled her gaze. She stiffened her neck and squeezed her eyes shut.

How far down was the Octalien hatch? Unimportant. They would go as far as they had to. "It's just like the ladder up top," he said. He'd used the same encouraging tone when his kindergartener nephew had swung his bat at a tee ball and missed.

"It's not. The gap. Don't you see the gap?" She slid a few inches over and opened her eyes where she could only see Jaeger. "The gap?"

"I'll get you down there. Ulanovas, take the lead. Annike," he said, and had he ever used her given name before? "Take my hand."

She wrapped graceful fingers around the stubby ones of his left hand. He went slowly forward, giving her time to shuffle her feet.

At the top of the ramp, his headlamp panned over black matte rock that smothered reflection, and the glinting surface of the Octalien hull. A glance up did not reveal the ceiling.

He guided her next to the wall. He paused with his feet close together and close to the edge of the alloy sheet. Unease squirmed inside his torso until he rested his free hand on the ancient alloy. Cool to the touch and rougher than it looked, gouged by micrometeorites and infinitesimally corroded by the dry, low-oxygen air for a thousand millennia.

Ingvarsson's warm hand shifted its grip.

Down they went, a gentle slope. The alloy sheet curved gradually to the right, following the curves of wall and Octalien ship, and flexed with each step. He resisted the bleak urge to look down at the gap. Instead, his gaze tracked the reflection of Ulanovas's headlamp off the glinting alloy. Glows in the corner of his eye came from d'Arbaud and McIlroy behind them.

Around ragged breaths next to Jaeger's ear, Ingvarsson asked, "How much farther?"

"Not far at all."

Ulanovas stood sideways, back to the rock wall, facing the ship. He held out his hand to them, *stop*. "Found the airlock."

Jaeger stopped about five feet from the Lithuanian. A glance past Ulanovas showed why he'd bade them halt. The alloy walkway ended, hanging over an empty space five feet wide and no telling how deep.

He pressed his right hand harder against the hull and with his other gave Ingvarsson's hand a squeeze. "Told you it wasn't far."

A slight nod, but her face remained scrunched.

"How do we open it?" Ulanovas asked. He lifted his helmet with one hand, and with the other cleared sweaty bangs from his forehead. He seemed as blithe as an ironworker about the long fall near his feet.

"I'll send you instructions," Ingvarsson said, voice pinched. She subvoked commands to her wearable. A pickup patch, the same shade as her fair skin, flexed on the side of her long neck.

"Got it." Ulanovas squatted to the airlock's right.

The outer hatch was larger than an Octalien. About the size of the entrances to the measuring chambers inside the Vault. Jaeger's eye made out two tones of metal, with one cladding about the top and left three-fourths of the hatch surface. In the remainder of the surface, a small circular recess held a grab handle.

"They rebuilt their airlock to accommodate larger species," Jaeger said.

"Left the controls where they were," muttered Ulanovas. He sat cross-legged now, knees over the edge of the alloy sheet. He swung up from the hull a hinged, smoke-brown cover. A snap sounded, dust trickled down the gap, and the cover came off in his hand.

After a Lithuanian curse, Ulanovas glowered at the broken cover, then set it down.

"Hopefully we don't need that," McIlroy said.

Ulanovas waved his hand, dismissing the needling comment. His head swiveled between a set of piezoelectric buttons and the place he'd pinned a virtual instruction window on the hull above them.

"Here, and here," Ulanovas muttered as he pushed buttons. He double-checked the virtual instructions, then scooted on his rump over to the circular recess. "Hold, twist counterclockwise, and pull." Another curse, Jaeger guessed from his tone. "If I could get my fingers in there.... Yes."

Ulanovas tugged. Hinges groaned, roaring off the hull and stone walls. But the hatch swung open.

The Lithuanian scrambled to his feet. He crouched and jumped into the open space.

Jaeger lifted his hand locked with Ingvarsson's. "Room for us?"

Ulanovas looked like a kid asked to wait to open presents on Christmas morning. "First I get the inner hatch, okay?" Then he took another look at the Swedish woman's pallid face. "Yes, there's room, come."

He held out his hand for Ingvarsson. Together, the two men helped her into the airlock. The three of them stooped under the low ceiling and crowded the interior. A metal box, like every other airlock of Jaeger's experience, except for Octalien symbols in shades of yellow and green. He studied the inner door, looking for welds or alloy seams, and finding one similar to the one on the outer.

His heart quickened. *They rebuilt this ship for us.*

While Ulanovas kneeled next to the inner hatch controls on the side wall under a long-dark bioluminescent panel, Jaeger patted the back of Ingvarsson's hand. "A moment more."

"Be careful," d'Arbaud said from outside. She stood with her back against the stone wall. "If the atmosphere inside is poisonous…"

"It won't be," Jaeger said.

"You cannot be so certain."

Ulanovas pressed a spot on the side wall. Suddenly, light glowed on the panel above him. A sickly yellow tinged his features. "What's this?"

Ingvarsson's face relaxed, but her eyes remained closed. "From your voice you are near the controls?"

"Above them."

"There is an atmosphere status display."

"Atmosphere where? Inside the ship or out?"

"What are the symbols?"

"I studied their math, not their writing, okay?"

Ingvarsson gave Jaeger's hand a stronger squeeze and took a long breath in. She squatted near Ulanovas, pulling Jaeger down with her. He didn't mind. He bent his fingers on the frame of the outer hatch.

Another deep breath and her eyes opened. Jaeger shifted his body to block as much as he could of her view through the open outer hatch.

"Half the pixels are dead," she said. "But I think those symbols together mean inside the ship. There, nitrogen—"

"Forty-nine and two-eighths." Ulanovas angled his head at a dark-spotted symbol group. "I think."

"—oxygen—"

"Fourteen and one-eighth. I'm certain of that."

"—argon, neon, carbon dioxide, all traces?"

"Yes." Ulanovas raised his voice. "Just what you ordered, d'Arbaud. I'm opening it now."

His fingers jabbed pressure-sensitive zones on the wall. He slipped his fingers into a recess on the inner hatch and twisted with a grunt.

Ulanovas pushed. The inner hatch swung open.

Their headlamp beams passed over bare walls. An overpressure of air wafted toward them.

Jaeger inhaled. After months in the low-oxygen atmosphere of Bravo Charlie, the air coming out of the open hatch felt like coming home to Earth.

CHAPTER 23

ALPHA CENTAURI B SYSTEM | BRAVO CHARLIE | GAGARIN STATION

26 AUGUST 2127 (EARTH REFERENCE FRAME) | 27 OCTOBER 2125
(CONCORDIA REFERENCE FRAME)

THE AIR WAS EARTH NORMAL, but much else about the ship plainly
showed its alien origin. A twisting, up-and-down path wound about a
quarter of a mile toward the center of the ship. There, alloy walls, still
warm to the touch from shifting shape, formed a mazy collection of
twisting hallways and spiraling ramps, and rooms of odd proportions.
This one had too high a ceiling, that one was too long and narrow.

In one spot, the alloy failed in the middle of shape shifting.
Between a thin section that reached the ceiling and a thick, chest-high
section at a right angle to the first, curves of metal reached jagged
fingers toward each other across a three-inch gap. One of the fingers
snagged a pocket flap on Jaeger's sleeve and ripped out half the seam.

McIlroy created virtual yellow caution signs, and slathered them
on both sides of the gap for all to see. He also added a sticky note.
Grind down or cover.

"A reminder when we get around to it," he said. "I reckon it'll be a while."

They continued exploring. Every two or three yards, metal bars the size and shape of tennis racket grips and hinged at one end lay flat against the walls. Each bar about a foot long, a tug on the free end would flip the bar out to a right angle with the wall. Some hinges wouldn't pivot, and those that did worked with a shriek of metal and a trickle of dust.

The walls themselves ran at odd angles. At the ceiling, they cut across bioluminescent panels. Maybe a third of the panels still worked, and those spottily. The explorers kept their headlamps on in the dim and uneven light.

One level above the airlock, they found a double-height chamber, cubical or close enough to fool Jaeger's eye. The walls were cool to the touch. Nineteen bioluminescent panels in concentric rings on the ceiling. An alloy tree with twenty-three metallic branches running from floor to ceiling along one wall. The stringy plasticky foliage had long since crumbled to a yellow dust drifting toward the corners of the room.

Around a balcony connecting two doors halfway up the other walls and ladders leading down to where Jaeger and the others stood, faded murals showed life-size Octaliens holding hands in a jungle clearing, watching the first stars of twilight.

"Who had temple, not fitness room, in the betting pool?" Jaeger said in a tone far more reverent than his words.

"Beautiful," Ulanovas said. "But we cannot fly a ship by prayer."

McIlroy scratched his beard. His gaze trailed over a second door at floor level. "The control room's around here somewhere."

Not through the second door, as it turned out. The control room backed up to one of the other side walls, the only muraled one without a door. A cramped and narrow space, Jaeger and Ulanovas stooped to enter. A solitary bioluminescent ceiling panel emitted flickering light, and not enough of it for Jaeger's eyes. Another panel covered the upper two-thirds of the front wall.

They had to sit on the floor, sideways like kids in the back seat of a sports car, to examine control surfaces and half-dead displays fixed at Octalien height. Most looked built-in, but one filled the corner and trailed a thick cable up the wall to a small port in the ceiling.

The two men spent most of the next three days in the control room, with Ingvarsson in the corridor outside. Days—the lighting from the ceiling grew brighter and dimmed on a twenty-four hour cycle. She poked her head in when asked to assist in reading faded Octalien print and displays splotchy with dead pixels. They soon covered the control surfaces with virtual sticky notes like mushrooms on a fallen log.

Ulanovas had the easier job. A pilot could only make a ship pitch, roll, and yaw. For it to go anywhere, the engines had to generate thrust.

As the nearest thing to a physicist on board, figuring out how to do that fell to Jaeger. In addition to time in the control room, he took multiple trips to the lower levels of the ship, usually accompanied by Ingvarsson, to figure out how the vacuum energy extractors worked and how to couple their output to the propulsion system.

The Octaliens' shape-changing alloy had barely touched the narrow accessways and sharp corners leading to the extractors. Sixteen of them formed a ring, each one a metal drum big enough to swallow the main tent at Gagarin Station. Conduits and giant magnets fed streams of virtual particles into a spaghetti bowl of machinery in the center of the ring. Nearly a kilometer in diameter. At first, every schematic Ingvarsson showed him gave him a headache. But eventually he began to understand. Some charged particles can be shunted *here*, to generate electricity. The rest flowed *there* to be flung out the bottom of the ship at relativistic speeds.

He proved the former by lifting an access panel and contorting to work hidden controls. An electronic hum rewarded him, followed by a sudden brightening of the overhead lights.

Ingvarsson smiled. "You didn't blow anything up."

He backed out of the panel grinning, full of false modesty. "I know a thing or two, Annike." *Ahn-i-ka*. If he botched the pronunciation in some subtle way, she let it slide.

A rare smile touched her features. "I never thanked you for helping me down the ramp."

"Nothing to it. We're all in this together."

She took his hand, gently. But something troubled her brow and her fingers soon slipped from his.

He found out what when the lights dimmed on their second evening on the ship. Second? Between fleeing from Varanathan's men, learning their way around the Octalien vessel, and the circadian shock of going from three shifts in ninety hours back to a twenty-four hour day, he had to think to be certain.

They sat on the rigid floor of a small room near the temple, backs against the walls, with food and refilled water bottles before them. They fanned themselves with their hands—the climate control must have slowly leaked refrigerant over the millennia—and talked shop.

While he, Annike, and Ulanovas worked on propulsion and navigation, McIlroy and Marie d'Arbaud tried decoding the ship's molecular fabricators and life support systems. No luck enhancing the food, yet. McIlroy emphasized the point by waggling his dinner, a sandwich of dry protein and gloopy fat between torn starch hunks. Edible but bland.

"What have you been doing all day?" Jaeger joked.

McIlroy's expression deflected the attempt at humor. "Watching for visitors."

Varanathan's men wanted the ship. The two easiest ways to get to it would be ripping open the hatch on the flat-topped formation, or digging down next to the hatch. Either way, they'd come down the spiral ramp and then a mile along the tunnel.

McIlroy and Marie set a hardhat on the tunnel floor at the foot of the ramp. Lamp on to distract anyone approaching, and hopefully obscure any reflection off the hull that might clue their visitors in on what exactly waited inside the vast chamber. The hardhat's cameras and microphones would give a 3d soundscape and views in visible light and infrared of anyone approaching. Every three or four hours, the active hardhat's battery ran out, so they always kept two spares charging by wearing them. The hardhats drew power from their movements.

"No sign of visitors?" Jaeger asked.

"Not yet," McIlroy replied. "But they could be fabbing excavating equipment at Gagarin Station right now."

Ulanovas wrinkled his nose. "It couldn't be a very good excavator, okay?"

"Doesn't have to be very good to be good enough," McIlroy said.

Annike tugged on her blond ponytail. "Varanathan's men will come to the ship eventually. What do we do?"

"If we can find specs for weapons in the ship fab's database, we could deny them access through the tunnel." McIlroy raised his hand to her. "I don't want to have fire on anybody either."

"But you're considering it," said the Swedish woman.

"They'll kill us all if they get here," Jaeger said.

Her brown eyes implored him. "We don't know that...." She shut her eyes and rubbed the side of her nose. "I'm fooling myself, aren't I?"

Jaeger ran his palm over the back of her hand. "Decent people don't know how ruthless ruthless people can be."

"If we can't fab weapons in time," McIlroy said, "then we'll have to button up. Lock the hatches."

"Could they force open the airlock?" Annike asked.

"No." Ulanovas sounded confident.

"They don't need one." McIlroy's voice carried through the room. "They could bring over laser cutters from the station, or fab a rotary tool with a diamond cutting wheel. It would take them a while, but they could get in."

"But that would damage the ship..." Annike trailed off.

"Varanathan wants the vacuum energy extractors in his control, more than the ship intact," Jaeger said.

"I don't see any way around it," McIlroy said. "We have to launch. Sooner rather than later."

Ulanovas nodded. "I figured out what the extra piece of equipment in the corner of the control room is. It connects to a laser array embedded in the lava bed, like what they used to open the rock formation to us. It will carve the ship and its wake shield free of the rest of the rock."

"Wake shield?" Annike asked.

"A cap of rock mounted atop the ship. To absorb impacts from micrometeorites when accelerating."

"The Bussard scoops on *Concordia* serve that purpose, in addition to pulling in hydrogen for the fusion reactor," Jaeger said.

Silence descended, broken only by chewing sounds and the glug of water bottles washing down the tasteless chow.

"And after we launch?" Annike's brown eyes landed on Jaeger. Her expression cycled through emotions faster than he could track. "Are we really going to pretend to be Octaliens and attack Earth?"

"The faction leaderships on Earth are just like Varanathan," he said. "Only more ruthless. We can't trust either side with the technology on this ship. Alone or together."

"Yes, I agree, but..." Her fingers flexed, as if gathering from the air the strands of a better answer. "We could stay in the Alpha Centauri system. Let *Concordia* return to Earth."

"And then the factions race each other to build ships for a return mission." McIlroy said. "To seize control of this ship."

Jaeger nodded. "Which puts us right back where we started."

"I follow your logic." Annike winced. "But isn't there another way?"

Jaeger looked in her eyes. "You're hoping for something this plan won't give you."

She grimaced at the misproportioned metal walls. "I want to go home. To see my friends and family. To start a family of my own. Don't you want these things?"

Memories panged him, of practice fields and lakes and his

nephew's fifth birthday party. "I do. But when we discovered this—" He lifted his hand and rapped his knuckles on the metal wall at his back. "Those things were off the table for all of us. All we were going to get from the Trad and Humanist leaders was a shallow grave, either here or somewhere on Earth. So were billions of others. Maybe including your friends and family, or mine."

Her brown eyes turned red. She sniffled and slid toward him. Her hands clasped one of his and she nestled her cheek against his shoulder. "We'll get home someday?"

Jaeger skipped false hopes and pep talks. He gave her hand a squeeze in reply. Near them, McIlroy and Marie shared a glance that showed they'd drawn closer together too.

Ulanovas showed no sign of resentment for being odd man out. He brushed crumbs off his shirt and onto a napkin of soft beige polymer resting in his lap. "The bad guys are coming and we got a lot more to do to get her flying."

Jaeger patted Annike's top hand with his free one. She nodded and disengaged her grip. Her eyes were a little puffy, but she didn't sniffle anymore. Voice level, she said, "Let's do what we must."

Must involved twenty more hours in the control room and below decks. Sporadic ninety-minute naps, tuned to the length of an REM cycle, took some of the bleariness from their eyes. So too did the coffee-like substance in ceramic vessels the size and shape of test tubes that Marie teased from the ship's fab. "It has caffeine and coffee flavorants," she said apologetically.

He sipped. One bitter, unsweetened flavor note. Worse than the swill out of the machine down the hall from his shared office in graduate school. Jaeger tilted the test tube nearly vertical. He swallowed the last drops. He held out the test tube. "More?"

They shared a laugh, then got back to work. Some controls had failed over a million years, forcing him to crawl back into the machinery with toy-sized wrenches from Octalien toolboxes to activate overrides. He mapped out a pre-flight checklist of which buttons to press, in what order, and when he had to wait for Ulanovas....

He fell asleep in the control room. The backs of Annike's slender fingers rasped down his beard stubble to wake him.

"Time for a dry run, okay?" asked Ulanovas. Days of work in tight quarters had given him a sweaty odor about as bad as Jaeger's own. The main display on the front wall glowed, splotchy like a skin disease.

"Right." Jaeger ran his gaze down the virtual checklist. A full simulation of the launch process would take forty-five minutes, give or take. "Step one, we—"

A siren went off in his ear. Ulanovas's too, from the way the Lithuanian winced and raised his hand to the side of his head.

Not external. Someone triggered an emergency override in the group channel.

The siren cut off. McIlroy spoke. "We need to change *sooner* to *now*."

"You mean?" Ulanovas said.

"Hostiles are coming our way."

ALPHA CENTAURI B SYSTEM | BRAVO CHARLIE | GAGARIN STATION

26 AUGUST 2127 (EARTH REFERENCE FRAME) | 27 OCTOBER 2125 (CONCORDIA REFERENCE FRAME)

Mouth suddenly dry, Jaeger turned to Ulanovas. "Can we do this for real?"

The pilot kneaded his forehead. "Looks like we got to."

Jaeger spoke in the group channel. "Mac, stall them."

"Any suggestions?"

"How many games of UltraHistory have you played in your life? You'll figure out something. Annike, Marie, stay on board and find a place to hold on."

Jaeger turned to the checklist. Nervous energy leaked down his arms, made him want to hurry. He stayed calm and followed the protocol. Blowing themselves up would deny Varanathan his prize, but wouldn't help anyone. Least of all themselves.

"Everyone's on board," said McIlroy. "The hardhat's speakers are synced to my wearable. I'm buttoning up."

"Share the hardhat's I/O," Jaeger said.

"On it."

A thumbnail window showed in an upper corner of Jaeger's vision. It might distract him, but if Varanathan's men came ahead of schedule, he wanted all the advance warning he could get.

If their choice was between the risk of blowing up the ship versus the certainty of ending up in a shallow grave with the ship in Varanathan's control, it was no choice at all.

The hardhat camera provided no distraction at first. The black walls merged with the darkness, showing nothing. Occasional sounds, muted bangs and clangs, were the only sign of visitors.

Then a tiny glow came from no telling how far away.

"We're halfway through the checklist," Ulanovas said.

Jaeger's gaze ran down the next items. "Almost halfway. With the more time-consuming steps to go." Nineteen minutes to warm up the dormant vacuum energy extractors. They needed eleven of them to work, maybe just ten in a pinch, to lift the massive ship and its rocky cap into Bravo Charlie orbit. Not including the one currently feeding power to all the other systems.

If six of the extractors had failed during their million dormant years...

The tiny glow slowly grew bigger and taller. Transient bulges on its sides and ripples at its bottom soon showed. As more dual-camera data came in, the glow resolved into multiple men speed-walking single file down the long straight tunnel. Tough to get an exact number. Five? Ten?

Soon, Varanathan's lead man came close enough to make out his arms and head. From the position of his arms, he carried a rifle across his chest. Not enough ambient light or heat emission to confirm the weapon.

Jaeger checked the time and mumbled a curse. Eleven minutes to fully warm up the extractors. His hands worked on one another, crackling knuckles one finger at a time.

"This is McIlroy," sounded from the hardhat speakers.

The man-shape in the lead halted. He moved his arms like he leveled his rifle.

"Don't bother," McIlroy said. "I'm talking from a remote, secure location."

Jaeger counted seven man-shaped blobs. They huddled together. Someone spoke aloud until the others shushed him. Most of them would have had military training, but like Jaeger and McIlroy, not much of it and a decade or two ago.

Over the group channel, McIlroy said, "Lot of transmissions between them. Encrypted."

"Good," said Jaeger.

Marie spoke with a hint of feedback echo. She must be in the same room as McIlroy. "How is that good?"

"Talking among themselves buys us more time."

The infrared blobs shifted. A different figure, shorter and with long arms, came forward. Between the man's helmet and the acoustics of the tunnel, Jaeger couldn't identify him by voice. "You're the spokesman, McIlroy?"

"Spokesman? I'm in charge here."

The figure loomed over the hardhat until only lower legs were visible. Then he stooped and extended his arms. The view lurched, then bobbed along. He'd picked up the hardhat and carried it fifteen or twenty feet back up the tunnel. "Thought you and Jaeger were co-leaders. Working together for all mankind."

McIlroy let the words hang for a moment, then said, "He thought that too."

"Ulanovas and d'Arbaud?" He mispronounced her name badly, *DEE-ar-BOD.*

You were supposed to ask how McIlroy got rid of me and why. Jaeger's timer counted down slowly, as if it had been reprogrammed to display Octalien seconds.

"I did what I had to," McIlroy replied.

A light flicked on. Washed out pixelation filled the hardhat cam for a moment before the image processing software in McIlroy's wearable caught up. Through the glare, it looked like the light was mounted on a standard spacewalk helmet. The gold-tinged reflective visor obscured the man's face.

"Just you and Ingvarsson inside the Octalien ship? Lucky you."

"She can read the writing on the wall."

The man's voice shifted gears. "What do you want?"

"To bring this ship home. For the Humanist Alliance."

"Small world, eh?"

McIlroy laughed. "Nice try, Kowalchuk."

Jaeger rapped his forehead with his knuckles. He should've placed the voice sooner. Kowalchuk, from the Canadian prairie. A second-tier geneticist on the Trad side.

"Had to try to get you to open. I'll be honest with you. We're here as part of a joint mission to secure the Octalien ship for both factions, against conspiracies we knew were trying to steal it for one or the other. Good job, by the by. We didn't know you were mixed up in the Humanist one."

"A joint mission? That shot Feng?"

"Feng? He was part of the Humanist conspiracy. Pretty cold of you to throw one of your own to the wolves to throw us off the scent. But shoot him?"

"I heard the rifle fire."

The light slid side-to-side. "Warning shots. He surrendered after we put a couple of bursts over his head. He's in protective custody on the surface. What do you want?"

McIlroy put a frantic hint into his voice. "If you're really a joint mission, put me through to Sandford."

"Sure, sure..." Jaeger's gaze roved the golden mirror for some hint of Kowalchuk's expression behind it. "You might have lost track, it's the middle of the ship's night. Might take a while to find someone who'll interrupt her beauty sleep."

"I've got time. If she tells me in her own words to open up to you, I will."

A broad shrug. "However you want it. I'm going to give my arms a break and put this thing down."

The hardhat's view lurched again, then showed nothing but mile-long empty tunnel. A ghostly zone of trampled-together footprints showed in the infrared, fading a little with each second.

In the group channel, McIlroy asked, "How much time do we need?"

On a panel in front of Jaeger's knees, blue lights popped on by ones and twos. Thirteen. He blew out a breath. "Ten minutes."

"Our stall is working, okay?"

"If we complete the checklist," Jaeger said firmly. Next, fire up the electromagnets in the particle and antiparticle beam collimators. Squint at the displays. Look for blue ready lights next to faded Octalien symbols. Yes. Next...

Kowalchuk's voice sounded from near the helmet, but out of its view. "Having trouble finding one of your people who won't mind getting their head bit off for waking her," he said.

"I'm not going anywhere," McIlroy said with easy confidence.

Moments later, he spoke in the group channel, voice pinched and words stampeding over themselves. "We're not the only ones stalling! The airlock!" The sounds of pounding feet followed.

"Airlock?" asked Annike. "They're coming through?"

"I reckon they're trying." McIlroy's breaths rustled long and deep over the channel.

Jaeger's stomach flopped. "Steady," he said, to Ulanovas and himself. Don't take a shortcut now and blow up the Octalien ship like an underground fusion bomb test. "Mac?"

"Almost there." The sound of his feet grew quieter. "Subvoking now. At the inner hatch. Listen."

Muffled sounds came over the group channel. Low male voices, close. A buzz, then a high-pitched keening.

"They're cutting the outer hatch?" asked Marie.

"We can fly without it if we have to, okay?" Ulanovas said.

Something clanged near McIlroy. Louder than before, a male voice cursed. A wave of shushes from other men around the man followed.

"Sounds like they're in the airlock," McIlroy told the others. "Jaeger, Ulanovas, how much longer?"

Jaeger's chest heaved. They could fly without the outer airlock, but the inner?

He stabbed a virtual checkbox with his finger. Two more items. Could it be? A frantic swipe down confirmed the end of the checklist. "Thirty seconds. Go!" he said to Ulanovas.

The Lithuanian twisted between a control board and the corner, to the extra piece of equipment hacked into place by the Octaliens. "Cleaving rock cap now!"

Distant crumps sounded somewhere above them. Jaeger felt the explosions through the seat of his pants.

In the feed from McIlroy's microphone, the male voices spoke from the other side of the inner hatch. Indistinct words, but a tone of plain confusion.

McIlroy spoke. Jaeger could tell he didn't subvoke anymore. "Y'all noticed a ways back, how the rock turned black?"

Kowalchuk's voice came through the feed from the hardhat. "What trick are you pulling, McIlroy?"

"No trick. I'm trying to save the lives of your men who are trying to break and enter this ship. They need to run like the devil is chasing them. Because even though it won't be the devil, the tunnel's going to get hot as hell."

Hunched over a control board, Ulanovas said something in Lithuanian. His tone made it a curse.

Jaeger wiped sweat off his forehead with the back of his hand. "Doesn't sound good."

"One charge didn't fire."

Jaeger swore. Maybe the same meaning, but now was not the time to compare translations. "If we put the pedal to the metal, can we break free?"

A puzzled look came over the other's face. "Pedal?"

"One way to find out. Everyone! We're launching now!"

Orienting a ship is easy. Roll, pitch, and yaw. Accelerating is even easier. Jaeger pushed back a brittle, smoke-brown cover that went flying across the room. On the panel, a thick green line surrounded a pressure-sensitive surface bearing green Octalien symbols for *increase thrust.*

A rumble sounded deep under the ship, like an earthquake shook the bedrock. The hardhat's view brightened.

Kowalchuk's voice sounded ragged. "Good God, McIlroy."

"I told you it was no trick."

"Get out!" Kowalchuk shouted to his men.

McIlroy's microphones picked up frantic voices and the pound of boots. Then Jaeger pressed harder. The rumble from under the ship deepened, like a million demons strained to escape the underworld. The sound filled the walls of the control room. The box next to Ulanovas rattled against one of the walls.

The brightness seen by the hardhat inside the tunnel grew. Jaeger squinted until his wearable dimmed the view. The tunnel still grew brighter, brighter than daylight. From light reflected off the chamber walls and the hull, sneaking up the tunnel, and bouncing off the polished walls. The figures of Kowalchuk and his men cast long, sharp shadows down the tunnel as they fled.

A massive crunching sound added to the cacophony from somewhere above them. With luck, not the ship dying, but the last connection between the rock cap and the wider lava bed breaking free.

The floor pushed on Jaeger's rump. The light from the ship's exhaust grew even brighter in the hardhat's view of the tunnel.

For the first time in over a million years, the Octalien ship flew.

CHAPTER 25

ALPHA CENTAURI B SYSTEM | CONCORDIA | BRAVO CHARLIE ORBIT

27 AUGUST 2127 (EARTH REFERENCE FRAME) | 28 OCTOBER 2125 (CONCORDIA REFERENCE FRAME)

EARLY IN THE ship's morning and Varanathan was already at work. In his office, door closed. A cup of coffee steamed on his desk, next to the still image of his childhood cricket field. He ignored it now. The first sips had turned into rancid oil in his stomach.

He leaned forward, elbows on the desktop. He wanted to scream at O'Daniel in one of the visitor chairs. *You damned fool, you cocked this up.* But screaming wouldn't be leaderly. He willed his face to be stern, like a disappointed father. "What are we to do now?"

O'Daniel relaxed against the chair back. He sat as tall as he could with his shoulders hunched toward his paunch. His forearms lay solidly on the chair arms. "We have to neutralize the Octalien ship."

"'Neutralize'? We cannot destroy it. Our whole purpose is to bring it home for the Coalition. Nothing else would do anyone a damned bit of good. 'Neutralize...'" He trailed off. O'Daniel had lifted his hand a few centimeters in the middle of the words.

"I know that sounds like a euphemism," the American said in his ghastly accent, "but it isn't. We want the whole ship, but all we really need is one energy extractor. Everything else is gravy."

Varanathan arched his eyebrow. Americans could no longer impose their slang on the world. "Gravy?"

"A bonus." O'Daniel bowed his head, but not far. "Sure, better if we could get the ship intact. I agree. In fact, I know how to do it."

Varanathan leaned back in his chair. The well-oiled machinery flexed silently under him. "We've tried soldiers."

"Not soldiers. We could deploy a squad on a small craft to intercept the Octalien ship in orbit, but Jaeger and the others would see them coming."

"There's not stealth in space, is there?"

"A life support system at 20° Celsius would glow like a beacon against the deep space background. And there's another problem with attempting a boarding party. Only a few trustworthy personnel would remain on *Concordia* to, ah, bolster our authority."

Muscles hardened around Varanathan's mouth. Yes, people grumbled about the official story of the deaths of Sandford, Lavin, and other Humanist loyalists in a gun battle. Whispers of disbelief trickled down the corridors. The Humanists sought to seize the Octalien ship for their faction, anyone could believe it. But Varanathan wanted to donate it to all of Earth? Especially when the only armed men on the ship were Traditionalists?

And flying over the planet's continent in nighttime, the yellow-orange lake of fresh lava, spoor of the Octalien ship's launch, caught the eye of anyone looking through a camera or a telescope. Something very strange had happened. Anyone could see that.

He could not tell the truth to mission personnel or to Earth. Even if he did not, his hold on *Concordia* could slip from his fingers any moment. Why, then, did the American seem so confident?

"What do you propose?"

With a flat voice, O'Daniel said, "A neutron bomb."

"A what?"

"It dates back about a century and a half, to the First Cold War. A type of fusion bomb engineered for maximum neutron output. A high enough dose of neutrons can kill instantly. It might be enough to hit them with a lower dose, enough to debilitate them immediately and kill them by radiation poisoning within a couple of days."

Varanathan squinted. The ins and outs of radioactivity were beneath his notice, but from the big picture, he knew enough to ask, "Even through whatever Octalien alloy makes up that ship's hull?"

"Turns out metals make pretty weak neutron shielding."

O'Daniel's placid confidence made Varanathan's fingertips claw across the polished desktop. "Would that we could. There are no instructions in the fab for a neutron bomb. Give me a real idea."

"Not literally a bomb. But we can generate more than enough neutrons."

"How?"

"The ship's drive. We can tune fusion conditions to spew out neutron-rich reaction mass. Then we make an orbital adjustment burn that runs them through our exhaust."

"We can target it so precisely?"

"Our satellites in synchronous orbit feed us their location all the time."

Varanathan lowered his gaze to the still image of the cricket field. It wouldn't do to appear eager to a subordinate. "Work up a solution and give it to me today."

"Took care of it already." O'Daniel rotated his wrist. A virtual file appeared above his palm, an archaic icon of manilla pasteboard spinning slowly, carrying the label *Proposed orbital maneuver* in and out of Varanathan's view. "It's good for the next transfer window. About eighty minutes from now."

Varanathan nodded at the file. O'Daniel flicked the icon. It drifted over the video loops of politicians on the desk. Varanathan grabbed the icon and dropped it on his desk. The file popped open and he skimmed the first paragraphs and a couple of data tables. Tedious details.

"The next best transfer window won't come up for another twenty hours," said O'Daniel. "They might decide to leave orbit by then."

"For where?"

"Elsewhere in the Alpha Centauri system? Back to Earth? We have no intel from inside the Octalien ship."

Varanathan swung his gaze back to the open file. Tedious details, but if O'Daniel seemed sure it would work, he had no need to micromanage the American. "I'll review for a few minutes. If I say the word, you'll prepare for action immediately?"

A nod jostled O'Daniel's jowls. "I'll drop everything else."

"Good. All for now." Varanathan made a show of reviewing the file while O'Daniel left. In reality, his gaze kept returning to the cricket field of his youth. After all of Jaeger and McIlroy's trickery, seizing the Octalien ship would be like scoring the winning runs in front of a crowd of billions.

Five minutes after the door shut behind O'Daniel, Varanathan sent a simple message to his subordinate. *Agreed.*

Two days in orbit, and Jaeger's stomach still flopped around his abdomen. Like *Concordia*, the Octalien ship was built for thrust, but the Octaliens hadn't bothered to configure the interior for spin-gravity when their ship coasted. Maybe free fall reminded them of jumping between branches in the rainforest trees of their homeworld.

At least they figured out the purpose behind the hinged bars on the wall. Handholds for free fall.Marie teased out enough secrets from the ship's fab to make fabric straps. Tied to the handholds, they made passable hammocks.

Stomach still uneasy, Jaeger, McIlroy, and the women crowded the break room, eating protein and fat sandwiches on starch cakes and squirting water into their mouths. McIlroy held an empty bottle to collect drifting starch crumbs.

Ulanovas pulled himself in. He moved through free fall like a seal with arms. He took a sandwich from Marie with a glint in his eye. His first bite muffled his voice. "It's ready."

McIlroy picked up crumbs. Annike turned her brown eyes between Ulanovas and the other men. "You're certain you can aim so precisely?"

"I got it."

Jaeger moved his sandwich closer to his mouth, but the bile in his chest from his previous swallow kept him from taking a bite. "And it's the only way to keep Varanathan from spoiling our plan."

"But if you're off by even a few meters...."

He found her empty hand and give it a squeeze. "To give the Alliance and the Coalition the common foe they need, we have to take the chance."

She sucked in a breath. Before she could speak, Ulanovas said, "We'll test the particle beam weapon, okay? On a smaller target and more distant target."

"What target?" Annike asked.

"The tunnel access on top of the rock formation."

Memories flashed, bright as the sun-baked surface. Five days ago? It felt like five lifetimes. Jaeger asked, "Where are we in our orbit?"

"Close."

"Do you have time to set it up?"

Ulanovas grinned. "Already did." He crammed a giant bite of the sandwich into his mouth, then twisted his feet to the wall opposite the door and pushed off.

Jaeger followed him to the control room. The others trailed after.

The red desert filled the functional stretches of the main display. Alpha Centauri B threw long afternoon shadows of rocky outcrops across the sands. The shadows bled into splotchy zones of dead pixels. Half-bent, Ulanovas floated in a corner of the room. The control box for the particle beam generators dangled on slack power and data cables.

Most of the generators broke apart when they carved the ship and its rock cap free of the lava bed. One had survived, though, shown by ready lights on the control board. Confirmed by a test fire two orbits ago. In the deep ocean three thousand miles from land, a circular shock wave had rippled out from the target site, and a column of steam rose into the sky.

The Lithuanian hooked his toes under an edge of a control board and pulled his torso closer, dragging the particle beam box with him. With one hand he worked the board while the other touched a tracking surface on the box.

A targeting reticle popped onto the main display. A bright green circle glowed against the long shadows and the rusty terrain. Octalien symbols appeared in the corner. "Dialing down the beam intensity, okay?"

Reflux smoldered in Jaeger's chest. "Where's the rock formation?"

"Coming," Ulanovas said. He jabbed his finger at the top of the screen. "See. Gagarin Station."

The cluster of tents on the rise looked tiny and temporary. The posts of the basketball goals cast shadows too thin to be seen, even at the highest zoom. Their home for months, never to be lived in again.

Jaeger glanced around the small room. This ship would be their home for years.

No. Wherever the other four were would be his home.

The view slid by. To the lower left, the two landing craft stood half a mile from Gagarin Station, each in the middle of radial scorches on hard rock. A moment later they passed from view. The energy absorbing formations dotted the terrain to the right.

Then the lava bed came into view. Flat black crept onto the screen. Had it resolidified so quickly?

No, Jaeger saw a moment later. A circular pit glowed orange-red in the middle of the lava bed. Rock, still molten from their launch. Like a pit mine dug down to Hell.

Ulanovas slid the targeting circle around the lava lake, then up and to the side. Beyond the lava bed, the rock formation showed its polished gray top. Metal glinted near the center, near a tiny shadow that had to be a hole Kowalchuk's men dug to get in.

"Here we go, okay?"

The view zoomed in. The center of the bright green reticle crawled up the jagged rocks and onto the polished stone, on a straight line for the hole.

Ulanovas tapped a surface of the particle beam box. He nudged it away from him. It bumped the control room wall while he tracked the camera view back.

The hole looked the same, except now a straight black line extended from it all the way to the alloy slab over the entrance. The black line ended at a nick in the slab's side. The nick's edges glowed as orange-red as the molten lava pool.

"Do you now trust me to slice off *Concordia*'s interstellar transmission antenna and particle spin magnets?" Ulanovas asked.

McIlroy broke the silence, hamming up his Texas accent more than usual. "I reckon we do."

"Good," said Ulanovas. The image on the wall display jump-cut. Red desert gave way to a blue arc of cloud-dotted atmosphere, melding into black space. Alpha Centauri B hung in the distance. "*Concordia* should be here. Four hundred kilometers on a crossing trajectory."

Jaeger squinted at bright stars all fixed in space. "Where?"

"No visual?" Ulanovas said, half to himself. The view panned to compensate for the dead pixels.

At four hundred kilometers, they should see a steadily moving dot. Nothing. "Lost in the sun?"

Ulanovas tossed his bangs away from his eyes. "I plot *Concordia*'s orbit. We should see it. I check infrared, okay?"

He pressed buttons. The display added false colors to objects in view. Blue tinted Alpha Centauri B and greener shades tinged the atmosphere's clouds.

Jaeger sucked in a breath. *Concordia*'s lifesystem and fusion reactor should have been pulsing with purple against the star field. Nothing.

"Did something bad happen to *Concordia*?" queried Marie from the corridor.

"An explosion?" Jaeger shook his head. "Wreckage would still be hot enough to glow in IR."

A scraping sound came from the hallway. McIlroy's fingers in his beard. "And I reckon we'd see some fragments in visible light."

"Looks like *Concordia* changed orbit," Jaeger said.

Annike said, "Varanathan would not have returned to Earth without his prize."

"I agree," said Jaeger. His blood suddenly ran cold. "He's gunning for us."

In Marie's voice, he could hear her shake her head. "Almost certainly, *Concordia* carries no fab blueprints for missiles."

"A missile would wreck what he wants, okay?"

Jaeger raised his voice. "He doesn't need a missile. He's got hot exhaust from *Concordia*'s drive."

Annike, Marie, and Ulanovas fell silent. McIlroy spoke. "We've got a rock cap for shielding."

"For something coming at us from the front," Jaeger said.

"The alloy on the hull will block radia—"

"Not neutrons." Jaeger's mind raced over output specs of *Concordia*'s drive and neutron scattering and activation properties of various materials. Too much math to do quickly, even with his wearable, but decades of experience gave him a hunch. "Some would get through to us, and much of the rest would turn metal atoms in the hull into radioisotopes. Varanathan could kill us with radiation poisoning and then board the ship whenever he wants."

Jaeger's skin went clammy. He barely noticed it, or anything else.

He swatted the back of his hand against Ulanovas's shoulder. "Check every camera. We need visual contact on *Concordia.* Everyone else, grab something and hold on. The ride might get choppy."

Feet scampered down the corridor to the break room and beyond. Jaeger extended his legs and rolled his shoulders forward, bracing his feet on the front wall under the display and his back on the wall behind him.

Ulanovas worked the camera controls with one hand. Slices of planet, atmosphere, sun, and black stars swept through the display, along with the Lithuanian's staccato commentary. "Aft? No. Starboard? No. Below? No."

The main display showed a red limb of desert hazing into the yellow of dry scrubland. The blue band of horizon melding with black. Stars.

And *Concordia* almost head on. The particle spin magnets around the inlet bulged like a trio of metallic warts. Backscatter from the drive silhouetted the ring of the six modules in ghostly white. The interstellar antenna poked toward them from the top of Mod 5.

The exhaust showed as a needle of heat shimmer roiling the horizon and the lowest stars.

"Is she on a collision course?" Jaeger asked.

"Two hundred klicks. Closing at ten klicks per second. Closest approach twelve klicks," Ulanovas said.

A little waggle of *Concordia*'s tail would lance the Octalien ship with a fatal dose of radiation.

"I'll fire the particle beam then turn us hard. On my mark, engines full."

Jaeger glimpsed the maneuver in a moment. Turn their ship perpendicular to *Concordia*'s exhaust and punch it away.

And hope you get clear.

"Got it."

The display zoomed in. The green targeting circle appeared,

dancing over the three particle spin magnets. Ulanovas's fingers hammered the control box like a manic pianist.

Particle beam slashes knifed across the magnets. From the red-orange gashes, metal fragments crumbled away. Puffs of coolant flash-froze into ice clouds.

"Good," Jaeger said.

The view slewed as a sudden force tugged at his feet and back. He gritted his teeth and pressed harder against the walls. Down the corridor came grunts and groans.

"Now!"

Jaeger punched up all the acceleration he could. An invisible giant sat on his chest, slammed him to the floor. The drive rumbled through his battered body. Spots swam in his eyes, clouded his vision. Amid flashing green lights and streams of Octalien symbols on the display, was that the symbol for five gees?

He pressed harder. He willed his diaphragm down and his chest out to get enough breath. Six gees?

The view lurched. *Concordia*, broadside, passing a mile from the Octalien ship's exhaust. Against the reds and yellows of Bravo Charlie. The interstellar antenna showed as a hefty parabola jutting away from the smooth curve of Mod 5. The green circle neared the antenna mount.

Ulanovas's fingers pounded the control box. Nothing happened. The hell?

And then *Concordia*'s acceleration caught up with the antenna, coasting as it rode the stump of Ulanovas's beam. The cut edges of the antenna mount glowed red like blood seeping from an amputated limb.

The antenna slowly tumbled away from them. Ulanovas slashed the beam across the parabola, breaking off mesh plates, slicing the inner gain antenna free from the parabola's focal point to drift from the rest.

Varanathan's voice could no longer reach Earth. Without the

particle spin magnets, he lacked the ability to refuel in flight for the journey home.

Varanathan could not stop them.

A faint relief from the crushing weight. Jaeger's rump and back ached like every hit he'd taken on the football field had come back all at once. He fought for breath. "No more." His fingers eased the ship back to three gees.

Blood pounded in his head. The aft view showed *Concordia* near the center, close to the hot particle stream of their ship's exhaust. If Varanathan tried to pivot *Concordia* to spew its drive's lethal radiation at them, his ship would die too.

The heat shimmer needle of *Concordia*'s exhaust flickered over the limb of the world below. A moment later it went out. The ship coasted onward in its orbit.

Jaeger dialed the engines down to 1.2 gees, but his fingers remained ready, in case Varanathan went irrational and tried for mutual destruction. He caught his breath and spoke through voice and wearable, "Everyone safe?"

All four said yes. "Though bruises don't heal as fast as they used to," McIlroy said. "How did you do?"

"We damaged the particle spin magnets and sliced off the interstellar transmission antenna. He's mute and can't chase us to Earth."

"What about our colleagues on the surface?" Annike asked. "Glenn and Yang Stations?"

She had a good heart, Jaeger mused. "They'll be fine. With their fabs and polywell reactors—"

"I know that. Should we tell them our plan before we leave?"

The main display tracked *Concordia* coasting in its lower orbit. The science stations on the planet were thousands of miles out of sight and would be too small to pick out anyway. Amundsen might be insufferable, things hadn't clicked with Regina Smalley, but would they agree with the logic of why Jaeger and the others had to pose as hostile Octaliens?

"We have to keep it our secret," Jaeger said. From their tones of voice, all the others agreed. He swallowed, awestruck by the audacity of their plan. *We come in war for all mankind.*

Would it work?

They had to try.

The drive rumbled. The Octalien ship climbed to a higher orbit, the first leg of the years-long journey back to Earth.

I'm **RAYMUND EICH.** I use my Middle American upbringing as a launchpad for journeys to the ends of the Universe.

Growing up in the Midwest prepared me for my academic career, culminating with a Ph.D. in biochemistry from Rice University. It helps me help inventors prosper from their progress in medicine, biotechnology, and computer hardware.

Above all, it inspires me to write science fiction and fantasy about ordinary people facing extraordinary wonders and horrors, battling enemies both foreign and domestic, and building better lives for themselves, their families, and their societies.

My last name has one syllable and is pronounced "eye-sh." I live in Houston with my family.

Connect with me at **www.raymundeich.com** or follow the QR code below.

Online and brick-and-mortar bookstores around the world list millions of books, with thousands more published every day. I'm glad you discovered this one.

If you'd like to know when I release a new book, instead of leaving it to chance, join my Readers Club. I'll email you every two months with publishing news, an off-beat patent, and a short personal update. Plus, I'll let you know about an older book of mine you might have missed.

Yes, please! I'll go to **www.raymundeich.com/mailing-list** or scan the QR code below.

No thanks. I'll take my chances next time I look for your books.

Earth barely survived the 21st Century.

Biotechnological and nuclear terrorism, civil war, famine, and ethnic cleansing killed billions. Thousands fled on warpdrive ships to colonize planets around distant suns.

In the 22nd century, after Earth unified under one world government, it opened wormhole links to the distant colonies, to prevent a repeat of the previous century's chaos on a galactic scale.

Enter operative Stone Chalmers. Spy. Assassin. Instrument maintaining Earth's dominion over all human worlds.

Opposing him are hostile forces on colony worlds... and within the Earth government itself.

When Stone clashes with those forces, Earth—and every human world—will be transformed forever.

Learn more about the Stone Chalmers series at
www.cv2books.com/stone-chalmers, or follow the QR code below.

The Progress of Mankind

To maintain order in the 22nd century, Earth relocates undesirables through artificial wormholes onto colony planets. Everyone benefits... except the planets' original colonists.

Now, the newly rediscovered colony of New Moravia learns Earth's plan and fights back.

The Greater Glory of God

Thousands fled the chaos of the 21st century on rogue warpdrive ships to settle colony planets. When Earth reunified in the 22nd, its fleets rediscovered the colonies and hunted down the warpdrive ships.

Every warpdrive ship but one.

To All High Emprise Consecrated

Unified Earth has rediscovered the colony of Minerva. Prosperous and technologically advanced, Minerva quickly submits to Earth supremacy.

Surprisingly quickly...

In Public Convocation Assembled

Earth's government controls all human colonies scattered through the galaxy by means of wormholes, warpdrive ships, and ruthless operatives. Operatives working to strengthen Earth's grip.

Or destroy it.

Take the Shilling

The Confederated Worlds implanted in his brain the skills to make him a soldier. Tomas Neumann had to learn for himself how to survive interstellar war.

Operation Iago

The Confederated Worlds lost the war. Can Lt. Tomas Neumann win the peace against elusive, deceptive foes out to turn the Confederated Worlds against itself?

A Bodyguard of Lies

Assigned to the halls of power, only Capt. Tomas Neumann can save the Confederated Worlds from the ultimate treachery.

The Blank Slate

Neuroscience entrepreneur Clay Shieffer must stop a tyrannical president... because he unwittingly gave the tyrant power over the human mind.

New California

After New California's founder committed suicide, two men vied to rule the colony.

Ashwin George, supported by the colony's elite and the Chinese company dominating half the settled galaxy.

Against him, Desmond Park, nanotechnology engineer, armed with the most formidable weapon of all.

A single idea.

The Reincarnation Run

Skeptical spacejock Landry Krieger knows exactly how to smuggle the "reborn" spiritual leader of an oppressed people past their conquerors... but the boy's priests—and governess—shake up his orderly plans.

Azureseas: Cantrell's War

Ross Cantrell joined the animal control mission on the newly-discovered planet Azureseas to earn the money to start married life together with his girlfriend.

Then Ross discovers the truth about the planet's "animals."

The ALECS Quartet

He had a month to learn the planet's mysteries—and Juliette's.

His cover story: return to Elard to dismantle his sect's missionary work to the planet's natives.

His true mission: investigate decades-old mysteries of love and death.

His objective: return to Earth with his discovery.

If he can.

A Mighty Fortress

Theodore and his team from the Lutheran Interstellar Terraforming Society would transform a barren, rocky world into a refuge of faith and life.

Or die trying.

Winner and the Poacher

A Portia Oakeshott, Dinosaur Veterinarian Short Novel

As a consultant to law enforcement, Portia confronts stark evidence of a rich young man's crime: the mounted head of a massive herbivorous *Wintonotitan*. A winner.

A dinosaur the company never granted a permit for hunting.

The First Voyages: The Complete Science Fiction Stories 1998-2012

From 21st century asteroid settlements to World War II Romania, from an Earth dominated by immortal aliens to Christ's empty tomb, a fresh, distinctive voice in science fiction will take you on journeys to the photosphere of the sun, the coding regions of DNA, and the complexities of the human psyche.

Stage Separations: The Complete Science Fiction Stories 2013-2018

In these pages, you can...

...race against time to solve mysteries hidden in a planet's vast desert—and in a woman's heart

...learn the true story of a president's assassination

...journey 14,000 miles to a high-tech fountain of youth

...win or go "home"—to an Earth you've never seen

and explore six other worlds created by a distinctive voice in twenty-first century science fiction.

Orbital Maneuvers: The Complete Science Fiction Stories 2019-2020

In these pages, you can join–

A mission to terraform a lifeless, rocky planet | A private detective uncovering the ultimate crime | A woman called by an ex-boyfriend... who's been dead twenty years | A President breaking his country's highest law | A star athlete discovering the true price of a championship

–and enjoy five more tales, in the latest installment of the Complete Science Fiction Stories of Raymund Eich.